# Cracks in the Wall

## Duke Southard

Published by Wheatmark®
1760 East River Road, Suite 145, Tucson, Arizona 85718 USA
www.wheatmark.com

ISBN: 978-1-62787-409-0 (paperback)
ISBN: 978-1-62787-410-6 (ebook)
LCCN: 2016937054

This novel is a work of fiction. Names, characters, places, and events are either products of the author's imagination or are used fictitiously. While some locations in the book actually exist, they are used only as points of reference and the events that occur in them are fictitious. While fiction often mirrors true life, it is not the author's intent to do so in this novel. Any resemblance to actual events, persons living or dead, or locales is coincidental.

Author's Note:
This novel is set in an era when sheriffs' departments still existed in Connecticut. For dramatic purposes, this jurisdictional system remains in place in the book even though county sheriffs no longer exist in the state. Also, some liberties have been taken with the duties of the sheriffs' departments in homicide cases during the time period in the book. I accept all responsibility for any errors or omissions.

# Acknowledgments

There would be no *Cracks in the Wall* or any other of my books without the support of so many special people whose insights, critiquing skills, honesty, and, most of all, patience with me, have helped me beyond measure.

My heartfelt thanks go out to Carol, Denise, Lise, the Green Valley Writers' Group, and the folks at Wheatmark for their help with this project.

To my family, especially my ever-supportive, understanding, and incisive critic and wife, Barbara, my love for all of you knows no bounds. I thank you for always being on my side of the wall!

# Part One

## The Murder

# One

COVINGTON COUNTY, A SPRAWLING rural area west of Hartford, Connecticut, had not seen a murder since early in 1990, over two years before. Despite the bucolic horse farms and forests to the west and north, the county was gradually falling victim to the encroachment of an imaginary boundary line, one which moved the city to the east inexorably closer with each passing day. While the city limits signs stayed in place, the appearance of bargain-priced housing developments, shopping malls, and automobile traffic threatened to destroy the quiet neighborhoods that served as an escape from the rat race that was the city. With the growth came the inevitable increase in crime, but thus far, the populace had been subjected to nuisance offenses like graffiti sprayed on bridges mixing with an occasional sliced tire or property vandalism. The possibility of violent crime remained just a niggling itch, the kind of worry that was easily scratched. For Linda Phillips, that trifling itch turned into horrifying reality. She had less than thirty-six hours to live.

Linda would not see the dawn of Mothers' Day on May 10, 1992. That festive weekend of celebration with special family gatherings were to be bittersweet for her. As the residents of Hampton Village relished the thank-God-it's-Friday moments and anticipated a relaxing few days of gardening and puttering around the

3

house, Linda could only look forward to a Mothers' Day weekend without her three young children. As only he could, Shane Phillips cajoled, pleaded, and begged with Linda to allow him to have them for the weekend. When all else failed, he resorted to his usual intimidation and threats. With their final divorce settlement hearing just days away, Linda would soon be rid of him and his influence permanently, so she finally relented. She would use the weekend to sort out the myriad personal problems that were bedeviling her in the eleven months since she separated from Shane.

SHANE JR. CAME BOUNDING through the door to the real estate office of Chambers and Stone, followed in rapid succession by Tonie and Jackie. All three ran directly to their mother sitting behind the receptionist's desk. She smiled as they jockeyed for position to give her the usual hug. At nine years old, Shane won the battle over his younger twin sisters and squeezed Linda hard around the waist.

"Do we have to go with Dad this weekend?" he asked, allowing the girls enough space to make the gathering into a group hug. "I don't want to."

"Your father has some fun things planned for the weekend. You'll have a good time with him." The hug broke apart and she looked at Shane. "He's looking forward to it and you don't get to see him that much."

"He's not always fun, Mom. Sometimes I feel like he doesn't even like us." Linda noticed the seven-year-old twins nodding in agreement.

"It's all arranged, and he'll be at the house in a little while so we better get going."

Steve Chambers appeared at the door of his office and greeted the children with a warm smile. "You take good care of your mom this weekend, and behave yourselves, especially on Sunday. It's Mothers' Day, you know!"

"Shane's taking them for the weekend. He's picking them up this afternoon. I'll be back to close up after he leaves."

Steve's surprise was evident. "Really? On Mothers' Day

weekend? Wow!" He hesitated as the words caused Linda to frown. "Listen, don't bother coming back. I'll take care of things here. You just enjoy your weekend."

"I don't want to go, Mr. Chambers," Shane Jr. whined.

"Me neither," Jackie added.

Steve's quick glance at Linda caused a blush to creep into her cheeks. "He's not always a fun guy, if you know what I mean. They're fine once they get there." She shrugged her shoulders in resignation, then directed her attention to the children.

"We've got to go, kids. And thanks, Steve. I'll take you up on your offer. I'll see you tomorrow morning. It's my Saturday to work." She hustled the three children out the door.

SHANE PHILLIPS, AS USUAL, was more than an hour late. Linda had the children ready to go on time and the four of them sat on the veranda waiting. When Shane roared up the driveway, spraying gravel and dirt behind, Jackie began to cry. She moved against her mother, clinging to her blouse while Shane Jr. thumped his small suitcase down each of the five wooden steps and dragged it toward the car. Tonie followed him and they both climbed into the car, silent, their father's presence ignored.

"Jackie, get in the car," Shane shouted through the open window on the passenger side. When all three children were in the back seat with their faces pressed against the window, he began to back down the driveway. After returning their tentative waves, Linda watched as they struggled with their seat belts. Shane had not said a single word to her.

The children would not see their mother alive again.

# Two

PAUL AND DOLORES FREEMAN traveled in the same social circles as Linda and Shane Phillips, a bonding that continued even after the initial divorce proceedings. Paul seemed to enjoy the time with the Phillipses more than Dolores, circling around Linda like a hawk over a wounded sparrow, swooping in for accidental contact at every opportunity. With his direct access to the high-end drug dealers in the town, he was guaranteed invitations to the weekly parties of a small and select group of wealthy young professionals, most of whom worked in Hartford. It was Thursday night when he made the call.

"DOLORES AND THE KIDS are off visiting her sister for the weekend," Paul said. "If there's any way you could figure out how to have Friday evening free, I think we could have a nice time together. There's nothing wrong with friends getting together for a dinner, right?"

"I'll have to wait to make sure I don't have the kids," Linda replied. "You never know with Shane. He's not very dependable."

They left it with the agreement that Linda would call him early Friday evening if she had no responsibilities.

LINDA WAITED A FULL hour after Shane left before making the call. There had been times in the past when he would take the

6

children for his regular visitation, then be back on the doorstep within minutes, making excuses for why he couldn't keep them. She was always happy when he returned, but since he seemed so determined this time, she believed with some certainty that he wasn't coming back. This would not be the first time she had accepted a dinner invitation with one of an increasing cadre of male friends since she filed for divorce. It would be the first time she would be alone with Paul Freeman, a thought that in turn excited and frightened her. He was a powerful business leader in town while also known to be able to supply his close friends with what he called "enhancers" of the mental human experience. If Paul was at your party, you could be assured that drugs of all levels would be available for those willing to pay for them. In the nine months since serving the divorce papers to Shane, Linda had attended numerous gatherings where the focus was how subtly the revelers could attain their relative highs. Paul was always more than ready to assist. Early in her newly found freedom stage, Linda had moved beyond her pot phase on two occasions, experimenting with the magic white powder while Dolores and Paul watched with amusement as the euphoria overtook her. The second time, Dolores did not notice Paul's hand slipping under the table to squeeze Linda's upper thigh after she was well under the influence, a state of mind that welcomed the touch that sent chills through her entire body. Having a handsome, influential man paying attention to her added to the building excitement from the drug. Now she would be spending an evening with him under the guise of a harmless friendship. As she stood facing the shower, the hot water cascading over her, she wondered if the evening might include a friendly sharing of one of Paul's expensive enhancements.

LINDA'S HAND SHOOK AS she pushed the buttons on her phone. "This is just a dinner with a friend," she said aloud, repeating "just a dinner, just a dinner" several times as she listened to the ringing of Paul's phone. After six rings, she was just about to disconnect when he answered.

"Is this good news?" he asked, a greeting which could be taken as a light-hearted joke if anyone other than Linda happened to be calling.

"I'm not sure if it is or not. I'm wondering if this is a good idea. I mean, this is a small town, and people talk, you know?" Linda's voice quavered but became stronger as she continued. "Not that we're doing anything wrong; it's just the appearance and perceptions I'm worried about."

"I understand completely." Paul chuckled. "I've got a reputation to uphold, too, you know. That's why I'll meet you at the rest area on I-84 just before Hartford, and we'll have dinner at a place I know in the city. Just so we don't have to explain anything, even if the anything is nothing." He laughed again. "I'll see you there in an hour."

"Okay," Linda said, and hung up.

PAUL EPITOMIZED THE PERFECT gentleman during the entire evening. Even when they were in his BMW in close quarters, his hands stayed on the wheel. For the most part, their conversation during dinner stayed in neutral areas like town politics, the real estate market, and the usual family and kid issues. It wasn't until they had almost reached the exit for the rest area to pick up Linda's car that he broached a previously avoided subject.

"So, are you okay to drive?" he asked. "You did have a couple of glasses of wine."

Linda responded with a grin. "That was a while ago. I can't even feel any effect from them. I'll be fine."

Paul turned onto the exit ramp for the rest area and pulled up next to Linda's car. Linda reached for the door handle, but Paul reached over and put his hand on her left arm. She turned to look at him.

"I've had a nice time, Paul; a really nice time and thanks a lot." She kept her hand on the handle as his grip tightened into an insistent squeeze.

"I've got some stuff you might want to try. It's a hell of a lot better than wine and won't give you a headache like that Merlot you were drinking." He was smiling. "You've had similar stuff before, but this is higher quality." His smile broadened as she put a finger to her lips as if in deep thought.

"I remember Dolores sharing something one night." Linda remained in the same pose, stretching out the decision that she had already made. "I guess it wouldn't hurt anything to try it again, if that's the sort of similar stuff you're talking about." The dim glow cast by the overhead lights in the parking lot provided proof that her smile not only could light up a room but the inside of a car as well.

"Your place or mine?" Paul asked.

"I'm thinking that since it's dark, we could go back to my house for a little while. My neighbors tend to go to bed early and you can park at the end of the driveway behind the house. Not that this has to be a big secret but, you know, discretion's the better part of valor, and all that."

"Great. I'll give you a five-minute head start and see you in a bit." He released his hold on her arm, slid his hand down to hers and patted it. "And no need to worry, Linda. I'll do my best to be the gentleman I've been so far."

TOMMY IVERSON LEFT THE bar just before the last call. The Red Sox were in the middle of a nine game road trip to the West Coast and were hopelessly behind. A fanatical fan, he had pounded several beers as the Angels scored seven times in the fourth inning. They were just catching up with his circulation system, clouding his brain, when he decided to call it a night. He slipped off the bar stool, stumbled, then negotiated through the single door, which looked like a revolving door to him, and made his way to his car.

After putting several key marks on the door in his search for the lock, he finally found the slot, unlocked the door, and tumbled into the driver's seat. His befuddled state of mind had him mumbling to himself as he fumbled with the ignition key.

"Wonder what Linda's doing tonight?" he asked aloud. Then, in typically inebriated fashion, answered himself. "Maybe I'll just do a drive-by and see if she's up for some company."

He weaved the car through the parking lot, passing the exit

drive once before finding it on the second try. A few seconds later, unable to see in the enveloping darkness, he switched on his headlights and headed for Linda's house, just minutes away from Sweeney's Bar and Grille. He drove by once, slowing to see if there were any signs of life in the house. The kitchen light at the rear of the house reflected onto the tall pine tree that acted as a canopy over the backyard. He made a U-turn the first chance he had, and a minute later, parked at the end of the driveway. After turning off the engine and lights, he sat for a full five minutes, mulling over the possibilities as well as he could. Except for the light filtering through the backyard, the house, a turn-of-the-century colonial, was dark. The untrimmed yews and rhododendrons crowded around the front windows, hiding the peeling paint around the lower portion of the clapboarding. In the darkness, it had an almost haunted look about it. Even the most desperate trick-or-treaters might be hesitant to approach it. He decided that she probably was having a late night cup of coffee and reading a book, activities he knew she enjoyed often after the children were in bed. He slipped out of the car, stumbled, and left the door open, the inside light reflecting enough to light his way for part of his erratic trip up the driveway.

Halfway to the top, the other car parked next to Linda's came into view.

"Shit," he muttered. "Dolores and Paul are here." He turned to retreat, but reconsidered. "Hell with it; I'm just an old friend stopping to say hello. So what if it's late?" He ended his one-sided conversation and continued up the drive.

"Amazing," Linda said, as she pulled her sweater up over her head. "That stuff is just amazing." She leaned back against the island in the center of the kitchen, leaving her arms outstretched as the sweater fell to the floor. Paul leaned into her, then reached behind and, with practiced deftness, unclasped her bra. She lowered her hands and the shoulder straps slipped down her arms, allowing the undergarment to flutter down, landing softly on her sweater. Paul slid to his knees, his lips brushing the valley between her breasts before he paused at her bared navel.

"No, you are amazing," he whispered as he found the zipper of her skirt and tugged on it.

Linda's piercing scream brought him to feet, shaking. "What the hell's wrong?"

"Somebody's at the window. I saw somebody looking in the damn window!" Linda stammered as she stooped to pick up her clothes. She brought them up to cover her chest, as though suddenly aware of her nakedness. The rapture of the drug evaporated in the fear as adrenalin surged through her bloodstream.

TOMMY LEAPED FROM THE porch and ran down the driveway, stumbling and almost falling headfirst several times, the residual effects of his alcohol consumption still disturbing his coordination. He jumped into the car and dug into his pants pocket for his keys. A quick glance up at the house told him that no one was yet chasing him. The car started and he yanked the shift lever into drive, flooring the accelerator pedal. The car lurched forward, leaving behind a long patch of smoking tire marks which would make any teenage male driver proud. He entered his house minutes later.

"Son of a bitch," he shouted, producing an echo in the empty living room. Then he picked up the phone and dialed Linda's number. It rang four times before the answering machine kicked in.

"Hi. You've reached Linda. Sorry I can't take your call right now but please leave your name and a short message and I'll return your call as soon as I can." The unoriginal recording turned Tommy's face bright red, the veins on his neck popping out. "I'll just bet you can't take a call right now," he hissed.

"I fucking hate you!" He slammed the receiver back into its cradle.

PAUL AND LINDA SAT on opposite sides of the living room. In the ten minutes since the appearance of the peeping Tom, which was how Paul referred to him, she had relaxed to the point that the effects of the drug she had snorted earlier were returning.

"Do you want me to leave?" Paul asked, as he watched Linda mellowing with each passing instant. She reacted immediately.

"No, please don't; I'd like you to stay for at least a while."

"You're sure you saw something, right?" Paul asked, rising from his chair and taking a seat next to her on the sofa. "I mean, sometimes the stuff can create a bit of confusion..." His voice trailed off as he inched closer to her.

"Positively; there was a man staring at us through the window. I couldn't see any detail, but he was there, no doubt about that." She leaned toward him. "I'm so sorry to interrupt...you know, um..."

Paul put his arm around her shoulder as if to comfort her. "Listen, that was a scary thing. What else could you do? You couldn't ignore it. I understand completely." He pulled her closer.

"That's really kind of you, and I appreciate it." She let her hand fall on his thigh and squeezed. "You've got nowhere to go tonight, right?" she said, sliding her hand higher.

Paul grinned. "Nope, nowhere at all."

The phone in the kitchen rang a minute later. "Let the machine get it," Paul whispered into her ear. Linda didn't object.

# Three

FIVE HOURS AFTER GOING to bed, Tommy Iverson was wide awake. He lay motionless on his bed, staring at the ceiling. Every time he awakened during the night, the images of Linda and Paul in the kitchen flashed through his head like a series of still photographs—Linda with her arms extended over her head; her sweater floating to the floor; Paul using one hand to unsnap her bra, then his face sliding down between her bare breasts; her mouth opening to produce a frightful scream. The actual recollections were bad enough but when his imagination filled in what may have happened after he left, sleep was impossible. If he slept even two hours, it would be a surprise. The question now was what should he do next?

LINDA NOT ONLY HEARD the pounding on the door but could feel the vibrations coming through the floorboards from the kitchen directly below her bedroom. The early spring sunlight splashed across the bed and reflected off the clock, making it impossible to read. Paul Freeman lay face down in the bed, showing no sign of awakening. She nudged him and when there was no reaction, she leaned over and hollered in his ear.

"Paul, wake up. Come on, someone's downstairs beating on the door." She tossed the covers aside and practically sprinted into the bathroom. When she emerged seconds later, she was carrying her robe and slippers. Paul sat on the edge of the bed, as naked as she was.

"I'll go see who it is. You've got to get dressed but don't come down unless I call you." She glanced at the clock. From her new angle, she could see the face. "Christ, it's only six o'clock in the morning. What the hell is going on?" She slipped into her robe, cinching it tightly across her waist and pulling it together so that the upper part of her body was well covered. She left a befuddled Paul behind as he scanned the room looking for his scattered clothing.

When Linda arrived at the bottom of the stairs and was able to see around the corner to the kitchen door, she stopped moving altogether and leaned against the doorjamb. "Shit! Shit, shit, shit!" she swore.

Tommy continued his attack on the door, hammering so hard that the dead bolt lock strained at its screws. Linda took a deep breath and entered the kitchen. Tommy saw her coming through the same window where he had watched the show the night before. He stopped knocking, smiled in at her and pointed to the doorknob, an obvious indication that he wanted to come in. Her grim frown pushed his smile into oblivion.

"What are you doing here?" she shouted through the closed door.

Tommy put his hands together in the prayer mode he learned in his brief sojourn into Catholic school, his fingers perfectly steepled together and thumbs crossed. "Please?" he pantomimed, his mouth exaggerating the word like an actor in a silent movie.

"This is completely ridiculous," Linda fumed as she unlatched the dead bolt.

Once Tommy gained entrance, his friendly façade evaporated.

"What the fuck are you thinking, Linda? I thought you were trying to get yourself straightened out." Tommy had Linda backing across the kitchen as he moved closer. "And where's Freeman? His goddamn car is still here."

As if on cue, Paul came pounding down the stairs. He had missed two buttons on his shirt, the fly of his pants was unzipped, and his shoes were untied. His appearance would have been comical in a different setting, the situation duplicating so many scenes in television dramas where a panicked lover tries to escape before the cuckolded husband gets home. In this one, his appearance fueled the anger of Tommy Iverson, especially with Linda standing there in her robe, which by now had a dramatic gap revealing that she had nothing else on.

"Get the fuck out of here, now!" Tommy's low growl left little room for argument but Paul tried to save face.

"You can't talk to me that way. Who do you think you are? You can't charge in here and start telling..." He stopped speaking as Iverson approached him with balled fists, rage contorting his reddened face.

"I'll tell you who I am," Tommy hissed. "I'm the guy who is going to beat the living shit out of you if you don't clear out."

"You've not heard the last of this, Iverson. You can bet on that," Freeman said as he put his hand on the doorknob. "I'll call you later, Linda, just to make sure this nutcase left right behind me."

The insult seemed to change Tommy's mind. "Wait just a second. I want a witness to this." He turned to Linda, who cowered in a neutral corner, looking around as if searching for a safe escape route.

"Right now, in front of him," he said, jerking his head in Paul's direction, "I want you to tell me that you don't love me, that you never want to see me again. Go ahead, tell me that it's over—that you're done with it. Just say it now in front of him and I'll never bother you again." Tommy had actually sunk to one knee, as though making a marriage proposal. "I just want to hear it, that's all. Freeman will be your witness."

"Why do you have to force me into this?" Linda's anger overcame her sense of decorum as she came out of her corner like a prize fighter in the first round of a title fight. As she crossed the room and entered Tommy's personal space, her robe fell open even further, revealing her ample cleavage. "Okay, if that's what you want, here you go." Her voice quivered. "I don't love you, Tommy. I'm not sure now if I ever did. Are you satisfied? Is that what you had to hear? And now why don't you get the hell out of here. Just go home, will you?"

LINDA STARTED THE COFFEE pot, then trudged up the stairs to her bedroom. The faint aroma of Paul's presence from the night before made her hesitate as she entered the room. "Tommy's probably right," she muttered. "What in the hell was I thinking?"

She threw her robe onto the bed. Her reflection in the full-length mirror hanging on the wall froze her in place. Since she had filed the divorce papers, she had lost almost fifteen pounds, all from the right places. "Not bad for a thirty-six-year-old," she muttered as she rummaged through her drawers for underwear.

Fifteen minutes after Paul and Tommy had left, still snarling at each other but with much of the intensity missing after her passionate scolding left both speechless, Linda sat at the kitchen table sipping a cup of coffee, trying without much success to calm down. The rest of the day stretched out before her with only her morning stint at the office offering any respite. It was only six-thirty on Saturday morning; she was alone, missing her children and the pure joy they brought into her life. With her work day not scheduled to begin until nine, she decided to combine one of her least favorite chores with a short visit with one of her best friends in the hope that they might set a more positive tone for the day. The first half hour had already drained her energy for facing the rest of it.

THE LOCAL LANDFILL OPERATION, especially early on a Saturday morning, was a busy place. When Linda arrived with her weekly allotment of two plastic bags of trash in the back of her station wagon, the gate was not yet open. She was fourth in line and sat tapping her fingers on the steering wheel for ten minutes while waiting for the foreman to walk out to unlock the entrance. She watched as the three pickup trucks moved forward. The first truck stopped at the dumpster and the driver got out. He was soon joined by the other two drivers, who seemed fascinated by watching the process of pitching trash bags into the huge bin. The thrumming of fingers on the wheel increased in intensity as the three men became engaged in a lively conversation. She moved her hand to the horn but the trio broke up just before she was going to lean on it.

By the time she pulled up to the bin, two of the employees stood ready to help her. They had been nowhere in sight for the pickup trucks. She lowered her window.

"Morning, Mrs. Phillips," one of the men shouted. "Give you a hand with this stuff?" He was already standing at the back of the wagon.

"Thanks, Jack, but I can manage." The other man opened her door and offered his hand to help her out. She ignored it and climbed out. Before she reached the rear of the car, Jack held one bag and a tug of war was going on over the other one.

"Nice that you boys want to fight over my trash," Linda said, winking, "but I'm really pretty capable."

The tug of war ended with her grabbing the second bag and hoisting it over the side. Jack threw the other one in, then backed away. "Always happy to help a beautiful woman," he said, elbowing his colleague in the ribs. They stood there staring, as she walked away.

"I hear them newly divorced girls are something else," he said as she drove off, throwing them an enthusiastic wave. "And I hear Mrs. Phillips is among the best of them."

"Hearing about her's about as close as you're ever going to get." The comment drew another poke in the ribs, mixed in with a chuckle as they returned her wave.

LORETTA JAMES STOOD AT her kitchen sink, washing the few dishes left over from breakfast. The two bird feeders hanging right outside the window overflowed with a flock of rose-breasted grosbeaks, going through their rotating turns at the sunflower seeds. The sight of them combined with the beautiful early spring morning had Loretta whistling. The slight chirp of skidding tires wheeling into her driveway startled her out of the pleasant reverie. She grabbed a dishtowel and dried her hands. Seconds later, she was outside and standing at the end of the long driveway.

Linda seemed to out of her car before it rolled to a complete stop.

After a clinging hug, they separated and looked at one another. Linda's eyes filled. "It's Tommy and Paul. It was just an awful scene." She stuttered to a pause, allowing Loretta just enough space to join the conversation.

"What is it? What's going on? Where are the kids?" Loretta's staccato questions left her short of breath.

"The kids are fine. They're with Shane for the weekend. I thought I'd told you."

"That's right, you did. I just forgot. But let's get back to why you're here," Loretta said, her patience almost exhausted.

"Look, I really can't stay long. I've got to work today, at least until one, but I've just got to tell someone. I was terrified that something terrible was going to happen."

"Now you're scaring me. Tell me," Loretta commanded, placing her hands on Linda's shoulders like an elementary school teacher getting the attention of a reluctant student.

Linda drew in a deep breath, then let it out with a heavy sigh. "Okay. I'm okay now." She sucked in another long breath, then began her story. It came out in bursts, with hesitations between each, as if she were picking and choosing what to include. As she finished, the tears started again.

"I've never seen Tommy so angry. His face was practically purple. I thought for sure there was going to be a big fight." She used the sleeve of her sweater to wipe her face, giving Loretta her first chance to react.

"So you went to dinner with Mr. Sleazeball, then had him come back to your house? What were you thinking?"

"Seems like I'm getting asked that question a lot lately. It was just two friends who were alone and decided to get something to eat. What's wrong with that?" Linda had recovered enough to slip into defensive indignation.

"You were so upset when you got here. I thought it had just happened but you've had a whole night to sleep on it. I can't imagine what you must've been like last night." Linda looked down at her running shoes, losing eye contact with her friend for the first time in the entire episode. "They both left at the same time," she mumbled. "Listen, I really appreciate your listening to my tale of woe but I'd better get going or I'll be late for work." She leaned into another long hug, providing

Loretta with the briefest of opportunities to whisper into her ear.

"You're not quite telling me everything, are you?"

Linda broke away from the hug and hurried to her car. "Thanks again, my good friend," she shouted, leaving the question hanging in the air between them.

Loretta watched the car glide back toward the street. She answered the perfunctory wave with one of her own.

"You're welcome," she whispered. "But, my also good friend, you'd better be careful."

STEVE CHAMBERS GREETED LINDA with his usual warmth when she arrived ten minutes early for work.

"How did everything go last night?" he asked.

"What do you mean, last night?"

Steve, surprised at the question and the tone that came with it, backtracked. "Sorry, didn't mean to pry. I meant with Shane picking up the kids. You've said he's not always dependable; I just wondered..."

"I'm sorry, Steve. I've just been on edge lately—too much going on in my life right now. You're kind to ask. Everything went well and I had a night off. Kind of quiet without the kids, you know?"

"Well, that's good." With an unsure grin, Steve retreated to his office.

Five minutes later, the first phone call of the day came into the office. Linda answered with her practiced professional response, a cheerful verbal smile welcoming a potential client. Her demeanor changed dramatically when she heard the voice on the other end.

"It's me. Listen, something's come up. I'm going to leave the kids at my mother's for today. They haven't seen her for a while and she's been bugging me to let them have a sleepover. You don't mind, do you? I'll still have them back tomorrow on schedule."

"What could have possibly come up between yesterday and this morning? Honestly, Shane, you really make me angry. They'll be fine with her, I know that, but you are just so damn irresponsible." Her rising voice left no doubt of her state of mind. "I could drive out there and get them if that would be better."

"No, don't do that." His harshness matched hers. "If you do that, then I'll have two women pissed off at me. Just pretend I didn't tell you. I mean, I didn't have to, right? I'll see you tomorrow, right on time." He hung up.

The rest of the morning crawled by with only a few calls. At five of twelve, Steve came out of his office and offered to cover the last hour of her shift for her. Linda, her stomach in aching knots ever since Shane's call, put up a token fight.

"You covered for me yesterday. I don't feel right about this again. How about if you take the afternoon off, play golf, relax. I've got nowhere to go and nothing to do."

Steve refuted her argument with the ultimate logic of a salesman. "It only takes one. At four this afternoon, someone might come in and buy that million-dollar place on the river. You just never know."

"Thanks. I guess I'll take advantage of your offer once again." She smiled and was out the door.

# Four

*Saturday Afternoon, May 9, 1992*

LINDA WALKED PAST THE blinking machine. An orange six flashed at her. "Six messages. Everybody knows I usually work on Saturday mornings," she murmured. With a sigh, she sat at the small desk in the corner of the kitchen and pushed the play button.

"First message: Friday, 11:35 p.m." the mechanical voice began. The first message brought her to a standing position, staring down at the phone. She glanced around, as if expecting someone to be peering over her shoulder.

The robotic voice droned on. "End of message. To erase this message, press delete. To hear the message again, press repeat. Next message: Saturday, 9:20 a.m." Linda pushed the stop button. Her hand shook as she started the messages playing from the beginning. The jarring first message played a second time.

"I fucking hate you!" Tommy's voice crackled with emotion. Linda's eyes filled with tears. Everyone who knew her would attest to the fact that she was a kind and gentle person who wanted to be liked. Some even saw this as a flaw in her character. "You can't keep everybody happy all the time, Linda," Loretta told her on more than one occasion.

The call from Tommy was obviously the one that Paul insisted that she not answer. She sat down again, recovering from the initial shock of the harshness of the first, and played through the remaining messages. The second and sixth were from Loretta, first calmly

21

asking that she return the call, then, with renewed urgency, insisting that she call her back as soon as possible. "I'm worried sick about you," she said as she closed the message.

The third and fifth calls were from Shane, both asking what she planned to do for the weekend. "All alone, without the kids. You'll probably be having a grand old time," he said during the first message. The second didn't mention the children but requested a return call so that he could know where she was, "in case I have to get in touch with you." Each call ended with an unnerving edge of intensity. The fourth call came from another friend, Yvonne DiMartini, a woman several years older than Linda but also a recent divorcée who traveled in the same social circle and shared her sense of freedom as they escaped from abusive relationships. Her message was simple. "Want to hit the Grille tonight?" she asked. "Girls night out!"

Linda placed her finger on the erase button, ready to eliminate all the calls, when the phone rang. The answering machine and phone formed a combination unit and she grabbed the receiver before the second ring. Loretta opened the conversation before Linda had the chance to say anything.

"God, I'm glad you're home. I was just going to leave another message. I've thought of nothing else since you left. Something's going on, Linda. And how come you're out of work so early?" Linda started to explain but her friend interrupted. "Never mind; that's not important but this is."

A stern five-minute lecture on the dangers of keeping what Loretta called her stable of men dangling on a string came to an end with a frightening admonition. "You have got to call it off with Tommy; I mean, no being nice, no being kind, no being compassionate. Tell him it's over. And don't pull that stuff about still being friends. That never works, especially with guys like Tommy. I think he's dangerous. I've seen his temper first hand." She was breathless when she finished.

"I did tell him exactly that this morning. I used almost those exact words and Paul Freeman heard everything I said to him." Linda vacillated between irritation at the personal intrusion and gratitude for Loretta's concern. "And, besides, he'd never do anything to hurt me. He's actually a pretty gentle guy."

"Yeah, I've known guys like that: pretty gentle except when they're not." Loretta went silent for a moment. "Hey, what did you mean about this morning? I thought all that stuff happened last night."

Linda, caught in a flat-out lie, blushed and tried to recoup. "I meant last night; not sure what I was thinking…"

"Bullshit, Linda. You spent the whole night with Paul, didn't you? You just didn't want me to know about it, right?" Her voice gave nothing away—it was impossible for Linda to tell if she was angry, pleased, or somewhere in between.

"Listen, I didn't intend to do it but the stuff he brought over was so good and the next thing I knew we were in bed. Plus, with that guy, who I'm thinking maybe was Tommy, peering in the window and catching us in the kitchen, I guess I felt better with him staying here."

Loretta's tone of voice underwent a transformation. "All I'm saying is that you'd better be careful. As much as everyone loves you, my dear, you are seriously pissing some people off. What do you think Dolores Freeman would do if she ever finds out? Shane's your almost official ex—what do you think he'd do if he knew about the stuff you're doing. He still thinks he owns you. You could lose your kids. As I said, and I mean this, you'd better be a little more discreet; if not, you'd better watch out." She hung up without giving Linda a chance to respond.

Linda sat with the phone in her hand as the dial tone morphed into the high-pitched wail used to alert homeowners that the phone was off the hook. Dazed, she let it slip; it crashed into the cradle and bounced off the table, dangling by the cord.

"What am I doing?" she said to the walls that now seemed to her to be closing in.

"WHAT DO YOU WANT, Shane?" After a lunch of two slices of three-day-old pizza and a cold beer, Linda had recovered from Loretta's lecture enough to respond to her soon-to-be ex-husband's call. In just two more days, the final hearing would be over and she'd be able to change the soon-to-be status to permanent. Her curiosity about his motive for calling increased as she realized they had nothing else to talk about. The arrangements for the children were all made; it wasn't as if they spoke on a regular basis anyway.

"Thanks for calling me back, Linda," Shane said after answering on the first ring. "I was just feeling bad about taking the girls away from you on Mothers' Day, you know?"

"Forget the apologies. Feeling bad doesn't fit your persona. Now, what did you really want?" She teetered on the verge of hanging up before he answered.

"You are one tough lady. I just hoped you'd be planning something big tonight so you wouldn't be alone. Are you?" Shane could operate on so many levels, ranging from charming and warm to vicious and vindictive. He was solidly in his charming mode. "Give me a break, Linda; I'm just checking in because I care about you. We were married for eleven years. You can't ignore that fact. So, what do you got going on tonight? A heavy date? What?"

"Nothing planned and certainly not a heavy date. Curling up with a good book and having a quiet Saturday night by myself is sounding pretty good right now. You're nice to ask but I've got to go. Don't forget to have the kids back here on time. And, by the way, Shane, I don't have to answer to you at all, and after Monday, I won't ever have to speak with you again. You'll be the loser. Bye."

Shane's answer echoed in the empty sound of Linda's disconnected phone.

"You are such a bitch. We'll just see who the real loser turns out to be."

ONE MORE FRIENDLY VISIT convinced Linda how she should spend some of her Saturday afternoon. Linda approached Nelson Thompson's house under a suffocating trepidation even though she knew Patty should be at work. A quick glance up the driveway showed no sign of Patty's car. She hurried up the steps to the side door and rang the bell. The surprise on Nelson's face when he opened the door drained her confidence immediately.

"I've made a mistake. I shouldn't have come here." She turned to leave but Nelson stepped onto the landing and grabbed her arm.

"Wait a second, Linda. What the heck are you talking about?" He relaxed his grip but still held her arm firmly.

"I really can't stay. I left the kids playing and told them I'd be right back. Junior's great for a nine-year-old but I don't want to push my luck." Enough of the tension emptied from her that Nelson let her arm go.

"You came for a reason, Linda, so let's hear it. If you want me to come back to your house, I'll do that, but something's going on."

FOR NINE YEARS, THE Thompsons had been neighbors in Hampton Village, Sally and Nelson living just two houses away, but their acquaintance consisted of a few waves and hellos over that span of time. Linda had heard that Sally Thompson had moved to California about two years before after reigniting a high school romance at a reunion, leaving Nelson and their seven-year-old daughter behind. Five months before, Linda had her first real conversation with Nelson Thompson at a New Year's Eve gathering. Since connecting at the party, Linda and Nelson had visited back and forth on numerous occasions, purely as friends and parenting comrades. Patty Hamilton, Nelson's live-in girlfriend for the last year, knew Linda. On the surface, she seemed not to object to the platonic nature of the relationship. Patty's outwardly calm acceptance of the friendship began to erode when the pair hired a babysitter for their four children and attended a dinner show in Hartford. Several weeks of almost daily phone conversations between the two finally led to a hostile confrontation on Linda's front lawn on Thursday, just a day before her dinner with Paul Freeman.

When Linda arrived home from work that day, she noticed Patty sitting in a lawn chair on the front porch. At first concerned that something had happened to Nelson, she instructed the children to stay in the car. She lowered all of the windows but was not out of the car before Patty had jumped down from the porch and stood with her hands on her hips, glowering. The presence of the children had no impact on her rage.

"Stay the hell away from Nelson. I'm warning you," Patty screamed, loud enough so that most of the neighborhood heard it through the open windows sucking in the first warm day of the spring. At first, Linda was so taken back that she could only stammer a reply.

"What are you talking about? We're friends, that's all. I..."

"Bullshit, Linda! It's pretty obvious when you're talking on the phone all the time. I can see where this is going and I'm telling you again. Stay away from him. You've got plenty more going on and you sure as hell don't need still another boyfriend." She turned her back, stomped across the lawn and disappeared around the corner of the house.

Tonie, Jackie, and Shane Jr. had unbuckled their seat belts and the open car window framed their shocked faces. "What's Miss Hamilton so mad about, Mom?" Shane asked.

"She's just a little upset, honey. It's really nothing to worry about." Relief flooded across all three young faces, the intrinsic trust in their mother and the knowledge that she had everything under control showing in their smiles. Linda herded them inside for their after school snack, hoping to suppress the incident with a heavy dose of cookies and milk.

Patty Hamilton had thoroughly frightened her.

ONLY FIVE MINUTES HAD passed when Linda finished her breathless description of the Tommy Iverson incident with Paul Freeman. "So, this all happened last night. Has Iverson come around at all today?" Nelson asked, his face a solemn mask of worry lines.

Linda turned her back to him, waited a few seconds as if gathering strength. When she turned back, tears streamed down her cheeks. "Oh, shit," she said. "You'll probably find out anyway. Tommy came around early this morning. That's when the whole thing started. Paul spent the night."

Nelson blanched as the significance of what she said washed over him. "You let that goddamned drug dealer spend the night with you? Jesus, Linda!" This time he turned his back on her.

"You've got way more problems than I can help you with," he said, the words bouncing off the wall. "I'll tell you one thing you've got to do and that's get Tommy Iverson out of your life."

Linda put her hand on his shoulder and gently turned him around. Her tears had stopped, leaving dried streaks of mascara behind. "I pretty much told him we were done this morning, but we know he hasn't taken hints before. He's a good guy but there's nothing there anymore. I'm going to see him one more time this afternoon and that will be it."

"Do me a favor and talk to him in a public place. I'll even go with you if you want. He might be a good guy, but his temper scares the hell out of me." Nelson stared at her, awaiting a reply.

"He'd never hurt me; if I ever wind up dead, it'll be Shane who did it." She broke eye contact and looked down. The next few words came out in a whisper. "I'm not scared for myself, but I'm terrified for the kids." She raised her eyes and looked directly at Nelson. "My biggest fear is not that he'll kill me. It's that he'll wind up with the kids."

"Now you're scaring me. What can I do to help?"

"Nothing, really. You've got your hands full with Patty. I'll take care of Tommy Iverson today, and it'll be on his turf so he knows I'm not afraid of him. Then on Monday, I'll finally be rid of Shane. My life turns around this weekend." She reached for his hand and gave it a gentle squeeze. "Thanks, Nelson. I appreciate your friendship. You're a kind man."

THE CALL SHOCKED TOMMY. When Linda told him that she wanted to meet him at his cabin at the hunting lodge that afternoon, he figured she had changed her mind. Why would she travel for over an hour just to tell him again what she told him that morning? The only possible reason he could imagine was that she realized afterward that she'd made a mistake. He was the one who had always been on her side. He was the one who had encouraged her when she said she needed to get away from Shane. He was always there to help with the house, the kids, and even the occasional shortage of cash. She had to be ready to admit that he was the one who helped her keep things together during the restraining order hearing that kept Shane away from her after the initial divorce filing. There was no other possible explanation for her request to meet him at an isolated cabin in the forest.

"Of course, I'll meet you there," he had said, without the slightest hesitation. "We could spend the night, if you'd like." The silence on the other end announced that he had overstepped the limits of the conversation.

"I can only stay an hour or so. If this is causing any trouble, we'll do it another time," Linda finally said.

"No, it's fine with me. How about meeting me there about three?" Tommy asked, wondering what the *it* in "doing it another time" meant.

TOMMY'S CABIN AND HUNTING lodge were situated more than a half mile off of Route 4, in perfect proximity to the open hunting lands of Housatonic State Forest. The dirt road into the compound wound through a stand of magnificent oak trees, their leaves in full bloom thanks to the unusually warm spring. Even with the bright sunlight, the foliage formed a canopy that darkened the road, giving it the ominous feel that venturing into thick forests often provides. The environment added to Linda's trepidation but also reinforced her determination. Her relationship with Tommy Iverson would end permanently today, in the same cabin where it had been consummated eight months before. There would be no ambiguity, even if she had to hurt his feelings. The romance had evolved quickly through the stages, turning from hot to warm to lukewarm to cool. As much as he had helped her, the proverbial spark necessary for sustaining a romantic connection was gone.

The huge clearing showed through the trees about a hundred yards ahead, and Linda felt her respiration and heart rate surge as she approached it. The log cabin came into view, a beautifully crafted home constructed of timber hewn from the property. With the warm sun splashing across the entire site, she expected to see Tommy sitting on the front porch in his rocker, waiting for her. The jitters increased as she got out of the car and approached the cabin.

Linda dressed down for the occasion. She wore no makeup;

her loose fitting jeans and sweat shirt provided no provocations; someone who didn't know her would have thought that she was rather plain in appearance. If Tommy had not already experienced her body in a wide variety of ways, he might have seen her as asexual. She walked up the wooden steps, fashioned from logs left over from the house, and knocked on the door. Tommy's greeting already had her mentally backpedaling.

"You look gorgeous," he announced when he opened the door. "Come on in and I'll get us something to drink."

"I don't think so. I'd rather we just sat out here on the porch," she said as she retreated a step backward.

Tommy's shoulders sagged.

"It's a beautiful day and we might as well enjoy it." She watched his reaction closely. Her excuse for not entering the house did not diffuse his disappointment and was far too transparent.

"Don't want to be alone in the house with me, huh?" he asked, but with a grin. He motioned toward the antique rocker, and Linda sat down. He pulled up a plastic lawn chair opposite her, arranging it so their knees were inches apart. "I understand completely after what you told me this morning, but, you know, as they say, 'hope springs eternal' or something like that. I thought maybe you'd had a change of heart. Like, maybe, you remembered how much I've done for you and the kids." The guilt trip approach was as obvious as hers had been.

"Look, Tommy, I came out here because I was pretty harsh with you this morning but the message really hasn't changed. We've both got to move on. I was vulnerable when we first met and it's not like I don't appreciate all you've done. You've been a Godsend for me."

Tommy picked out the only negative immediately. "So, if you hadn't been vulnerable, you never would have gotten involved with the likes of me, right?"

The conversation was deteriorating and Linda slid out of the rocker, nudging Tommy's knees in the process. He responded with a gentle pressure of his own. She recoiled and he stood as well.

"This was a mistake," Linda said. "I should have just let this morning speak for itself." She left the porch, two steps at a time, and was at the car before Tommy had a chance to respond.

"Linda! Come on, wait a minute," he called, but she had already slammed the door. With a single leap, he was off the porch; his next two steps brought him to the driver's side window. He leaned on the roof, waiting for her to lower the window. She finally let it down less than an inch.

"Just let me go, will you?" she shouted.

Tommy grinned. "Sure you don't want to hang around a bit longer? I'll bet I could show you a better time than Paul Freeman, but it would have been with a beer instead of coke." He continued to lean on the car, even when Linda put it in gear.

"I'm going and you'd better back off or you're going to get hurt." She began to inch forward and Tommy backed away, holding up his hands in an "I give up" sign. As soon as she saw that he was clear, she punched the gas enough to make the tires spin. Spraying dust and dirt behind, she careened back down the road, leaving Tommy standing in the haze. She could barely see him in the rearview mirror, unable to distinguish his gestures. His right arm was extended in what could have been a friendly wave, except for the middle finger jutting toward the sky in the universal salute of contempt.

THE RIDE HOME ALLOWED ample time for considering her predicament. The first items on her agenda were several phone calls to allay the concerns of her friends about her relationship with Tommy. Next, she would have to extricate herself from the clichéd tangled web of deceit she wove as she tried to keep her life in balance. Lying to her best friend about when the confrontation with Tommy had taken place troubled her, but she knew that Loretta would be upset, even angry, with her for allowing Paul to spend the night. Nelson's reaction verified that. If, as religious types were inclined to believe, everything happened for a reason, maybe the chaos of the start of the weekend would prove to be helpful.

"I'm leading a double life," she said aloud as she sped down Route 4 toward home, "and one of them is totally screwed up."

While not a true epiphany, her admission came close enough. The remainder of the trip home blurred as her mind churned with a jumble of thoughts and plans. This Mothers' Day would be a turning point in her life.

LINDA MARCHED INTO THE house, determined to take control of the life that threatened to destroy the relationships that she had worked so hard to establish. She was greeted, as usual, by the flashing numeral on the message machine. "Four new messages," she grumbled. She paused at the counter and pushed the play button.

"You have four new messages and six old messages. First new message..."

Shane's voice affected her like fingernails on a blackboard, sending enough chills to make her shiver. The content of the first two calls from him was virtually the same. When the second one ended, she responded as if he were standing in the room with her.

"Why the hell are you so interested in what I'm doing tonight?" she said to the machine. "It's none of your damned business anyway."

Nelson's voice on the third message had the opposite effect, calming her nerves with his gentle tone and considerate inquiry. "Hi, Linda. Just wondering how your visit with Tommy went and how you are doing. I'll talk to you tomorrow. We're on our way out for the rest of the evening. Take care." She heard Patty's voice screeching in the background, asking who was on the phone just as he disconnected.

Loretta's message simply said, "Just checking in. Call me."

At five thirty, Linda poured a large glass of Cabernet and sat in her favorite padded lawn chair on the veranda, savoring the warmth of the spring sun just settling into the oak trees at the rear of her property. The two brief but pithy conversations with Loretta and Nelson reinforced her determination. She had had her fun with her newfound freedom; she was ready to move on. Loretta's firm warning about her plans for the evening reverberated in her head after she hung up.

"You're not going to the Grille tonight, right?"

"No need to worry about that," she had said. She wouldn't be going to the Village Grille this Saturday night. Although confident that she could withstand the enticements that always were present in that environment, Linda would not bother with what the Catholic nuns of her long-ago past called occasions of sin. The easy availability of high-end drugs, alcohol, and casual sex defined an occasion of sin, a place where temptation could be overwhelming. She looked forward to an evening beginning with a pizza and a beer and ending with a favorite old movie and an early bedtime. Tomorrow, Mothers' Day, would truly be a cause for celebration.

# Five

*Saturday Evening, May 9, 1992*

"Hi, Mrs. Phillips. What can I do for you today?" Rob Kelly called out to her from behind the counter before she had closed the door. "Let me guess—starting your Mothers' Day celebration early with one of our delicious pizzas, right?" His infectious grin and always cheerful disposition made him such an asset to Kelly's Pizzeria that she never considered trying another shop.

"Where are those adorable kids of yours?" His innocent question surprised her, wiping away the euphoria of the good mood she had been riding for the last couple of hours. She turned away, struggling to keep her composure. She seemed ready to bolt from the store when Rob's call stopped her.

"Are you okay? Did I say something wrong?" He watched as she drew in a deep breath, then faced him.

"It's nothing, Rob. Don't worry about it. The kids are with their father and I'm just missing them. I'm feeling kind of silly right now. Not sure where this came from," Linda said, wiping her eyes with her sleeve. "I'll just have a plain old cheese pizza, the medium one, and I'll be back in about fifteen minutes to pick it up."

Rob's relief was palpable. He retreated to the kitchen to place the order while she left the store.

TONY LUPPINETTI, THE OWNER of Village Video, watched as Linda walked across the parking lot toward his store.

"She is one fine-looking woman," he remarked to Martha, who was standing right next to him. His wife just let loose with one of her patented patient smiles.

"You pretty much say that about most of the women who come in here. Lucky I'm not the jealous type." She called out a cheerful greeting as Linda entered the store.

Linda acknowledged her with a brief wave and proceeded directly to the comedy section. Within minutes, she was at the checkout counter, with Tony jostling his wife aside so he could wait on her.

"A double feature for tonight, huh, Linda? I'm surprised you wouldn't be going out somewhere special on a Saturday night. Maybe even the Grille. I hear that's a real interesting place these days," he said with a flirtatious leer.

"Nope, just a quiet night at home for me. It's been a real busy week and I'm ready for some down time." Linda looked at him and slid the two movies closer, trying to move the transaction along. Martha reached around Tony and picked up the VHS tapes.

"Two of my favorites, guaranteed to put you in a good mood. You've got about four hours of watching here," she said. She checked out the tapes and slipped them into a bag. Tony remained directly in the way until she swung a hip, jarring him aside. "Have a good evening, Linda."

Linda paid, then grabbed the bag with a mumbled thanks, and left the store.

Tony and Martha watched her all the way to her car. "Like I said, a fine-looking woman," Tony repeated, and absorbed the good-natured elbow in the ribs from his long-suffering wife. "Looks like she might not be watching those movies alone, though," he observed, as Tommy Iverson approached her car.

"SO, WHAT'VE YOU GOT?" Tommy's appearance at her car shocked her into silence, followed quickly by a hostile glare and an uncharacteristic response.

"What the fuck are you doing here?" Linda already was shaking, her anger apparent even to the interested spectators in the Village Video Store.

"Hey, come on, relax. I saw your car in the lot and thought I'd just see if everything was okay. There's no need to be upset." Tommy softened his voice and, as he so often did with women, switched her animosity to his advantage. "We're clearly just friends now and if friends see friends, they stop and chat, right?"

Linda looked around the lot. They were alone. She looked back at the video store but the one-way, reflective windows exposed nothing.

"So, what movie did you get?" Tommy asked, revealing that he must have been following her and knew that she had been in Village Video.

"Look, Tommy, I don't see this leading anywhere but a bad place so why don't you go on home or head to the Grille or something? I'm just not up to dealing with this."

Tommy didn't say a word. He just stared at her. After a full minute of silence, Linda relented.

"Okay. If this is going to be what you are saying it is, how about if I invite a friend back to the house to share a pizza, a beer, and a movie? Then, that friend goes home without so much as a good night hug." Linda had the car door open, ready for whatever might come next.

"Sounds like a good deal to me," Tommy said. "I'll promise on my Boy Scouts' honor to behave and do just as you want me to do."

"You are incorrigible, Tommy Iverson. You so much as lay a finger on me, I'll break your neck. Understood?"

"So, what's the movie?" He smiled at her the way he had months before, when they consummated their intimate relationship.

"Actually, it's a double feature tonight, but with no popcorn. I got *When Harry Met Sally* and *City Slickers*. It'll be good having the company of a friend to watch them. I'll pick up the pizza and see you back at the house." Linda got into her car, closed the door, and screamed. "What in the name of all that is holy am I doing!"

Rob had the pizza at the counter waiting.

"I saw you coming," he said, grinning and with the pizza box in hand. "Here you go," he said, "enjoy. And I'm sorry to have upset you." He looked her straight in the eye. "I can't believe he has your children on Mothers' Day."

Linda handed him a ten-dollar bill for the six-dollar pizza. "Keep the change, Rob, and thanks a lot. Your dad's lucky to have such a fine young man." She stopped at the door and looked back. "I guess I can't believe it either," she said over her shoulder, then she was gone, leaving a bewildered Rob staring after her.

THE FOUR HOURS PASSED in the strangest silence that Linda had ever experienced. The only words spoken came from Tommy midway through City Slickers, the second film, when he announced that he had to use the facilities. Linda pressed the pause button, resulting in a static picture which threatened to implode at any second. Tommy returned just before the player slipped out of pause mode, the implosion avoided. They continued to watch the movie to its philosophical conclusion.

"So, Linda, what would you consider your worst day?" Tommy asked, a question inspired by the character Mitch Robbins in the film. Billy Crystal, as Mitch, answers the question with the profound observation that his best day and his worst day were one in the same—the day his father walked out on his family. Tommy, apparently searching for some equally profound response, was disappointed.

"I'd actually rather not say," Linda announced. "Anyway, thanks for coming over and keeping me company for the movies. I appreciate that." Her dismissive message contained not the least bit of subtlety. She stood and walked him to the kitchen door, a door just a foot away from the large picture window facing the expansive porch surrounding the house.

It was 11:30 p.m. Twenty-four hours before, Tommy had peered through that very window, watching a live porn show starring Linda and Paul Freeman. Now, here he was, in the same room with her, doubtless wishing to repeat the show with him in a starring role. Almost as if she could read his thoughts, her body tensed and she inched further away from him. Her stiffness informed him that he might be dreaming, or, more realistically, hallucinating.

"I guess I'll be going," he said, as if he had a choice. "I'll check in with you tomorrow."

Linda just looked at him without saying a word.

"And you're sure you're okay?"

"Yes, actually, I am." She reached around him and opened the door.

She had less than three hours to live.

# Six

*Sunday Morning, May 10, 1992*

LINDA CLOSED THE DOOR behind Tommy, giggling as it tapped him on his rear.

"And don't let the door hit you in the butt on the way out," she said to herself, her giggle evolving into a chuckle. During the movies, she heard the phone ring several times, but knowing how pausing a movie on a VHS tape player usually caused issues, she allowed the answering machine to pick up the calls. The flashing orange number in the window of the machine showed the total number of calls as thirteen; she hadn't erased any all weekend and wasn't about to go through them at midnight. The first new message was from Loretta James, and listening to it shook her so much that she stopped the playback after she heard it.

"I just drove by your house and saw Iverson's car in the driveway. I almost stopped to check on you. I have to say that I am shocked that you have him over there. What was all that bullshit about ending the relationship? I'm hoping that he's not a welcome guest. Call me if you need help. I'll come right over, no matter what time it is." Linda tried to read the emotion in her friend's voice but couldn't separate the mix of anger, disappointment, and concern.

"I'll need to straighten that out in the morning," she said to the machine.

She looked around the kitchen and decided that any cleanup could wait until morning.

"What a day this has been," she said aloud, rubbing her temples. "Great! Now I'm talking to myself."

She flipped the kitchen light off, went into the living room, and turned on the television. On the rare occasions when she was alone in the house overnight, she liked having the white noise of the downstairs television as company. After selecting the CNN cable news channel, one that assured her of talking heads for the duration of the night, she dimmed the overhead light and climbed the single flight of stairs to her bedroom. Her nighttime routines were simple. The safe environment of Hampton Village precluded any need for locking doors, the house wide open to anyone who might want to enter. Once in her bedroom, she turned on the television, again not to search for a favorite program but to cover the creaks and groans of the old house and the occasional tree branch scraping the siding or a window. A person sleeping in the house for the first time would spend much of the night deciphering what the various noises were, but for Linda, the soft, monotonous sounds of the television worked as well as any sleep remedy she had ever taken. Often, the twins would appear at her bedside somewhere between one and two o'clock; when they did, she gathered them into her bed, where they would curl up like two kittens against their mother. With them gone for the night, she knew she would awaken around the same time, waiting for them to arrive, until she realized that she was alone for the night. The complexities of her life appeared to now be under her control. Would they still be when she awakened to a new day?

By twelve fifteen, she was asleep, the ambient light from a lamppost outside and the glow from the television combining to cast enough light to create strange shadows across the wall. She slept soundly for more than an hour, and then awoke to a different sound that somehow penetrated the monotonous drone of the two televisions. The soft click was unmistakable, unique enough to bring her to a sitting position in bed. The universal questions of anyone alone in a house in the middle of the night began their pummeling.

*Did I imagine it? Was it a dream? Is there someone in the house? Should I investigate?* Her one-sided debate ended after she listened intently for several moments and heard nothing more than the usual sounds of an old house. She lay back down, staring at the ceiling until her pulse rate returned to normal. The draining effect of her day overcame any concern and soon she was asleep once more. She didn't hear the soft swoosh of the door to her bathroom being pushed open.

THE KILLER KNEW THERE was no margin for error. Every risk factor had been calculated precisely, leaving nothing to chance. The grass muted the soft footfalls along the edge of the long driveway. The end of the paved section brought the trek to a standstill. There were no unexpected vehicles in the parking area. A glance up, first at the veranda which circled the east side of the house then upwards to the second floor, showed no signs of movement. The flickering bluish haze from one of the front rooms indicated that a television might be on. Other than that, the darkened house simply stared back.

Fifteen minutes were allotted to accomplish the mission. After that, everything would fall into place. If there happened to be one of Linda's lovers sharing her bed, he would have to go too.

Efficiency was the key to success.

The route to Linda's bedroom through the old-fashioned attached barn was the safest. The side door of the barn, always unlocked, was standing half open. The killer squeezed through the opening, avoiding any potential squeaks or groans from the rusted hinges. An uneven staircase with narrow wooden steps led to the second floor. Easing up the steps with the bundle proved easier than expected. The sports bag wasn't as bulky as it soon would be. Avoiding any of those things that tend to create an unusual sound—a loose floorboard, a protruding banister, a baseball bat carelessly left leaning against the wall—was crucial so that any light sleepers would not be awakened.

At the landing on the second floor, the muffled sound of a television drifted across from Linda's bedroom. Dressed in a white, hooded Tyvek protective suit replete with booties, an outfit designed to accommodate regular clothing underneath, the killer arrived at the door separating the attic of the barn and the master bathroom. Just a closet-type door with a push button lock separated the attic from the bathroom. A small screwdriver clicked into the lock, the soft sound exacerbated by the surrounding silence and darkness. The killer froze in place, like a young child in a game of freeze tag. After a momentary hesitation and satisfaction that the noise had not attracted anyone's attention, a gentle push sent the ineffective barrier falling away as easily as a gossamer spider web. Another hesitation at the bathroom door, then another gentle shove opened it with a barely audible purring across the carpet in the bedroom.

Just enough light filtered in from the streetlights to illuminate the bathroom. Once inside, the bed showed clearly through the open door to the bedroom, the flickering television casting an eerie light over Linda. She was sleeping alone this night.

At the bathroom doorway, the attacker slowly set the bag down and reached into it, extracting the freshly sharpened knife.

"WHAT THE HELL . . . ?" LINDA'S final words ended with a soundless scream as she managed to turn her head toward her attacker. A hand slammed against her mouth, stifling any chance to call out. A thumb and forefinger clamped her nose shut. Instinct took control, but before she could raise her arm in defense, the narrow blade penetrated the back of her neck. She was limp and unconscious in seconds. There was no fighting back as the murderer stabbed and slashed at the body. The life of Linda Phillips bled out on the floor of her bedroom, contaminating the month old carpet with a spreading red stain and a stigma that could never be washed away.

# Seven

*Sunday Morning, May 10, 1992, 7:30 A.M.*

TOMMY IVERSON PERFORMED A perfect three-point turn at the top of the driveway so the car faced the veranda and the kitchen windows. He flipped the ignition switch and the engine sputtered to a stop. His palms moistened the steering wheel as he squeezed it as if the car remained in motion. The huge old house radiated a foreboding starkness despite the rising sun glinting off the windows facing the east. Tommy sat staring at the house, contemplating his next move. Linda was sure to be sleeping.

"What am I doing here?" he whispered.

Drawing in a deep breath, he removed his hands from the wheel and wiped them across the front of his shirt. He exited the car, catching himself before his habit of slamming the door behind him took control. He held the door as it closed, careful not to allow it to make so much as a click. Almost on tiptoe, he approached the wooden steps leading to the back of the veranda and heading straight at the kitchen door. Several of the stairs sagged and groaned under his weight even as he tried to tread lightly. He did a slide step to the right and leaned into one of the stained glass panels that framed the door. Although the colorful window was opaque, a crazed, fun-house-style view of the kitchen was possible through a red, diamond-shaped section in the center. He cupped his hands against his forehead, reducing the glare from the sun, and peered into the room.

The distorted scene still allowed him to see the coffee pot centered on the kitchen counter. It confirmed his expectation that Linda must still be asleep. Early in their relationship, he discovered that the first thing she did every morning was come downstairs and start a full pot of coffee. If the coffee was not brewing, Linda was not awake. Tommy reached for the doorknob with his left hand, knowing that it was sure to be unlocked. He turned it, gave a light push, and the door swung open with a shrill screech.

"Shit!" he exclaimed. "I'm going to scare her to death." He remembered another trait that became apparent the first time he had spent the night at her house. Linda, always aware and protective of her children, slept lightly. He listened for any sound coming from upstairs, especially from her bedroom. After less than a minute, he made a decision.

"Hey, Linda, come on! Time to rise and shine. It's Mothers' Day. You don't want to waste your whole day sleeping." His shouting up the staircase toward her bedroom produced no perceptible reaction. He walked to the old wooden door separating the barn, where she always parked her car, from the kitchen. A quick check revealed that her car was there. Tommy hollered up the stairs a second time with the same message almost word for word and waited again, this time for a full minute. Again, his boisterous outburst generated no reaction.

"Okay, Linda, ready or not, here I come," he called out and bounded up the steps. When he reached the doorway, he called again, loud enough to be heard over the drone of the television.

"Linda, come on! I know you're in there. Are you teasing me?"

The lack of a response created a fluttering of butterfly wings in his stomach.

"What's going on?" he said, as if asking the question of an obviously upset friend.

The door to the room stood wide open. Tommy leaned just enough to peek around the jamb. Linda's bed was empty. He took two steps into the room, then the large, dark-red spot on the bottom sheet froze him in place. "Oh, Christ!" The exclamation came out so loud that it startled him. His whole body shivered as he crept toward the foot of the bed, driven by an insane curiosity even as the significance of the red blotch struck him like a physical punch in the jaw.

Linda lay on the floor next to the bed; the twisted top sheet wound around her body as if someone had deliberately arranged it to expose the hideous wounds to her upper torso and head.

Tommy's legs buckled; he caught himself but stumbled against the wall behind the bed, his shirt smearing a few large drops of slowly drying blood.

With bile rising in this throat and his stomach roiling, he turned and fled. A minute later, he was on his knees behind his car, the minimal contents of his stomach splattered across the driveway. His retching gradually subsided into dry heaves, leaving him alternately gagging and gasping for air while his eyes watered from the effort, overflowing and streaking down his cheeks. Still partially blinded, he reached out and rested his hand on the rear bumper as he crawled closer. With a deep-throated grunt, he pulled himself up to a standing position and looked around, his face as white as a cattle skull after months in the desert sun.

"Son of a bitch," he said aloud. "I've got to get out of here."

Route 4 early on a Sunday morning was deserted. Tommy's eyes locked into a routine, glancing first forward, then to both side mirrors, and finally to the rearview mirror, with the process repeated over and over again. The speed limit sign of fifty-five went past in a blur as the speedometer crept over seventy. Realizing that exceeding the speed limit might attract attention, even at that time of the morning, he pulled his foot off the gas pedal, slowing to just under the limit. About halfway to his cabin, he slowed for an intersection and made a decision. The Chevron gas station on the corner had only one car at the pumps and the public phone booth sat in an inconspicuous corner of the property. He turned into the station but slowed quickly, avoiding the attention of the lone customer. Within a minute, he found the number for the Connecticut State Police in the phone book hanging precariously by a chain from a graffiti-covered shelf. He fumbled through his pockets and came up with three dimes and a nickel. His quivering hands inserted all four coins, even though the call required just ten cents. The dial tone produced a sigh of relief. He punched in the numbers and almost instantly the dispatcher answered.

"There's been a murder," he shouted. By the time he gave the address, sweat had dampened his forehead. He slammed the receiver down but walked calmly to his car, unnoticed by the man who seemed focused on squeezing every last drop of gas from the nozzle.

Even with the stop, the trip to his cabin consumed less than fifty minutes compared to the normal hour. As he turned into the entrance to his hunting lodge, the right sleeve of his flannel shirt pulled tight against his elbow and he felt a stiffness in the material as it brushed against his skin. A tentative twist of his arm provided a brief look at the cause of the sensation. The smeared red blotch on his shirt could only be one thing. His stomach, completely empty, churned once again when he realized what it was. It was the same elbow that struck the wall as he careened away from Linda's body and down the stairs from her bedroom. He unbuttoned the cuff and pulled the sleeve around for a closer look as he brought the car to a skidding stop a hundred feet short of the lodge. The dried patch of congealed blood was on the outside of the sleeve. It had to be Linda's.

"Oh, my good Christ! I am so thoroughly fucked!" He left the shouted exclamation ricocheting around the car as he trotted toward the cabin. By the time he reached the steps, the offending shirt was off. Ten minutes later, a wood fire heated the interior of the cabin, the pine kindling quickly igniting several well-seasoned oak logs. Tommy waited until the hardwood crackled and popped as the last of the moisture evaporated from its center. Sweat shone on his face, reflecting the fire just a few feet away. Satisfied that the blaze was capable of disintegrating any flammable material tossed into it, he shook his shirt so that it was a single layer and floated it onto the top of the now fiercely burning logs. It burst into flame even before fully settling into the fire.

Two hours later, Tommy returned to the cabin after a lengthy stay at the Empire Diner several miles north on Route 4. The thought of eating even the blandest of breakfasts caused his stomach to clench in rebellion. He chose a booth at the rear of the diner where no waitresses would be passing by with plates trailing the delicious aromas of fried eggs, bacon, or sausage—all menu choices that on a normal Sunday morning might have him salivating. Instead, he ordered a cup of coffee and an English muffin and spent his time staring out the window. An occasional sip from his cup allowed the waitress to return for a warm-up, but the butter-ladened muffin grew cold with not a single bite taken from it.

"Are you okay, Tommy?" Alicia, the waitress, finally asked. "I've never seen you not eat before." The diner always was a favorite with his hunting clients and the shapely Alicia never failed to send the men off to the woods with enough fantasies to last them through a long morning on a stand.

"Thanks for asking, Alicia. Just a bit under the weather this morning. Too much wild partying, you know." Tommy made the joke without his usual smile and Alicia just shook her head and walked off. The Sunday morning crowd was long gone when he decided that the fire would probably have died out. He left a five-dollar bill on the table and headed back to the cabin.

A thin wisp of smoke drifted from the chimney but there were no accompanying shimmering waves of heat. A quick check of the hearth inside confirmed his expectations. Only a few glowing embers remained among the smoldering ashes. He grabbed a poker from the ornate set of cast iron fireplace tools and stirred the remnants of the fire. Confident that any proof he had entered Linda's that morning was gone, Tommy left the cabin and started back toward what was certain to be a chaotic scene in Hampton Village.

# Eight

*Sunday Morning, May 10, 1992, 11:45 A.M.*

FROM SEVERAL BLOCKS AWAY, Tommy could see the activity in front of Linda's house. He counted three police cruisers with bubbles flashing red and blue. Other cars scattered in disheveled fashion on both sides of the street would surely have received tickets on most days. With his eyes locked straight ahead, he drove by the scene, his peripheral vision catching the bright yellow tape strung across the driveway and across the front yard. He circled the block and on his second pass glanced up toward the house. What appeared to be a huge motor home covered the entire parking area at the top of the driveway. Tommy snapped his eyes front again and continued to drive by, the residual image of the vehicle with the writing emblazoned on the side fixed in his mind.

CONNECTICUT STATE POLICE
MAJOR CRIME UNIT

On his third trip around the block, he made a decision. He parked in the first open space he could find and walked back toward the house. The yellow crime scene tape across the entry to the driveway fluttered in the breeze, stretched enough so that it practically touched the ground. The insistent buzz of conversation drifted down to him from the veranda at the front of the house. He looked up to see Loretta James, Yvonne DiMartini, Shane Phillips,

47

and the three Phillips children herded into a corner, seemingly guarded by a sheriff's deputy. One step over the tape and another three into the yard brought the deputy bounding off the porch.

"Can't you read the sign?" he shouted to Tommy, whose attention was directed up at the small knot of people, the adults now glaring down at him. "Which part of *do not cross* don't you understand?"

Tommy continued to walk forward until he entered the deputy's personal space.

"You got to look at me. It's going to happen sooner or later so it might as well be now." His curled fists, threatening to become balled, forced the deputy to reach out his right arm and thrust a finger into Tommy's chest.

"You'll leave this place right now. No one enters. This is a crime scene and it's not going to be wrecked by someone who doesn't belong here. Now turn the hell around and get out."

"What about them?" Tommy pointed to the gathering on the porch.

"Look, Iverson, I know who you are and you can be sure that someone's going to be in touch, but for now, you'd just be getting in the way. And don't worry about them. The Staties said to let them stay. It doesn't concern you anyway."

A brief stare-down ensued before Tommy turned his back and walked toward his car, pausing at the yellow tape to glance up at Shane Phillips one last time. Eye contact was made and broken almost immediately as Shane looked away.

"Bastard!" Tommy hissed as he stepped across the dividing line between the madness of what had happened in the house and the sanity of the quaint and quiet Hampton Village.

PARKER HAVENOT ESTABLISHED HIS relationship with the Connecticut State Police during his second year with the Covington County Sheriff's Department. Under extreme pressure and desperate to find the rapist/killer of a young woman in a park just outside of Hartford, the state police requested assistance when their investigators ran out of clues. Havenot's successful career in his years as a detective with the homicide division of the City of

Philadelphia Police Department was well documented. When the call to Jim Corbett came in asking if Parker could consult on the case, a Cheshire cat grin spread across the sheriff's face. The same grin was plastered on his face when he informed the detective that the state police needed him.

"Just imagine, Parker," he had said. "They're actually asking for our help. Some of those guys think all the sheriffs' departments in the state should disappear. Maybe we're not such local yokels as they think. Now, get on over there and solve that murder, will you?"

The loan of Parker lasted just ten days. Jim Corbett and his detective watched the morning news conference from the Connecticut State Police Headquarters in Hartford as the arrest of the killer was announced. The second most delightful part of the broadcast, the first obviously being the announcement regarding the arrest, was the mention that Detective Parker Havenot of the Covington County Sheriff's Department played a crucial role in the case.

"Should've had you standing up there with them, Parker. They'd still be looking if it weren't for you."

"I've always found that people love to take credit for what they haven't done and not take the blame for what they have done. I don't need to be standing up there with them, Jim. I know where the credit lies and that's enough for me. Besides, it never hurts to have the state police on your side if you should need them. They owe us." Parker smiled. "I came up here from Philly to escape the stress and I'm enjoying myself immensely."

PARKER WATCHED FROM THE murdered woman's bedroom window as Tommy Iverson was confronted and turned away from the house. Linda's body still lay on the floor next to the bed in a tangled mass of bloody sheets. He had lost track of how many murder scenes he had witnessed but this one matched any in his experience for its sheer brutality. The crime scene investigators from the Connecticut Major Crime Unit were preparing to expand their work outside of the room where the murder occurred. A brief consultation with Parker confirmed their conclusion that all of the action in the murder happened in Linda Phillips's small bedroom. No evidence pointed to the body being moved from another location.

A simple nod by Captain Harry Townsend as he left the room gave the waiting EMTs permission to enter with the body bag and transport the now late Linda Phillips to the morgue in Hartford.

"Make sure you have all of the sheets," Harry instructed, "even the one she's not gripping."

Parker continued to stand by the window, waiting with bowed head for the murdered woman's body to be removed. The entire process took less than ten minutes. Linda left her house for the final time in a nondescript, black plastic body bag covered with a blanket, carried past her disbelieving children and friends on a stretcher. Across the street, knots of neighbors gathered, their quiet conversations stopped in mid sentence as the gurney rolled down the driveway and was loaded into the waiting ambulance. It was as if the air had been sucked out of the neighborhood and those observing the event couldn't even muster a deep enough breath to gasp at what they were seeing.

"Time to get to work," Parker said aloud as he watched the ambulance pull away. The group on the porch should be his starting place but an irritating uneasiness kept him staring out the window for another minute.

"Shit! This is Mothers' Day," he whispered.

Harry Townsend was wandering around downstairs when he heard the call from the bedroom. The shakiness in Parker's voice sent Harry bounding up the steps, taking two at a time.

"What's up, Parker? Is everything all right?" Harry asked, sucking in deep breaths from the exertion.

"I need you to hold the fort for about a half hour, if you don't mind. If you can keep everything just the way it is, I'd really appreciate it. I've got to take a quick run home to check on something important but I'll be back as quickly as I can." The grim set of Parker's tight, thin lips told Harry that his unusual request should be granted.

"You got it, Parker. But this sure isn't like you to leave a crime scene. Are you sure you're all right?"

Parker just nodded on his way out the door. Then it was Harry Townsend's turn to watch from the window as Parker jogged across the lawn to his car and drove off.

JOSIE HEARD THE SLIGHT squeal of tires as Parker pulled into the driveway. She flung the front door open just as he arrived on the landing.

"What are you doing home..." The unfinished question stuck in her throat as Parker pulled the screen door open, revealing the sadness filling his eyes. "What is it, Parker? What's wrong?" She reached for his hand and pulled him inside. "Talk to me, please."

He continued to hold her hand and guided her into their living room. "Sit down, Jos," he said, indicating the over-sized sofa. He sat beside her, taking her other hand. "I need to apologize, Josie. Here it is, Mothers' Day, and I left this morning without ever acknowledging it."

Josie stared at him. "What are you talking about? I'm not a mother so there's really nothing to acknowledge."

Parker let go of her hands, stood up, and began pacing. "Josie, I've seen your reaction whenever we visit Brad Jr.'s grave. I know it was a stillbirth and it all happened a long time ago, but you still had a child. That's makes you a mother and your husband should be thoughtful enough to help you get through the day. Instead, I just rushed out of here this morning without saying a word. I'm sorry, Josie."

Josie got up and threw her arms around him. "You are really too much, Parker Havenot. Leaving a murder scene to come home and tell me that."

"I'll tell you something else. I know you would have been a wonderful mother. But then comes the what-ifs like, what if Brad Jr. had lived—I probably would have never met you. I can't imagine my life without you, Josie."

With tears flowing down her cheeks, she kissed him. "Thank

you, Parker. Now, don't you think you'd better get back? The crack detective isn't doing much good here."

Josie's chastisement captured his attention. "You're right. The poor woman...absolutely brutal. It's astounding what one human being can do to another."

"It's like you always tell me about how you're never surprised by people's behavior, only disappointed. I'll just bet you'll find a lot of cracks in the wall this lady built to shield her from the past." Josie started the process of moving the two of them toward the front door. "Go back to work, Parker, and find out who did this awful thing. And I love that you came home to see me. You're a special man and I'm lucky to have you."

Ten minutes later, Parker greeted a worried Harry Townsend with his familiar smile.

"Thanks a lot, Harry. I'll take it from here."

"Let me know what you need from us and glad everything's okay," Townsend said, the relief at having Parker back in control palpable in his voice.

"Just bag up that answering machine and log it in. I'll listen to it later today."

# Nine

*The First Forty-Eight Hours*

PARKER GLANCED AROUND THE room one last time. The blood-stain on the carpet had turned a darker red and a surreal quality enveloped it, as if denying that just hours before it was coursing through the veins of a living human being. A veteran of so many homicide scenes, he could only shake his head at the strange sensation of being in the presence of such vivid proof of man's inhumanity to fellow man.

"Well," he announced to the empty room, "now it really is time to get to work."

He turned from the scene and hurried down the stairs.

As Parker approached the group on the porch, he noticed that each one seemed to be rooted to the same spot where they had been when he first arrived. Shane Phillips was speaking in a hushed voice. Two of the three children faced Parker. Even across the veranda, he could see the tightness in their facial expressions as they stared up at their father. The slight sag of their shoulders and sideways tilt of their heads made them seem to be cringing but that appearance clashed with the tension evident in the rigid posture.

"They're terrified of him," Parker whispered to himself as he approached. The three adults noticed him at the same time. Shane stopped speaking in midsentence and glanced away as if embarrassed by what he was saying.

"Detective Havenot, Covington County Sheriff's Department," Parker announced. He reached out to shake hands with the women first, then took Shane's unwilling hand, who tried to match the firmness of Parker's grip without success.

"I'm very sorry for your loss," he said. The clichéd phrase served as an opening for the conversation with the adults but it did nothing for the depth of confusion and fear apparent in the children's eyes as they gazed up at him. He knelt down on one knee and, in a soft voice while looking at each one in turn, asked them their names. When they finished stuttering out a response, he started to rise, changed his mind, and knelt again.

Moved by the dreadful situation the children were facing, Parker stifled the emotion in his voice and, almost in whisper, said, "I'm really sorry about your mom," followed quickly by a "are you guys okay?" Shane Jr. nodded, but Tonie and Jackie cast an upward glance at their father as if asking for his approval.

"Of course, they're not okay!" Shane exclaimed, loud enough to startle everyone. "Their mother's just been murdered, and you ask them if they're okay? You must be fucking kidding me."

Parker's reaction was swift and decisive. In a single motion, he was standing and glaring down at Shane from his four-inch height advantage. As the detective moved further into his personal space, Phillips inched backward but was stopped as Parker reached out and grabbed his arm. The pressure of the crushing squeeze threw a grimace across Shane's face.

"You watch your mouth around these kids and these women," he hissed through clenched teeth, his face just inches away.

Shane mumbled an incoherent response and stared down at his shoes. Loretta and Yvonne, Linda's two best friends, looked at the detective, a hesitant expectation in their eyes accentuated by their tear-stained cheeks.

Parker relaxed his grip on Shane's arm but didn't relinquish it completely. "I'm going to have to talk with all of you at some point, but for now, can you two watch the kids for a while? I need to speak with Shane and it's better done where it's quieter. Shouldn't really be too long, if that's okay." Both women were nodding before he finished the request. He released Phillips completely and glowered at him.

"That's not a problem for you, is it, Mr. Phillips? You can either follow me or meet me down at the department. You do know where it's located, right?" Shane was back to staring down at his shoes. Without raising his head, he responded. "Yeah, I know where it is, but I sure as hell don't know why you're doing me first." After a long pause, he finally picked up his head and looked straight into Parker's eyes. "It's got to be Tommy Iverson. He's the goddamned psycho that's always stalking Linda."

Havenot took a step closer and whispered something that the women couldn't quite hear despite both of them leaning toward the two men as if trying to catch a conversation through a thin wall.

"Sure, Detective, whatever you say." Shane turned towards Yvonne and Loretta with a crooked grin on his face. "Hey, girls, sorry about the language, but I'm sure you've heard a lot worse. I'll be back shortly to take the kids."

PARKER HAVENOT PAID LITTLE attention to the gossip, determined not to allow a political issue draw his focus away from his job. Josie was right. He had to find out who killed Linda Phillips.

The Covington County Sheriff's Department was no different than all the others throughout the state of Connecticut. Many of the deputies already had job inquiries out to local police departments around the state and a few who felt they had the chance contacted the state police in the hope of landing a job there when the sheriffs' departments phase out started. The officers' gossip line indicated that within a few years, five at the outside, the legislature would eliminate what they saw as a duplication of effort. Under the guise of saving the taxpayers of the state considerable money, a plan to incorporate the duties of the sheriffs' departments into the state structure was rapidly taking shape. At the moment, the issue was not on Parker's list.

As he turned into the parking lot of the department complex, he glanced in the rearview mirror. Shane Phillips, who had tailgated him since they left Linda's house, veered in behind him as if afraid to lose sight of Parker's car. When the detective parked in his spot, designated for official use only, Shane stopped directly behind him and lowered his window.

"You'll have to park over in the visitors' area," Parker called to him as he exited his car. "I'll wait for you at the front desk." Without a word, Shane pulled away with enough speed to kick up a slight spray of dust and gravel. Parker just shook his head as he walked toward the impressive brick building looming before him.

THE STAFF ON SUNDAY afternoons couldn't even qualify as a skeleton crew, with just a dispatcher and greeter at the front desk and a few deputies in the break room, sipping vending machine coffee from cardboard cups.

"Looks like a typical busy Sunday for you guys, Carlos. Hope I didn't interrupt your card game." Parker smiled as the expected reaction came back at him.

"You glamorous detectives have no idea how hard we peons work." Carlos smiled back at him. "I heard the staties let you have this murder case. Probably 'cause they'd have trouble catching the guy. They only take the slam dunks, from what I'm told."

"Don't be too hard on them. This is really just about in my backyard and I figure that's why they let us have it." Parker winked at him. "Of course, you could be a little right about that. Hey, the sheriff should be here any minute. Just send him down to the interview room. I'll wait for him before I start."

Shane watched the interchange without the slightest trace of amusement, instead shifting from one foot to the other like a nervous schoolboy who needed to find a restroom.

Parker escorted Shane down a long corridor past a series of offices, all dark with doors closed but enough ambient light to reveal the universal austerity of their interiors. Near the end of the hall, he paused at the only door without a name or designation on it, pulled his key ring from his pocket, and flipped through it.

"We'll talk in here. Like I told you, this shouldn't take long. A lot of routine stuff that we do to eliminate possibilities, you know what I mean?"

Shane's unintelligible answer blended with the jingling of keys as Parker fumbled through the process of unlocking the windowless door. The door creaked open, creating a sound effect straight out of

*Psycho.* He led the way into the sparsely furnished room. A square wooden table, only slightly larger than a card table, sat centered in the room. A few cigarette burns marred the faded, distressed finish. Two matching chairs faced each other across the table, looking equally distressed. Two padded folding chairs leaned against the rear wall; each had a slight cut in the fabric, the stuffing threatening to dribble out. One wall had a large opaque window, which drew Shane's attention as soon as he entered the room. The other walls were bare, painted an institutional beige that sorely needing refreshing.

"Is that like TV or something, a one-way mirror?" he asked, the first words he had spoken since entering the building. "I thought you said this was routine."

"Yeah, it is, for your protection more than anything. There won't be anyone back there today anyway. The sheriff'll be sitting right here in the room with us; like I said, all customary stuff."

"Whatever you say, Detective. This is all new to me. Where do you want me to sit, or do I dare pick my own seat?" The signs of Shane regaining some of his earlier swagger were not lost on Parker.

"I brought you here instead of the state police barracks so you'd be more comfortable," he said. The knock on the solid mahogany door kept him from explaining further. Sheriff Jim Corbett entered before Parker could call out to him.

A twenty-six-year veteran in law enforcement, the sheriff knew that he was in a similar position to what his parents used to tell him when they visited friends and relatives. "Children are to be seen but not heard, James," his mother would say, and he knew she meant it. When Parker Havenot was conducting an interview or an interrogation, he was to be seen and not heard. Only when Parker gave him the signal was he to enter the process.

"Sheriff Jim Corbett," was all he said as he shook Shane's hand. He didn't wait for a reply as he immediately grabbed one of the chairs, unfolded it, and sat in a corner of the room. He told Parker regularly how much he appreciated his talents as an investigator. This was an interview he couldn't wait to see.

THE TWO MEN SAT across the table from each other, their postures almost mirror images. Each had his hands folded and resting on the table in front like first graders facing their first nun. Shane sat up straighter in his chair, his right heel dancing in nervous anticipation. Suddenly, he started to look around the room as if sensing something missing. "Where's the recorder?" he asked. Parker simply flicked his glance toward the mirror and nodded.

"Now, why don't we cut to the chase, as they say," Parker said, while grinning and glancing over at Jim Corbett. "Why don't we start off with the oldest cliché in the police interrogator's manual?" He watched for Shane's reaction before continuing and was rewarded with the same strange smirk he had seen earlier with the women at Linda's house.

"Where were you on the night of May 9 and the morning of May 10, 1992?" Shane's smirk broke into a wide smile. "That's it, right?"

Parker could only smile in return and shake his head, waiting for an answer to the question. It was obvious that Shane was ready for it.

"Camping. Actually, out scouting for a good deer spot for this fall."

"Camping? Camping in May to find a good spot to hunt deer in November? I mean, I'm not a hunter but don't deer change patterns over the course of three seasons?" Parker noticed Jim Corbett lean forward in his chair. It was early but it still seemed like time for him to enter the conversation.

"Is something wrong, Jim?" Parker asked.

"Best time I know of to scout is late summer; at least you're closer to the season and you won't spook them too much then." Shane continued to look at the detective while the sheriff's comment penetrated.

"Any answer to that, Shane? The sheriff's pretty avid about his hunting."

"Sure. But can't we just put this to rest? I was camping with two hunting buddies from late yesterday afternoon until I got back late this morning and heard about Linda. There is no way I could be in any way, shape, or form responsible for what happened to her." His voice had risen in volume and intensity as he spoke. "Now why don't we end this and you can go get Tommy Iverson."

"Let's have the names and contact information. That should get you off the hook. As I told you earlier, process of elimination." When Parker stood up, Shane did the same, adopting the bearing and attitude of a man who had just received the best news of his life.

Parker waited while Shane rooted around in his wallet, finally coming up with a business card. He glanced at it, turning it over in his hand, before giving it to the detective. "This is Johnny Stanton's card with his information. Will Comfort's name and phone number's on the back. It was a great overnight; I probably drank a little too much but that's what camping out with drinking buddies will do."

"Convenient," Parker remarked. Shane looked at him. "Having both names on the same card. Almost like you came prepared."

Jim Corbett joined them at the table before Shane had a chance to respond. He made eye contact with Parker, who shrugged his shoulders. Corbett took the cue.

"So, were you happy with the results?" he asked.

"What results? What do you mean?" Shane seemed perplexed.

"The scouting results; you know, where you're going to get your deer in six months."

"Oh, yeah, that Monongahela National Forest is overrun with them. One of the few left to issue deer hunting permits. We'll have ours on the first day, guaranteed." Shane's smirk had returned. "Can I go now, Detective? I'd like to get back to the kids."

Parker nodded and waved his arm in the direction of the door. Just as Shane pulled on the knob, he took three steps toward him and reached out for his arm. "Just one more thing if you don't mind. What's the status of your divorce from Linda? I understand it's been difficult."

"Final hearing was going to be next week. Damn lawyers are bandits and hers is the worst of any of them. She was going to get a sixty-forty split and the house. How fucking fair is that?"

The topic set an edge in his voice that hadn't been there before. The two lawmen glanced at each other.

"But I guess none of that matters now, does it?" Shane said.

"Here's another cliché for you, and you could probably guess this one as well but I'll beat you to it. Don't leave town without checking with us first. Best if you keep yourself available."

"Sure, Detective, wouldn't think of doing anything stupid. Do you guys have a book of those things or what?" Shane laughed out loud at his lame joke, then he was gone.

Parker and Jim Corbett stared at the door after it slammed shut.

Jim broke the extended silence as they both mulled over the brief interview. "Not much of a grieving husband, ex or not," he commented. "Didn't even mention the kids in the settlement."

"Hmmm. Let's go see his hunting buddies," Parker said. "I want this part out of the way before we go any further. You know what they say: look to the husband first, or, in this case, the almost ex-husband."

THE STORIES MATCHED. BOTH Will Comfort and Johnny Stanton declared without question that Shane Phillips was with them the entire night. When Jim Corbett mentioned to each of them how unusual it was to be scouting out a fall deer-hunting trip so early in the spring, their answers were remarkably similar.

"Great excuse to get away from the wife for a while," Johnny Stanton had said. "Never too soon to make plans. Plus, a good night of drinking with friends is better than a night in front of the TV with the family." Will Comfort, who was divorced, left out the wife part but used the exact phrase "never too soon to make plans" and mentioned the drinking and the boredom of watching television by oneself as reasons for the unusual camping expedition.

The interviews, as brief as they were, confirmed one inescapable fact. Shane Phillips had a solid physical alibi. As they drove back to headquarters, Parker articulated what both were thinking. "Their stories check out but it sure seems as if they got together on what they were going to say. Almost rehearsed, wouldn't you say?"

Jim Corbett looked over at his passenger and simply rolled his eyes. "Loyal cohorts," he whispered.

THE PARKING LOT, WHICH had been virtually empty when they left to interview Comfort and Stanton, now had only a few spaces left. A news van from WFSB out of Hartford parked diagonally across three spaces. An attractive young woman, obviously the on-air talent, stood in front of the building interviewing another woman, whom Parker immediately recognized as Yvonne DiMartini. The single camera operator jousted with a crowd of spectators as he tried to capture the interview.

"What the hell is going on?" Jim Corbett guided the cruiser through the small knots of people gathered in the parking lot and found his assigned space, thankfully unoccupied. Parker opened his car door first and no one scattered around the lot seemed to notice him. When Jim Corbett exited the car, his imposing presence in full uniform and wide brimmed hat did attract the attention of most of the people, and conversations died, seemingly in mid sentence. The silence was broken only by the voice of the television reporter, but her discussion ended abruptly when she realized who the two men were. In seconds, she and the technician had scurried to a position where they could intercept Parker and Jim before they entered the building.

"What did you find out? Did those friends of Shane Phillips back him?" She called out the questions in such a loud voice that most of the people gathered nearby could certainly hear them.

Parker motioned for the sheriff to keep going as he stopped and stared at her. After a brief moment, he approached her. She instinctively took a quick step backward, knocking into her cameraman who followed on her heels like a puppy after its new master. He recovered his balance after nearly dropping the camera to the concrete steps. Parker allowed his intimidation factor to continue to work to his advantage.

"Miss...I'm sorry, I don't know your name but..."

"It's Teresa, Teresa Wainwright, with WFSB news."

The pout on her face made Parker smile. How could anyone not know who she was?

"Okay, Miss Wainwright, for the record, this case is just hours old and as you professional journalists know, we can't be releasing any information at this time. We can assure you that the public will be informed as we make progress, but for now, we need to proceed with the investigation in a timely and efficient manner." Parker smiled again, engaging enough to disarm even the toughest reporter.

Teresa Wainwright's face was tinged red with the remnants of a blush. He found it impossible to determine if it was caused by being called a professional journalist or being in the presence of a charismatic and confident detective. "Of course," she stammered, "I understand completely and thank you for your time." She turned to the cameraman. "Turn it off for now," she said.

The minute Parker heard her order the technician to shut down, he moved closer again.

"Where did you find out about Shane Phillips's friends?" he demanded.

"I don't think I have to reveal my sources, Detective Havenot, but I guess in this case, it really doesn't matter. Shane himself told me that's what you'd be doing."

Without another word, the detective turned on his heel and entered the building. Teresa didn't hear the whispered exclamation as he disappeared. "Damn it!"

Carlos was out of his chair before the door closed. He leaned toward the barred window and motioned for Parker to come over, but his anxious state had him speaking before the detective was within hearing range.

"You've got two people waiting in your office. The sheriff escorted them down there, mostly to keep them from beating each other up. It's been a crazy afternoon here, Detective, and I have a feeling it may get a little crazier." The deputy ran out of breath, paused to recover, then continued. "They've been in here standing around waiting for you two to come back for over an hour."

Parker asked a question with his eyes, but Carlos answered with a shrug. He had no idea who they were. "Thanks, Carlos. And sorry your quiet afternoon has been disturbed." The hint of sarcasm was not lost on the dispatcher.

"I didn't mean to complain..." Carlos's voice trailed off to nothing as Parker hustled down the hall to his office.

PARKER ENTERED HIS OFFICE without knocking and did a classic double take as he glanced around the room. Jim Corbett had brought in a plush extra chair from his own office and rearranged the other two into a boxing ring layout. The detective's modest desk anchored one corner of the ring. Corbett's chair sat near the door, facing Parker, while the other two straight chairs made a perfect square. Tommy Iverson sat in one corner while Loretta James sat opposite him. They glared at each other like Mike Tyson and Evander Holyfield just prior to the opening bell of a heavyweight fight. All three started to speak before Parker was two steps into the room. He held up his hand and extended two fingers, looking like a Cub Scout Leader asking for order after an especially wild game of hide and seek in the woods. The gesture had the desired effect and silence enveloped the room.

"Okay, you first, Sheriff. You want to tell me what is going on here?" Parker kept the impatient edge from his voice. Known as a methodical and efficient investigator, he was not one to encourage interruptions in his routine. He had formed a plan in his mind on the trip back from the interviews with Shane Phillips's alibis. The crowd out front, along with the news truck, was disruption enough. This unexpected visit presented a challenge, an unanticipated test of his tolerance. In his usual imperturbable way, he met the test head on. He circled around behind his desk but remained standing as Jim Corbett began his lengthy explanation. By its end, Parker was seething, but once again, his anger dissipated as he looked at a distraught and grief-stricken Loretta James.

"How are the kids, Loretta?" he asked. "I take it Shane is with them now."

Loretta seemed to be expecting another question. She was silent and dropped her head while raising a tightly clutched handkerchief up to her eyes. Her head bobbed up and down while stifled sobs escaped through her mouth. Parker let the scene run its course, knowing that she would eventually give her side of the story as to why she was sitting in this office. After a full minute, she finally regained her composure enough to speak.

"I came here to tell you that you should arrest that man right now." She pointed at Iverson across the room. "He's the one who killed Linda." She was trembling and a sudden shiver shook her entire body. "You've got to do something now! She just dumped him and he can't take it." Her exclamation brought Tommy Iverson out of his chair.

"Look, Detective, I'm telling you that you have to look at me because I was the last one with her last night, but I didn't kill her." He glanced over at Loretta. "You are fucking wrong and you know it." With that, Parker slammed his hand down on his desk, causing the large photo of Josie to crash to the floor. Somehow, it managed to bounce without breaking.

"I'll tell you what we're going to do, and this better be the way it is. You both are going home. You're getting in the way of this investigation and taking up valuable time. You can count on us being in touch, but for now, you will leave this office without another word, especially to each other. You'll go to your cars and go home. Wait for us to contact you. Do you understand that?" Parker left no room for interpretation. The harshness of his voice only reinforced the content of the message.

A meek "yes, sir" came from both of them, almost in unison. Tommy Iverson was the first to leave, cutting in front of Loretta and almost closing the door in her face. After they both were gone, Jim Corbett walked over and pulled the door closed.

"So, what's our next move, Detective, sir?" he asked, smiling.

"Would you run out front and see if that woman who was talking with the reporter is still around—her name is Yvonne, last name Demarco or something like that? If you find her, bring her in. I'm going up to the evidence room to get the answering machine from the house."

WHEN PARKER RETURNED WITH the plastic bag holding the machine, Jim Corbett had Yvonne DiMartini sitting in the chair still warm from Tommy Iverson. Her rigid posture and tapping feet telegraphed her mental state.

"Thanks for helping with the kids, Yvonne. That made things easier from my end." His calm voice and genuine expression of appreciation visibly relaxed the tension in the air. "You've been friends with Linda Phillips for a long time, right?"

The question produced a loud sob and Yvonne buried her head in her hands. "I can't believe she's gone," she mumbled through her handkerchief. Parker waited until she cleared her throat and looked up at him. "Yeah, Loretta and I and Linda were like the three musketeers. I've got one daughter, Loretta has two and Linda had to outdo us with three kids. Oh, Christ, what's going to happen with those kids?" she asked, sniffling.

"I know this must be terrible for you and I'm sorry to take your time. This will only take a few minutes but I wanted to follow up on something that Loretta said." Parker leaned forward in his chair and began the interview.

Ten minutes later, he was escorting Yvonne down the hall. When they arrived at the front entrance, he advised her not to speak to any reporters again, "for your protection," he told her. "They'll twist everything you say so you'd never even recognize it."

"Thanks, Detective. I sure hope I was a help to you and please call me anytime. I loved Linda and I want the bastard who did this strung up by his balls."

"Don't sugar coat it, ma'am; you might as well tell me how you really feel." He grinned as she blushed furiously and hurried out the door.

Jim Corbett had donned rubber gloves, had the answering machine out of the bag and plugged in by the time Parker got back to his office.

"If even half of what she said is true, we've got a hell of a lot more potential suspects than we thought. Linda surely seemed to be enjoying her newfound freedom over the last nine months or so." Parker sat at his desk and pushed the play button on the answering machine. The first message had both men standing straight up.

"I fucking hate you!" the voice of Tommy Iverson screamed.

"I HAD TO EAT anyway so it might as well be with my wife, who just happens to be the most important person in my life," Parker explained. "It's probably going to be a long night, and I didn't want you to have dinner alone on Mothers' Day."

Moments before, Josie had greeted him at the door, astonished that he had left his murder investigation behind for the second time that day.

"You really are sweet, Parker, but I completely understand if you need to be away. Hampton Village doesn't exactly have a murder every day." She put her arm around him and they made their way to the deck at the rear of the house. "I've got some leftover potato salad and ham from the other night. That'll be quick. I assume you'll be going back, right? You probably don't want a glass of wine but I think I'll have one, if you don't mind."

Parker grinned as he refused the offer. "Very tempting, but I'd better not. I will be going back after dinner and meet with Loretta James and Yvonne DiMartini again. It turns out this is going to be much more complicated than I thought."

Josie disappeared into the kitchen and a few minutes later emerged with two plates—Parker's heaped with potato salad, several slices of baked ham, and a garden salad of greens and sliced tomatoes, while her portions were half the size. When Parker looked at her, she answered the question in his eyes. "Starting a diet tomorrow but might as well work my way into it slowly," she said, her eyes twinkling. "Gotta keep myself svelte and in shape for my dashing police detective." They both giggled and Josie left to get her wine and a tall glass of ice water for Parker. When she returned, she found Parker standing at the railing, staring out toward the cemetery in the distance.

"I guess that's where she'll be buried," he said. "Pretty much everyone is around here." When he turned to Josie, her hands were trembling hard enough to slosh some of the water out of his glass. "What is it, Jos? Are you all right?"

"Yeah, I'm fine. It's just that…you know, Mothers' Day and all, the cemetery…that poor woman…those kids…" She set the glasses on the picnic table and raised the hem of her apron to her eyes, covering her face. "Sorry, Parker, I'm feeling a little foolish now." The words came out muffled through the material.

"Oh, shit, Josie, that was so thoughtless of me." He strode across to her and hugged her tightly. "I don't know what I was thinking."

Josie escaped from his hug. "Come on, let's eat so you can go do your thing. This murder must have shaken the town to its foundations." She slid into the bench seat attached to the table and he followed her, sitting on the same side and as close as practicality would allow.

"So, if you can tell me, what did you mean by much more complicated?"

"Do you remember your profound declaration, the one I thought should be one of those motivational posters, the one about cracks in the wall or something like that?"

Josie laughed at first then thought for a moment. "Yeah, I kind of do recall that but I'm guessing it's never going to make the bulletin boards in any school rooms."

Parker struggled with the exact wording but decided that a paraphrase would suffice. "I found out part of it this afternoon, and will probably find out a lot more tonight. If Linda Phillips was trying to build a wall between her present and past, she wasn't too successful. As you predicted this afternoon, her wall has a lot of cracks and I know she was looking backward through them. I just have to find the crack that will let us know who killed her."

# Part Two

## The Wall

# Ten

## *The Foundation*

SHANE PHILLIPS DIDN'T KNOW it but he had laid the first bricks in the foundation of Linda Phillips's wall early in their marriage. His courtship of Linda McCormick had been fast and furious, fueled by the demands of his job and the natural restlessness of a young woman ready get out of the house and move on with her life. His proposal came just a month after their first date and the wedding was on the fast track immediately thereafter. On June 14, 1980, Linda left the McCormick name behind as Hampton Village Community Church hosted the enthusiastic couple and small gathering of friends and family. As usual, Linda McCormick Phillips pushed her desire to keep everyone happy to the limit. That personality trait presented the only test of the close relationship she shared with her mother.

"Your supreme niceness is a character flaw, Linda," her mother admonished on numerous occasions. "You can't keep everybody happy all the time. If you keep trying, you're going to have some serious problems in your life."

"What's wrong with making people feel good?" Linda often remarked when her mother would kid her about her empathy for a friend or her refusal to hurt another's feelings, even if the hurt might have been justified.

"People are going to walk all over you, Linda," she would

say, repeating the ominous warning on her wedding day. "Shane Phillips is not good for you, Linda. You're going to be sorry."

"He's a good guy, Mother, you just wait and see."

DURING THEIR SHORT ENGAGEMENT, Shane often spoke about how his long distance trucking job would mean extended absences, and he joked about how a beautiful blonde like her would handle the inevitable attention of the young men around town who knew he was gone. At times, his teasing assumed a sharpness she found uncomfortable, but once they were married, she was confident that any potential issues would disappear. For the first few months of their marriage, Shane was away from home for ten days to two weeks at a time. When he was home, the couple used the limited time as newlyweds were inclined to do, alternating between lengthy lovemaking sessions and adjusting to life in close quarters with another person. Linda arranged her work schedule so that she could be home on the occasional weekdays when Shane was home, and for several months they led as idyllic a life as was possible with so much separation.

On a Saturday morning at the end of their first three months of being together and two days before Shane was scheduled for a two-week cross-country assignment, the phone rang. For an insane moment, Shane remembered a famous comment by Marshall McLuhan, the guru of mass media in the turbulent Sixties. He had said that the telephone is the only device that can interrupt a couple engaged in sexual intercourse, an observation proven once more that morning in the Phillips bedroom.

"Shit!" Shane whispered as he caught his breath. "Let it go."

Linda worked her way out from underneath him. "Steve said he might need me today. I'd better get it." She continued to wiggle and squirm, finally breaking free from his weight. She stood up next to the bed, staring down at him. He grinned up at her, his smile an unsettling mixture of disdainful scorn and genuine affection. Before she could react, he reached out and grabbed her arm.

"Don't answer the fucking phone, Linda!" His voice echoed around the room. With a sudden and sharp motion, he pulled her back into the bed. "You're not going anywhere," he hissed, and, like a professional wrestler, pinned her face down on the bed with one arm behind her back. Linda's ineffective protests became just muffled noises as her face was forced deeper into the mattress.

Not more than a minute later, he groaned with pleasure, then rolled off of her. "A little more cooperation and you'd enjoy it more," he said as he lurched on shaking legs into the bathroom.

A dazed Linda pushed herself up, went to the bedroom extension phone and dialed the office of Chambers and Stone Realty. Through the partially open bathroom door, Shane heard her say, "Sure, Steve. I'll get there as soon as I can."

After a hesitant knock received no response, Linda called out. "I'll need the shower pretty quick. They need me at the office to cover this morning. It'll just be for a couple of hours." Still, nothing but silence came from the bathroom. "Shane, did you hear...?" Linda's question was cut short by Shane's sudden appearance filling the doorway.

"Of course I heard. You're taking off during one of the few days we have together. A couple of hours'll turn into three or four, if previous experience tells me right. Why can't you just tell him you can't come in?" Shane pushed past, his naked body brushing against hers. Her involuntary recoil was not lost on him.

"Look, Linda. I'm sorry about what happened just now. I just got pissed off at the phone and took it out on you. Come on, don't go to work." The harshness of his voice softened with each word until the final plea had her considering calling Steve Chambers back. Then her main reason for working rose to the surface of her mind.

"We can use the money, Shane, especially if we're going to be thinking about kids, you know." Linda smiled. "Do you realize we're conducting this argument, if you could call it that, standing here in the nude." Shane looked down as though just grasping the fact himself. The ludicrousness of the situation soon had both of them laughing, the tension of moments before relieved.

"Go get your shower and then get out there and rake in those bucks," he said. "I'll have lunch ready for you when you get home." They moved toward each other at the same time, meeting after a few steps in a full body hug. Shane was the first to break away.

"You better get going before I don't let you out of this room," he said, a suggestive leer plastered on his face.

"By the way, that's the first time, you know." She placed her hands on her hips in the classic pose as if about to chastise a child. Her nakedness eliminated any need for her to gain his attention.

"What do you mean? I told you I was sorry about the uh…the uh…" His stammering brought a soft giggle from Linda.

"What? The wifely rape? From what I hear, that happens all the time. I'm talking about the f-word. It's the first time you've ever used that word in my presence." The conversational tone softened the content and Shane answered with what he thought was a humorous response.

"Well, my dear, so sorry to have offended your tender little ears," he said in a voice tinged with sarcasm. "I am a truck driver, you know. What do you expect?"

Linda's comeback was swift, almost as though practiced. "Respect, Shane. I expect respect. That's not too much to ask, right?" Without waiting for an answer, she went into the bathroom and gently closed the door.

The incident faded into the youthful idealism that allows new-lyweds to believe that all will be well. It was, for six months.

Shane had called from the road only once since her early week visit with Doctor Steven Capaldi, the local OB/GYN recom-mended by her new friend, Loretta James. Linda decided that the special news provided by the doctor should be delivered in person. At the outset of the call, Shane announced that he only had enough change for the first three minutes, automatically placing time parameters on their conversation. A pregnancy announcement would not fit into those parameters, even if Linda had planned to tell him. She failed to hide her forced casualness during the hurried call. As he usually did, Shane recognized the nervousness in her voice and misinterpreted it.

"What's going on there, Linda? Not trying to hide anything, are you?"

Neither of them had spoken about the incident in their bedroom six months before. When Shane was home between trips, the newlywed euphoria captivated them. His insecurity in their relationship surfaced only when he was on the road. Every phone call included either an outright interrogation about her every activity or an implied suggestion that she might be having affairs. Most of the time, the calls ended with Linda asking the standard question of "Don't you trust me?" and Shane answering "Of course I do, but I just worry about you. You must have guys after you all the time." Linda's rejoinder to that always varied slightly from call to call but the connotation was the same.

"What about you? On the road all the time. I know how horny you always are, plus you're handsome and can be really charming. You could have a girlfriend in every city and I'd never know the difference."

The phone seemed the best place to raise the fidelity concerns as neither one of them seemed to want to disturb the peace when they were physically together.

"No, Shane. Nothing's going on and I'm not trying to hide anything. Just can't wait to see you, that's all." The call ended with the usual "love you" from both parties.

LINDA'S SPECIAL DINNER PLANS were postponed as she expected they would be. Shane arrived home at four in the afternoon on Friday as planned. They showered together and were in bed by four fifteen. An hour later, they enjoyed a cocktail on the veranda in the unusual warmth of a late March day in Connecticut. Linda waited until Shane's double Beefeater martini was down to the olive before clearing her throat. He hadn't noticed that her gin and tonic was lacking any gin.

"I've got some news, Shane, and I hope you'll be as excited as I am."

He was jiggling his upside down glass to shake the olive into his mouth but stopped the process and put his glass down. "You finally got that promotion. Well, that is good news." He eyed the olive again and picked up his glass.

"I'm pregnant, Shane," she announced, her eyes glistening. His puzzled look forced her to follow with an obvious statement. "We're going to have a baby."

Linda noticed the glass shaking in his hand. His eyes seemed to go out of focus as he stared at her for a few seconds then looked around as if searching for an escape route. He drew in a deep breath and appeared to come to a decision.

"No, we're not having a baby, Linda," he announced in the authoritative, I'm-the-man-of-the-house tone he was adopting more and more frequently. "What we're going to have is a fucking abortion." He stood up abruptly, so quickly that he staggered sideways for a half a step before regaining his balance. "I'm going to get another drink. Do you want anything?" Her disbelieving stare glanced off his back as he left the porch without pausing for an answer.

Shane remained in the kitchen long enough for Linda to have absorbed what he said. Her initial shock dissolved, replaced by as intense an emotional response as she had ever felt. She ripped the screen open with such force that two screws pulled out of the top hinge as it slammed against the wall. Shane stood with his back to her, gently shaking his new batch of martinis. She took his arm and spun him around, knocking the metal shaker from his hand and sending it careening across the floor.

"What the hell are you doing?" His face turned a deep shade of red and he cocked his arm as if to throw a punch.

"Don't you dare!" Linda's fury escalated with each passing second. "You just listen to me and don't say a word." The passion in her voice had Shane backing into the counter, his arms falling to his sides as she moved to within inches of his face. "You're going to tell me what you meant out there and we're going to straighten this out." Her adrenalin rush slackened and she took a step backward. "I'll be on the porch after you clean up the martinis. And don't make any more until after we talk." She turned on her heel and strode out through the screen door, which now hung crookedly on its one remaining good hinge.

Several minutes later, a chastened and empty-handed Shane quietly sat down in the wicker rocker facing Linda, who sat rigid in a matching straight-backed chair, hands folded in her lap. She remained silent, waiting for him to open the conversation. He finally broke the uncomfortable silence in a voice so quiet that Linda had to strain to hear him.

"I don't know what I was thinking. My mind goes a little crazy on the road, you know, imagining all kinds of stuff, plus I thought we were waiting a while for kids. Saving some extra money and all that..." As he spoke, his shoulders slumped with each word. "I guess the whole idea scares the hell out of me. Plus, I thought we were protected from, um, you know..."

Linda had been watching him closely, her powerful anger unsustainable in the face of his obvious regret. She pulled her chair over next to his and clasped his hand.

"We usually are protected, Shane. I try to see to that, except when you're drinking and refuse to use anything. If you remember, that's happened more than a few times lately." She reached up with her free hand and turned his face toward her. "So what are you imagining as you travel the highways and byways? It would seem like a good time to clear your head, not clutter it."

His answer brought a blush of annoyance back into her cheeks. "I think a lot of what you're doing back here while I'm gone. I mean, like I've said before, you're good looking, sexy, and..."

She stopped him by clamping her hand over his mouth. "That's the last I want to hear of that. I married you because I love you. Now we're going to be parents. I've got everything I want right here and right now, with you. So, that's the end of that, right?"

Shane looked at her with his impish grin. "Well, I guess you told me. Can I have my second martini now?' He waggled his finger from side to side. "Nothing but flavored water for you, though, Mom." They shared a generous laugh and he went inside to fill the shaker once more.

Linda turned her chair toward the expansive backyard where the warm spring day teased a light green tinge out of the still hibernating bushes. The excitement of sharing the news with Shane had been obliterated by his first reaction, and regardless of his second reaction, the harsh words came back to her.

"No way I would have a 'fucking abortion,' not ever," she whispered. "No matter what he'd want."

She went into the house, wondering which frame of mind Shane would be sharing as they ate the special dinner she had prepared.

# Eleven

*Bricks and Mortar*

A SIGNIFICANT EVENT OCCURRED on Election Day, 1981, just one year after the momentous election of Ronald Reagan to the presidency of the United States. While the off-year election carried no major news on November 3, the birth of Shane Phillips, Jr. brought special meaning to the Phillips household. Shane Phillips was in Seattle, Washington, about as far away from home as he could be and still be in the lower forty-eight, when he called Linda from his Super 8 motel room. Once every trip, he treated himself to a night spent in a real bed instead of the foam mattress in the back of his truck. After five rings, the answering machine clicked in with the message Linda had recorded, one that Shane thought was obnoxious but tolerated anyway.

"You have reached the home of Linda and Shane and the soon-to-be home of Shane Junior, whenever he decides he's ready for this world. Please leave a message and I'll get back to you as soon as I can."

"Choose your battles wisely, Shane," his father advised him on his wedding day and the phone message was one he decided not to fight, even if she did use the pronoun "I" instead of "we." Their discussions about who was captain of the home ship were becoming more frequent when he was home, but even he had to admit it was hard to be a captain when you are thousands of miles away. He'd have to be content with being firmly in charge when

78

he was home, especially with this new responsibility coming along.

After leaving a message, he called Loretta James, who agreed to be the news source if he couldn't get Linda.

Loretta picked up on the first ring, relieved to hear his voice. "I was hoping it'd be you, Shane. I left a message at your next stop but wasn't sure when you'd get it. She's in the hospital. I took her in this afternoon. The doctor said everything's fine, even if her due date is not for two weeks. He expected it to be just a matter of hours."

"Shit," Shane said. "I scheduled my vacation around that date. I can't get back for at least five days, probably six." After giving Loretta the phone and room number where he was staying, he hung up, then immediately dialed another number, this time local.

He didn't wait for the party he was calling to even say hello. "Hey, I'm free for a few hours. You have a little time? I mean, I know you're not free, but you're not that expensive either. Room 105, Super 8, as usual." The response from the other end was a soft giggle and a "be there in fifteen." Shane smiled as he set the phone down gently in its cradle.

Two hours later, the phone rang five times before Shane managed to disentangle himself and cross the room, trailing the top bed sheet behind him. An excited Loretta James cut his hello in half.

"Congratulations, Dad. Shane Jr. has arrived!" she exclaimed. "Baby and mom are doing great and she can't wait to talk to you." Her bubbly enthusiasm wound down as she waited for a response.

"Thanks for letting me know. I'll give her a call later." He abruptly disconnected the call, leaving Loretta pondering the cool answer and wondering when the thrilled new father might surface.

"Somebody else was in that room," she said to herself.

Six days later, the 18-wheeler rolled into Hampton Village. Shane turned left onto Lewis Street and coasted down the steep hill, using his engine brakes to slow the vehicle and annoy every resident who was home at the time. The municipal parking lot at the end of the street was certain to be virtually empty, and he found an easy-in, easy-out place to park at the rear of the lot. After a short walk back up the hill to the center of town, he entered Baker's Flower Shoppe, the only florist within miles. Shopping for a bouquet fell far out of Shane's comfort zone, but JoAnn Baker, the proprietor and an attractive woman in her early forties, greeted him by name. Her warmth set him at ease as did the second part of her greeting.

"Good afternoon, Mr. Phillips. I heard your truck go by, it really can't be missed, you know, and figured you were back home. Congratulations on your boy—you must be really excited." JoAnn saw the questioning look flash across his face and answered it before he could. "Your house probably smells like this shop. I think Linda received five or six sprays—a huge one from Steve Chambers down at her office."

Shane stood there bewildered for a moment, and JoAnn realized the situation. "You haven't been home yet, have you?"

"Actually, I haven't. Just got back from a two-week trip and wanted to bring Linda a little something. Looks like some people have beaten me to it." A note of explanation, taking the form of an unnecessary apology, slipped into his voice.

"It's my job, you know. I wasn't planning on the baby coming early and I was so far away and couldn't get back. Just beyond my control…" Realizing how lame he was sounding, he switched to an aggressive posture. "What have you got in the fifteen dollar range? I was thinking about a dozen red roses."

JoAnn made a decision she instantly regretted but couldn't take back. "It's a tough season for roses. They're usually two dollars each, but for such a special occasion, I'll make an exception. I'll make them up right away; it'll take about fifteen minutes, if you want to wait."

Shane thanked her, saying he had one shopping stop and would be back in a half hour. Three minutes and a block and half later, Shane was sitting at the bar in the Village Grille, and a minute after that, was sipping on his trademark Beefeater martini. Tillie, his favorite bartender, had seen him pass by the window on his way in and had the order in before he settled into the stool.

"Great to see you, Shane. And congrats on the baby boy," Tillie said. "Heard from some of Linda's friends that he looks just like you."

Shane changed the tilt of his glass from sipping to gulping and downed half of the drink in one swallow. "Wouldn't know about that. I haven't seen him yet." An acquaintance whose name he couldn't remember called out from three stools away.

"Just better not look like the mailman, right, Shane?" he bellowed, following the old joke with a guffaw.

"Damn sight better look like me," Shane muttered into the remaining portion of his martini before guzzling it, olive and all.

"Come on, Shane. Lighten up. You should be really happy right about now." Tillie assumed her best bartender/psychologist persona. "Why aren't you home, anyway?"

Chastened and mellowing quickly as the martini made its way into his bloodstream, he sighed. "Just waiting for some flowers to be made up. Sorry, Tillie, the long trip has made me a tired and grumpy old guy." He took out his money clip and pulled a ten-dollar bill off the bottom of the folded stack. "Thanks and I'll come back in a better mood next time," he said as he slipped the bill under his glass. "Keep the change. I'm off to buy some cigars and see my boy."

She hadn't seen such a smile from him in a long time.

A quick stop at Louie's Village Tobacco and Candy proved to be a disappointment. His search for the cheap cigars with the "It's a boy!" wrappers, the kind that no one ever smoked, was fruitless. "Not enough guys do that anymore," Louis explained when Shane confronted him demanding a reason. "But I've got some other cheap ones in the back. I'll get you a box."

Shane answered with a nod and shrug. While the storeowner was gone, he wandered over to the candy counter and selected a package of Altoids, advertised as the "curiously strong" peppermint variety. Anytime he mixed drinking with driving, he used several of the powerful mints.

"You really should carry those labeled cigars, Louis," he said as he paid his bill. "At least one or two boxes, you know?"

Louis grunted, leaving little doubt that the unsolicited advice was not going to be taken seriously. "Congrats on your boy," he called as Shane hurried out the door.

"THE ROSES ARE GORGEOUS, Shane. You really shouldn't have done it. They must've been expensive this time of the year." Linda ignored the wisp of gin blending with the breath mints as Shane bent over her chair and kissed her.

"Nothing too good for the mother of my son," he said, straightening up and gazing around the room. "Speaking of which, where is he?"

Linda got up and led him into their bedroom. "I put the bassinet in here so I can kind of keep an eye on him. We'll move him when he's older. I'm scared to death of that sudden infant death syndrome." She folded the top down. "Here he is. Hope you like him" she said with a giggle.

Shane peeked over the edge of the tiny bed at his sleeping son. "God, he's so small. He does sort of look like me, though, doesn't he?" He made no move to reach in to touch him, instead standing there staring down in rigid fascination, but his question seemed to require an answer.

"Everybody says so. Not as cute right now but he'll get there." Her infectious giggle made him smile. "You could hold him, you know." Linda bent over as though to reach for the baby but was stopped by Shane's reaction.

"No, not now. Maybe later," he said, his protest sharper than expected. "I mean, I should get cleaned up or something, right?" He stepped back, an almost involuntary response.

"You're right; maybe just go wash your hands in the kitchen and sit down in your favorite chair. I'll bring him in and get a picture—first one with your first born. Kind of cool, isn't it?"

Shane backed out of the room, as if afraid to take his eye off the bassinet. A few minutes later, he was stretched out in his recliner, his legs fully extended. "I'm ready," he called out. Linda laid Shane Jr. gently between his legs and Shane began to rock him from side to side. "This isn't so bad," he said, reaching for his drink.

"He's not going to break; I hear babies are pretty tough," Linda said, standing off to one side so she could frame both of them in her camera. After several shutter clicks, Shane stopped his rocking.

"You can take him now, Linda. I'll get used to this gradually, okay?" Linda put her camera on the coffee table and picked the little boy off Shane's lap and snuggled him into the crook of her left arm.

She sat down in the chair and began unbuttoning her blouse. "What are you doing, Linda? I thought we'd decided against breast feeding." Shane pushed against the leg rest and the recliner snapped into upright position. He leaned closer, emphasizing his disbelief.

"I changed my mind, or maybe I should say that Dr. Capaldi changed it for me. He said it's the most natural thing in the world. It's a little soon for his feeding but we'll see if he's hungry."

She smiled down at the baby as she snapped the bra flap open, exposing her left breast.

Shane sat straight up, his eyes directed everywhere but at his wife. "Don't you think we should have talked about this? Isn't this supposed to be a mutual decision?" His flitting glances finally settled on her chest, where Shane Jr. showed that he was certainly hungry as he settled into a contented sucking mode.

"This is not a big deal, Shane. It truly isn't. Mothers nurse their young. That's the way Mother Nature works." Linda struggled to stay calm, a requirement for successful nursing, according to Steven Capaldi. She stared at her husband, who looked away toward his glass on the end table. He grabbed it, and, after two deep swallows, he responded.

"What's that do to us, Linda? I mean, for God's sake, what am I supposed to do? How long do you have to do it?" Another swallow left only a few drops in the bottom of the glass. He stood up and paced back and forth. "Did the good doctor have any advice about how we're supposed to be like, uh…uh…?" He stammered into silence.

"First of all, I don't *have* to do anything, but this makes me feel good. Besides, if you think about it from your usual financial perspective, it saves money. Formula's pretty expensive, you know!"

Shane's pacing stopped when he stood over her and their son, his physical dominance causing her to sink deeper into the chair.

"Ask your special doctor about how you go about weaning him off your breast and onto a bottle, like I thought we had talked about using in the first place. And I want that bassinet in the second bedroom, the one closest to us. We'll be close enough to watch him but he won't be right next to us. Our bedroom is for us, period!" He turned and went into the kitchen. The clinking of ice cubes was followed by the unmistakable gurgling of a liquor bottle as its contents emptied into the glass.

Linda lifted the baby up to her shoulder and gently patted his back. After a loud burp, she stopped patting and laid him on her lap while she fastened the nursing bra flap.

"Sorry, Junior," she said in a low voice. "We must keep the master of the house happy."

The dozen roses did not prevent a few more blocks from being added to the foundation of Linda's wall.

# Twelve

## *The Pattern*

THE TRANSITION FROM PASSIVE manipulation and control to emotional abuse occurred gradually, so subtle in its nature as to almost go undetected. Linda Phillips observed it as if watching it happen to someone else, until the pattern became so ingrained that she could no longer deny it. The niggling guilt of feeling happy when Shane left for his long trips clashed with the reality that she loved him. By the time Shane Jr. was a year old, the blueprint for the four or five days Shane spent between the road trips was established.

Shane always had a gift, either a stuffed animal or some small toy, bought in one of the huge truck stop gift shops and usually not age-appropriate for his young son. Linda's gift invariably came from one of the adult boutique stores which were just beginning to appear on the interstate highways. Shane expected the apparel items to be worn during their first sexual encounter, which always occurred at the first opportunity after he arrived home. Before Shane Jr. the occasions were immediate; after the baby was born, the sessions ceased to be spontaneous, instead squeezed in during naps, or between feeding times when the playpen became the babysitter. Those times seldom worked, much to Shane's dismay. Linda was usually distracted, her attention on the baby, and they had to resort to waiting for bedtime, which presented its own set of problems. The fatigue factor of motherhood couldn't be

85

denied; when coupled with Shane's penchant for martinis before
and after dinner, the eagerly anticipated encounters often disappointed both of them.

One night, after a particularly frustrating attempt to make love,
Shane waxed philosophical and surprised Linda with an observation gleaned from his high school English class days.

"Shakespeare was right," he said. "Drink provokes the desire,
but it sure does take away the performance." The next instant, he
fell sound asleep.

The first two days were usually calm. Shane seemed content
to watch television all day as Linda tended to the baby, cleaned,
did the usual housework, and prepared the meals. By nightfall
on the second day of his being home, irritation at the one-sided
competition for Linda's attention set in. Although going through
the motions of being the attentive father, his patience eventually
wore down. The schedule became predictable. The cocktail hour
started earlier, usually about the same time as Shane Jr. awakened
from his afternoon nap and began to dominate the household the
way firstborns so often do. After his feeding came play time; after
play time came quiet time in the playpen. The quiet time lasted
no more than five minutes before he decided he'd had enough
of the imprisonment and separation from the other humans in
the house. He did what any baby would do in that situation; he
began to cry. Linda reacted to the crying in similar fashion as most
new mothers. She went to him, spoke softly, and, when the crying
didn't stop, ultimately picked him up. In the arms of his mother,
Junior usually calmed down. The first few times this occurred,
Shane sat staring at the stuffed olive in the bottom of his glass,
seething at the interruption in his routine. Each of these disrup-
tions ended with a silent, tension-filled house for the rest of the
night, lasting through the next day, when Shane would apologize
before leaving on his next trip. The escalation occurred when
Shane Jr. was three months old.

VALENTINE'S DAY IN 1982 brought with it an old-fashioned
New England blizzard. Shane returned from the West Coast
early Saturday afternoon, just as the first flakes swirled around

Hampton Village. After parking his rig, he made his ritualistic stop at the Village Grille. In several rapid swallows, he downed the drink Tillie had prepared, thanked her, and threw his usual ten-dollar bill on the bar. After a quick stop at the downtown IGA, he headed home with a packaged bouquet of assorted flowers. The snow began to fall in earnest before he arrived home. A light coating had already accumulated on the driveway, and he stamped his feet on the porch to shake the slush from his shoes. Linda heard the stomping and hurried to meet him.

"I'm so happy you're home," she said, throwing her arms around him. "This is supposed to be quite a storm."

Shane held out the bouquet. "Happy Valentine's Day a day early," he said. "Where is the little guy?"

Linda just smiled at him. "He's over at Loretta's for the afternoon. When you told me on the phone you'd be home this afternoon, I thought that maybe you'd like some quiet time; you know, just the two of us." Her smile turned seductive. "That is, if you feel like it."

When Loretta knocked on the door two hours later with Shane Jr. bundled in blankets in her arms, there was no mistaking the glow on Linda's cheeks. "So, did you have a nice afternoon?" she asked, winking. Linda blushed a deeper rose.

Shane appeared behind her. "We sure did, didn't we?" He wound his arms around Linda's waist, his right hand straying up under her breasts and pushing with enough force to pull the material of her blouse taut across her chest. Loretta looked away.

"I've really got to get going; the snow is coming down hard now. Anyway, such a darling little boy. He was great!" She passed the bundle to Linda, who had moved out of Shane's grasp. Shane reached around her for the diaper bag, filled to overflowing with the usual baby paraphernalia.

"Thanks, Loretta, We really appreciate it," he said, adding with a smirk, "Especially me."

"Enjoy the long weekend! Good old George's birthday Monday, you know." She turned and walked gingerly over the snow to her car.

"This is great, Shane. We've got an extra day together and you haven't seen your son for two weeks." Linda walked into the living room, gently laid Shane Jr. on the sofa, and began the unwrapping process. She looked back over her shoulder, expecting Shane to be right behind her. Instead, the sound of the liquor cabinet opening drifted through the doorway.

THE SNOWSTORM INTENSIFIED BEYOND any meteorologist's expectations. By Sunday afternoon, Hampton Village and the surrounding towns had already cancelled schools for Tuesday, adding an unexpected bonus day to the long weekend for the children and a predictable scrambling of working parents to find solutions to their babysitting problems.

Loretta James was the first to call. Her two daughters, ages six and seven, obviously could not be left alone. "I can get off early, maybe by two," she explained, "but I've got to work after the long weekend, at least just until I catch up."

Linda, remembering Loretta's giving up a half of her only weekday off so she and Shane could have time together, didn't hesitate. "I'll be fine. Your girls are sweethearts. Just drop them off here on your way and you can work as long as you like."

Loretta just giggled. "Thanks a lot, but I think I'll try to cut it short on Tuesday."

No sooner had Linda hung up then the phone rang again.

"This is Yvonne DiMartini. I was wondering if you could help me out." Linda ran the name through her memory bank but came up blank. The pause caused Yvonne to stammer out an apology. "Oh, jeez, I'm sorry, Linda. We just met that once at the Grille. I'm a friend of Loretta's." Yvonne's face came into focus in Linda's mind.

"I remember you now. You were with Loretta." Linda's memory of Yvonne placed her in the "she's nice, maybe good friend material" category. "What do you need? I'm sure I can help."

"I know you don't know me but Loretta said you were going to watch her kids for a while during the snow day, and I wondered if I could impose on you. My mom usually cares for my seven-year-old daughter in these situations, but she's been under the weather for over a week now, and I don't want to ask her..." Linda interrupted the lengthy explanation.

"I'd be happy to help out—the more the merrier, as they say. Bring her over whenever. It'll be fine."

When the conversation ended after profuse thanks from Yvonne, the Phillips household was committed to having three visiting children on Tuesday. Shane did not take the news well.

"Here we go again, Linda. You really have to get a backbone and say no to people, you know that? The last day of my break and I'll be falling over kids the whole damn day." Following the pattern, the tension increased with each passing hour after her announcement, culminating with a stress-filled early breakfast on Tuesday morning before the children arrived.

"I thought you could help out with Junior today," Linda said as she served him a perfect ham and cheese omelet. "It would be a perfect time to get to know him better."

"I'm not bailing you out. You're the one who made the decision to babysit so now you can figure out how to handle four kids. I'm going to make sure that my truck is clear of the snow so I can get out of here on time tomorrow." He was still chewing the last bite of his omelet as he ripped his hat and coat from the mudroom rack and headed out the door. "What time do those kids get picked up?"

Linda remained in her chair, staring at him. "They'll be gone by two for sure," she said.

"Then I'll see you about three." The slamming of the door shook the entire first floor of the house, startling Shane Jr. into a loud wail. A moment later, Linda was pacing the kitchen floor trying to calm him down before their visitors arrived.

"Thanks a lot, Shane," she hissed as she watched out the window at his car disappearing down the driveway.

THE ANTIQUE GRANDFATHER CLOCK, a prized wedding gift from Linda's grandmother, let loose with four of its melodious chimes just as Shane opened the kitchen door. Linda heard him tromping through the house as she rocked Junior in the upstairs nursery, an unfinished project with two walls painted a calming azure and the other two retaining the gaudy, flowered wallpaper fitting for a 1950s motif. She didn't answer when he hollered up the steps, but just kept feeding Shane Jr. his almost empty bottle.

"Where in the hell are you?" Shane shouted from the living room.

The heavy footfalls on the steps told Linda that he hadn't removed his boots, certain to be dripping snow and slush all through the house. She remained silent, waiting for him to make his appearance. Without even seeing his face, Linda knew exactly what his state of mind would be.

"Why didn't you answer me?" he asked as he entered the nursery, the pseudo hurt look on his face stirring no apparent sympathy from Linda. She cringed as he crossed the room toward her, his boots grinding moisture into the newly laid carpet. He leaned over and kissed her on the cheek, immediately exposing where he had spent most of his afternoon. With a still-gloved hand, he chucked the baby under the chin. "And how's the boy?" he asked. The response to the cold, gritty scrape of the glove was instantaneous. Shane Jr. pushed the bottle away and began to cry, first softly then building toward a crescendo.

Linda stood up from the rocker, alternately jiggling and swaying. "Where have you been? You said you'd be home about three. Have some trouble clearing the truck or just killing time to make sure the kids were gone?" The sharp tone of her questioning without even first saying hello to her husband had its desired effect and drained away some of Shane's aggressiveness. He quickly adopted his contrite mask.

"So, how'd it go with all those kids, anyway?" he asked. "I've been wondering about that all day."

"You obviously had some time to wonder at the bar. Look, let me get Junior calmed down, then we'll talk. Why don't you go downstairs and get out of those wet boots and gloves, maybe even get a towel to wipe up the mess you made on the rug?" Linda turned her back to him and continued to pace while the baby's crying showed no signs of diminishing.

"Nice fucking welcome home," Shane whispered as he descended the stairs.

SHANE WAITED UNTIL THE sobbing subsided in the nursery before starting up the stairs. He unrolled several paper towels from the freshly opened roll. Linda was back in the rocker, cradling their son in her right arm while her left draped over him in a protective mode, appearing to be shielding him from some impending assault.

Shane ripped off the towels and knelt at the doorway. After wiping the first splotch of dampness, he crawled across the room, daubing now and again at the small, rapidly drying spots he had left behind on his first trip, his efforts ineffective. Linda watched as he approached on his knees. She smiled more broadly with each forward movement. When he reached the rocking chair, he patted the last damp area and stood up.

"What so funny?" Shane asked, an annoyed edge creeping into his voice.

Linda's smile stayed in place. "It's just fun to have you come to me on your knees," she said. "I've got you just where I want you." A nervous giggle escaped from her mouth. "Only kidding, you know that, right? And thanks for trying to clean up."

"Yeah, that is funny, as long as you remember who's boss in this house." He reached down and lifted her arm away from its protective position across Shane Jr.'s chest. The baby was now staring up at him. "Hey, little guy, you agree, right? Your daddy runs this ship." Similar to his earlier attempt but without the glove, Shane put two fingers under Junior's chin and began to tickle him. The effect on the child was immediate. First came the typical baby frown which always precedes a quivering lower lip, followed inevitably by the first rumbles of a crying jag.

"What the hell!" Shane exclaimed as he watched his son break into full-fledged howling.

Linda jumped up and started her calming routine once again. "He's just a little afraid. He doesn't see you that much. Why don't you try to rock him? He likes that." She started to hand him to Shane, who first recoiled, but then accepted the challenge.

"I'll tell you what we're going to do, Linda. We're going to put him in his crib and let him cry it out. He's not going to be in charge here and he's not going to be a spoiled brat." He held Shane Jr. at arm's length, his hands under the armpits with the baby dangling, legs kicking fiercely. In two strides, he stood beside the crib and placed Junior into it, then pulled his legs out from under him so he was lying flat on his back, crying harder than ever.

Linda was frozen in disbelief, paralyzed for a few seconds, then reacted. "Shane, you can't do this; he's just a baby, for God's sake." She started to move toward the crib but Shane met her halfway. He gripped her arms and pinned them to her sides.

"We're going downstairs and let Junior do some growing up." He released his grip on one arm but squeezed the other so hard that she let out a yelp. "No discussions on this, Linda. We are going downstairs. NOW!" Retaining his hold on her arm, he turned her toward the door, forcing her through it. With his other hand, he reached behind him and slammed the door shut, leaving Shane Jr. screaming, hitches in his breath coming at regular intervals.

Without relinquishing his crushing grip, Shane directed the awkward trip down the steps, the two of them stumbling and almost falling twice during Linda's futile attempts to resist. With a single swinging motion, he flung her into her favorite living room chair. "I'll make the drinks and you just sit there," he growled. "And I mean it." She sank deeper in the chair as the fire in his eyes drove out any thought of fighting back, at least this time. Tears came to her eyes as the crying from the second floor continued.

As they worked their way through the first drink, the clamor from the nursery progressed from crying to blubbering to whimpering, and finally, to blessed silence.

"See, I told you, Linda. You really need to establish your authority, otherwise you lose control. He'll remember this lesson, and, trust me, he won't hold it against us."

Linda ignored his self-satisfied smirk. Shane's off-day pattern was established and more of Linda's wall fell into place.

# Thirteen

## *Control*

"WHY DON'T YOU JUST get another job, Shane?" Linda's now familiar question, one she asked about every other time he prepared for a long distance trip, was met with his standard vacant stare, like she was speaking a foreign language. "You could get something around here; you know, be home every night like normal people."

"That's bullshit, Linda, and you know it. Sure, I could work at the local IGA, or, worse yet, McDonald's, but trucking's about the only way I'm ever going to make the kind of money I'm making. It's not like I'm going to go back to school or something. Christ, I barely made it through high school." The argument he presented in answer was just as familiar as the question itself. The interchange had become as much of a ritual as exchanging disingenuous "love you's" as he left the house for one of his trips.

"You're always saying how much you miss me when you're away, and I miss you too, but I get a little tired of hearing about it when it's really your choice. I'd even move if we had to."

"Why do we always get into these discussions just when I'm about to leave? We're not moving anywhere. We've got the house; Hampton Village schools are about the best around; we've got some good friendships going. We're in a good spot, so let's make it work. Sure, I worry about you being by yourself so much. I see the guys salivating every time we're out anywhere..." Shane's voice softened as he glanced at the tea kettle shaped clock above the

93

stove. "I've got to go. Wouldn't you know another Valentine's Day snowstorm's coming in, just like last year?" He moved toward the kitchen door. "Give Junior a kiss for me when he wakes up. And you behave yourself while I'm gone."

Linda glared at him, then tempered her rising anger and wedged herself between him and the door.

"You behave yourself and drive carefully, especially if you don't beat the weather on the way out." She moved against him with a full body hug, pressing her pelvis hard against his. "I'll miss you and so will Shane Jr. He's fifteen months old, old enough to know when his daddy's gone now."

"Kid hardly knows who I am and what he does know is that I'm the only one who's not spoiling him rotten." Even as his voice rose in harshness, he reached low around behind her with both hands, each cupping one of Linda's shapely cheeks. "And don't you ever forget that these are mine, and mine alone," he said, deeply kneading her buttocks as if they were bread dough. Then he kissed her on the cheek and was gone.

"Love you," she said, but the slamming door eliminated any chance that he might have heard her.

"Not even three years and we're acting like an old married couple," she whispered as she climbed the stairs to fetch Junior, sure that the door slam had awakened him.

"When's the last time you had some free time to yourself?" Yvonne asked the question, but Loretta was nodding in agreement.

"Yeah, you know what they say. All work and no play makes Linda a dull girl," she said, flashing her trademark smile.

The three friends giggled like school girls. Their Saturday afternoon tea had been going on for over an hour as Junior napped and the other three children romped about in the snow in the backyard. The gatherings were fast becoming a tradition. Over the past year, any time Shane was on the road on a Saturday, Linda invited Yvonne and Loretta over for what she jokingly called "high tea," lending the event an air of United Kingdom authenticity, even though she knew the term was incorrect for what they were doing. While both of them were single mothers with all of the difficulties that status implies, the regular get-togethers revealed that Linda had much in common with them and the friendships deepened with each gathering.

While Yvonne's question momentarily caught Linda off-guard, Loretta's follow-up comment secured her attention. Since Shane Jr.'s birth, she couldn't remember the last time she went anywhere without him. Shane still didn't feel comfortable being alone with him, although she told him on numerous occasions that she thought that was ridiculous. Linda finally sputtered an answer to both the question and the comment in one sentence.

"Since before Junior was born, I guess, and you're right, Loretta, it's been pretty much all work and no play. My job used to at least get me out of the house but we've decided that I should stay home until he's at least three. So, I'll be housebound for maybe another couple of years, at least."

Her friends saw through the forced smile.

"Okay," Yvonne said, "here's what we're going to do. My mom is watching Sarah tonight and she loves toddlers so why don't I bring her over here with Sarah and we can have a girls' night out?"

Loretta joined in, adding her opinion and squashing Linda's reluctance before she could even express it. "You're going—end of story. My sitter is all set as well. We'll pick you up when we drop off Sarah and Yvonne's mom about six."

Linda laughed out loud. "Okay, I'll go but it would nice if one of you would tell me where we're going."

"The Grille, of course! Saturday special is an all-you-can-eat fish fry and happy hour's extended to seven. And they have a great DJ. As they say, it's a happening place." Yvonne reached over the table and squeezed Linda's hand. "It'll be good for you." Her place as the worldly leader of the group left no more room for discussion. She was a Village Grille veteran, her fiery Italian personality and bawdy sexuality making her a favorite of the regulars.

The conversation ended as the sound of children laughing drifted in from the mudroom. "I'll heat up the milk for the hot chocolate. The kids will surely be asking for that after being outside all afternoon." Linda went to the refrigerator, opened it, then stopped and turned around.

"What will I tell Shane? He probably won't be too happy with me." Both of her friends stared at her in astonishment.

"What—you can't go out with friends for dinner? What the heck is wrong with that?" Yvonne asked, a strong note of incredulity in her voice.

Linda's answer to Loretta's question was to turn back, reach in and get a half gallon of milk. She avoided looking at them as she hustled to the stove, grabbed a saucepan out of the overhead cabinet, filled it to within a half inch of the top and began the heating process.

"He doesn't like me going out without him, you know," Linda said. "He just likes to know what I'm doing pretty much all the time." She hesitated, as if uncertain she should finish her thought. Finally, with a resigned sigh, she murmured what she knew to be an understatement. "I guess he gets a little jealous sometimes."

Her two friends looked at each other and nodded. "Well then, don't tell him," Yvonne suggested, as if the solution to the dilemma was obvious.

LINDA SPENT MOST OF the evening at the Village Grille glancing around the room as if feeling guilty, not because of what she was doing but because she was having such a good time. The wine-enhanced conversation with her friends led to more hearty laughter and sharing than she had ever experienced before. The beer-battered fish filled her with more fried food than she had had in a year. When she announced that "I should have a liquid Maalox chaser," the lame joke sent her friends into paroxysms of alcohol-induced, over-reactive laughter. By the time the DJ began to spin his magic, every table in the restaurant was taken, and patrons at the bar stood two to three deep, jostling for attention from the bartender.

Loretta and Yvonne seemed to know everyone, frolicking away one dance after another with different partners as Linda sat on the sidelines, watching. When the DJ finally chose a slow number, her friends lost interest and returned to the table. They arrived simultaneously with a man Linda had noticed staring at her from a corner stool at the bar.

"Would you like to dance?" he asked, his eyes focused on Linda and ignoring the cool reception from all three of the women.

"I'm married," Linda blurted out, much to the delight of Yvonne.

"Does being married mean you can't dance?" Yvonne giggled through her response, looking straight at Tommy. "Not that Tommy here would be my choice, either."

Tommy Iverson glared at her, then turned his attention to Linda once more.

"She doesn't like me much but she did ask a good question. Can you dance?"

Flustered almost speechless, Linda blushed. "Of course I can dance, but my husband gets a little upset when it's with someone other than him."

"So where is he? No harm, no foul, I always say. What people don't know, can't hurt them, right?" Tommy had edged his way around the table so that he was standing next to Linda, leaning close enough to brush against her arm.

Linda pushed her chair back and stood up. "Maybe some other time..." She stuttered as she tried to recall his name. He caught her hesitation.

"I'm Tommy, Tommy Iverson." He held out his hand, which she refused to acknowledge. "I know, I know, Tommy sounds like a kid's name but I'm stuck with it. Wouldn't even answer if someone called me Tom." He grinned as he looked her up and down. "Sure would like to dance with you if you ever change your mind."

She didn't answer him, instead turning her back and walking away. As she passed by the bar on her way to the restroom, Tillie, the bartender, called out to her but the surrounding din drowned her out.

"Never seen Shane's wife here without him before," she said, mostly to herself.

"HE CALLED ABOUT SIX thirty, then called about every half hour until nine. I told him you were out to dinner with Yvonne and Loretta. I'd have to say that by the last call, he wasn't sounding too happy."

Linda rolled her eyes. "Sorry you had to put up with that, Mrs. DiMartini. Shane sometimes gets lonely on the road and just wants to talk to me, like, *right now*, if you know what I mean."

Louise DiMartini smiled. "Not to worry, dear. I know all about men away from home. My husband was in the Merchant Marine for years before he died. Sometimes by the end of a voyage, he'd be almost crazed." She reached out and touched Linda lightly on the shoulder, an impish glint creeping into her eyes. "But those reunions sure are fun, aren't they?"

Yvonne laughed out loud. "Mom! I am truly shocked."

Her mother just shrugged. "No, you're not," she said.

SHANE ROLLED THROUGH HAMPTON Village earlier than expected on the following Friday afternoon. He followed his regular ritual, parking, then separating the trailer in the Riggins Trucking storage lot and driving back into town. The only choice for his tractor in the town parking lot was at the very rear, a spot where leafless bushes and tall weeds invaded through the chain link fence, making parking there a precarious proposition.

"Damn town's getting too many people," he muttered as he climbed down and started his longer than usual walk across the lot toward the Village Grille.

Tillie greeted him warmly, as she always did, and apologized for not having his drink ready. "Didn't see you coming, Shane. Sorry," she said as she began to mix his usual.

"Not a problem as long as I have it in the next minute. It's been a long week." He smiled at her as she glanced back over her shoulder. "Hey, by the way, were you working last Saturday night?"

"Seems like I work eighty hours a week here, but yeah, I was working. If I'm not being too curious, why did you ask?" She finished mixing his martini and brought it over to the bar. He waited until she finished pouring to answer.

"Just wondered if you happened to see Linda in here that night. She was out with some friends for dinner. I think she said they came here." His casual inquiry relaxed her natural bartender's reticence to provide any information on the clientele. Unlike some of her customers, Linda had given her no instructions about letting anyone know about her presence at the Grille.

"I did see her, although it was just in passing when she was using the rest room. Place was packed that night, like always on fish fry night."

"So, they just ate dinner and left, right? Didn't stay for the dancing or anything?" The nonchalance of his questions had disappeared. Tillie's instincts kicked in and she resorted to the mental reservation technique of providing information.

"Like I said, only saw her going to the restroom." She turned and busied herself with rinsing glasses,

Shane persisted, asking the next question to her back. "What time of the night was that, Tillie? Had the DJ started to play or not?"

"Couldn't rightly say, about the time, but, yeah, I guess I remember the DJ was playing. Those friends she was with were sure dancing up a storm." She grimaced into the sink. "Oh, shit," she whispered, "too much information." In silence, she washed the same glasses several times before finally turning around. Shane's drink was drained and the usual ten-dollar bill was tucked under his glass, but he was gone. She looked out the window to see him hustling along the sidewalk toward the town parking lot.

THE UNMISTAKABLE RUMBLE OF Shane's truck backing up the driveway had Linda running to the upstairs window. Junior was about fifteen minutes into his afternoon nap, unlikely to awaken for at least another hour, probably more. She had expected to have more time to get ready for him but his early arrival excited her. She scurried into the bathroom, splashed some water on her face and ran a comb through her hair. "This'll have to be good enough for now," she said aloud.

She hurried down the stairs and opened the kitchen door leading into the mudroom. Shane had removed his coat and dropped it on the floor. He had the heel of one foot wedged in the bootjack and looked up at her.

"Hey, you're home earlier than I thought," she said.

After a few seconds of silence, he pulled his foot loose and the boot fell to the side. He put his other foot in the device. "Yeah, not interrupting anything, am I?" he asked as he yanked his foot out of the second boot.

"No, I just put Junior in and he'll be asleep for another hour or two. I'm excited that you're home already. Can't wait to hear about your adventures in the snow storm on the way out of here."

Linda picked up his coat and hung it on a hook then approached to hug him. He sloughed off the hug, grabbed her right hand and pulled her through the doorway.

"We're going upstairs, now," he announced as he dragged her through the kitchen.

"Well, my, my, I guess you missed me, huh?" she said, laughing. "But seriously, don't you want to get showered or something? We have plenty of time." No answer was forthcoming as he continued to haul her up the stairs. The silence continued as they entered the bedroom. He turned her toward him and she made another attempt to embrace him in a hug but he put his hands on her shoulders and shoved her hard, backwards toward the bed.

"Take off your clothes. I'll be back in a minute." He disappeared into the bathroom. She listened to the familiar sound of a man urinating into a toilet bowl and undid the buttons of her blouse. She was working on the snaps of her slacks when he returned.

"Are you angry with me, Shane? You haven't said two words." His answer was to reach for her partially undone slacks and rip out the last two snaps. She raised her hips, and he wiggled her out of the pants and her underwear. He hadn't zipped his fly after his bathroom visit and he didn't bother to undo his belt and drop his pants.

Their lovemaking sessions often lasted more than hour, but this one was over in less than a minute. Shane climbed off Linda, stood, zipped up, and started to leave the room. Linda lay on the bed, legs still splayed out as if she was willing and wanted to continue.

Shane stopped at the doorway. "Get dressed and come downstairs. We're going to have a little chat." The harshness in his voice left any response she might have had stuck in her throat.

Dazed and shaking, Linda picked her underpants off the floor, made her way to the closet and picked out one of her plain, work-around-the-house dresses. She took her clothes into the bathroom and leaned on the sink, staring into her eyes reflecting back from the mirror as if searching for answers to what just happened. The quest was fruitless. After dressing, she peeked in at Junior, whose gentle breaths indicated that he remained sound asleep. She pulled the door closed, and with hesitant steps, started downstairs, not looking forward to her little chat with Shane.

As she expected, he sat in his favorite recliner, the martini glass on the end table next to him virtually empty. His first maneuver took her completely by surprise. He stood up quickly and crossed the room toward her just as she came through the doorway. She stopped, even recoiling slightly at his approach, adopting what was close to a fight or flight position. Stopping short of entering her personal space, he shrugged.

"Look, Linda, I'm really sorry about what happened up there. Could you sit down so we can talk about it?" His apparent sincerity disarmed her.

"Sure," she said, relieved at his composure. Their chairs faced each other but the positioning of them gave the appearance of being in neutral corners of the room.

"You start, Shane. You're the one who wanted to talk so I'm listening." The distance across the room made eye contact easy, and her glare forced him to shift his gaze to the photo montage on the wall behind her as he squirmed in his chair. He spoke for a full five minutes, explaining his stop at the Village Grille where he discovered that she had stayed well into the night, not just gone there for dinner. The mention of Tillie's assertion that her friends were "dancing up a storm" with a variety of partners brought the first interruption of his monologue from Linda.

"They were, and they were having a good time, but I don't see what that has to do with me."

"It has everything to do with you, Linda. I don't believe you're going to sit there and tell me that guys weren't hitting on you left and right. I've told you how I feel about you going out without me." Shane's voice developed a tinge of anger as he finished. "You're not to do that again. It's that simple."

"Let's see if I have this straight; you're telling me I can't go out for dinner with friends. I'm supposed to stay home and be bored while you're traveling all over the country. Right?" Linda rose from her chair and began to move toward him but backpedaled when he came out of his recliner.

"You do have it straight and that's the way it's going to be. We're married with a kid, and his mother is not going to be out gallivanting around the town and hanging out in bars till all hours of the night." The rapid shift in his mood and increasingly hostile and threatening body language had her withdrawing until she backed into the wall. Being pushed into a corner delivered an extra jolt of courage fueled by adrenalin. It wasn't quite the final corner that Stephen Crane meant when he said that all men can develop teeth and claws when pushed into final corners, but it was enough to send her back in Shane's direction.

"We'll talk about this more when you calm down. I thought we were going to have a little chat, not a one-sided lecture. I feel like I'm back home with my mother, for God's sake!" Linda's mildly defiant tone combined with a finger waggling in his face sent heat streaming into his cheeks. Linda had no time to raise her arm in defense before his solid backhand sent her reeling backward toward the corner once again. She lost her balance and sprawled hard on the floor just before she struck the wall. He followed her like a fighter follows an opponent after a knockdown, his furious expression daring her to get up again. She glared up at him, but the fire in her eyes was gone.

"Like I just told you, Linda. You did have it straight. I'm calling the shots from now on. Now get yourself together. I'm going up to get the kid so we can have some family time together. I'll fix us some drinks when I come down." He turned and she waited until she heard him stomping up the steps to struggle to her feet. She rubbed her right cheek, now aflame from the sting of his blow. A passing glance in the decorative mirror over the couch confirmed what she already suspected. She'd be wearing extra makeup for a few days.

"Bastard!" she muttered as she heard Shane Jr. crying upstairs.

THE NEWS COULD NOT have come at a worse time. Linda made

the appointment with Dr. Steven Capaldi just five days after her period was due. Each day, her apprehension increased until she couldn't stand the suspense any longer.

"The doctor probably won't be able to tell anything yet, Mrs. Phillips. "I'm sure everything will be okay. You said it's been how long again?" Sheila Murphy, Capaldi's longtime nurse, recognized the anxiety in Linda's voice as soon as she heard the first request for an appointment. She adopted her most professional demeanor to deal with a fragile situation, one she had experienced on numerous occasions in her professional life. Research into the level of stress an unwanted pregnancy produces abounds, and the effect it has on anyone involved is thoroughly documented. "I'll speak with Dr. Capaldi and see what he thinks and call you right back."

After hanging up the phone, Linda buried her face in her hands, and began to sob. She was barely under control a few minutes later when the phone rang. She grabbed it before the first ring ended.

"This is Sheila at Dr. Capaldi's office. He says he'll try it under the circumstances but can't promise any definitive result. Just go to the same lab we've used for your blood work before. I'll call ahead so they'll be expecting you. I'm sure they'll agree to put a rush on it and will call later this afternoon with the results." Linda's boisterous "thank you!" interrupted her for a moment but she pressed on. "I really must emphasize that we may not be able to tell you anything yet."

"I understand completely and I truly appreciate this. I'll just wait for you to call, right?" After a lengthy pause, the nurse responded.

"I have a feeling that Dr. Capaldi will want to talk to you, Mrs. Phillips. He's a little concerned over your anxiety about this. But, yes, you'll hear from us later today if you can get to the lab sooner rather than later."

Five minutes later, Linda and Shane Jr. were in her car. As promised, her arrival at the lab, just several miles away, was expected and the technician greeted her with a warm welcome. The two other women sitting in the waiting room glowered at first when he announced that she'd be taken right in, but a wide smile from the toddling little boy holding his mother's hand turned their unhappy frowns upside down. "Mommy needs a test," Junior said, his pronunciation perfect. "Me watch." The technician escorted Linda and her wide-eyed son through the door, glancing over his shoulder at the two women. A brief gesture told them this would not take long; they just grinned and sent a dismissive wave back at him.

LINDA HATED TO PUT Shane Jr. down for his afternoon nap. When he was awake, the time passed so much faster and the two hours he would be sleeping would be interminable. When she heard him stirring just an hour and a half later, she rushed up the steps to catch him before he drifted back to sleep. By four o'clock, she was sitting at the kitchen table watching him cram Silly Putty into a variety of plastic animal molds while the ticking of the clock announced each second. Anxious glances at the time put everything into slow motion. The call from Steven Capaldi's office came just after she had poured a generous glass of Merlot. "I can't be pregnant," she whispered, as convincing as she could be and effectively assuaging her guilt as she slurped down several swallows of the wine. Sheila's promise of a late afternoon call had been met, but just barely.

"Hello," she answered, the phone wet and slippery in her sweaty palms.

"This is Steve Capaldi. The lab was able to get the results of your test over to us. Are you sitting down, Mrs. Phillips?" The doctor's voice was strong yet gentle. His question caused a weakness in Linda's knees, as severe as if she was coming down from an adrenaline rush after a near high speed collision on a super highway.

"Actually, I'm not, but I will if you think I should." The quiver in her voice matched the wobble in her legs. She sat in a straight back kitchen chair and put her wine on the table. "What is it, Doctor?" she asked, in a tone that told him she was reluctant to hear the answer.

"If the test is correct, and we have to remember that it is preliminary and could be wrong, although I doubt it, you are pregnant.

The hCG count is just beginning to show but there's no question that it's there and elevated. A retest in a week would confirm but I think we could set up an appointment now." Capaldi waited for his words to settle, then continued. "I'll confess to a bit of worry about you. Sheila thought you sounded very upset on the phone this morning. Are you all right, Mrs. Phillips?"

"No, I'm not, Doctor. This is not good news at all. My husband will not be happy and I have no idea how he'll react to this. I'll have to call you back for an appointment." The panic in her voice echoed in his ear as she disconnected the call. Shane wouldn't be home for several more days, but the cloud of dread had already formed and threatened to envelope her.

The cloud turned out to be prophetic. The surprising news created a more dramatic reaction than even Linda had anticipated.

SAM OLDEN DREW THE proverbial short straw. It was his turn to respond to the next Code 53, a domestic dispute, surely at the top of the list when it came to the least favorite duties of any cop. More times than not, answering this kind of call resulted in becoming a common enemy for both parties, who seemed to forget their dispute and transfer the hostility to the innocent third party trying to assist. The timing of the call made Sam a little more anxious. Most of these disputes came later in the day, usually fueled by alcohol. An early afternoon call often meant that the argument had a rational basis, which did not necessarily lead to a rational con- clusion. "Almost always a lose, lose situation," Sam muttered to himself as he pulled into the long driveway of the Phillips's house. He decided to park his cruiser at the bottom and walk up to the house, making his entrance less dramatic and not as threatening. By the time he reached the veranda that wrapped around the rear of the house, Shane was standing on the porch.

"My wife told me she called you guys. She apologizes for bringing you out here. Everything's okay, Officer. We just had a little disagreement but we're all good, now. Thanks a lot for the prompt response," Shane hollered. A sly yet forced grin crept in. "You know how these women are, right? Can't live with 'em and you can't live without 'em. Hope you're not going to charge for a house call." Shane's phony chuckle died away as Sam climbed the steps.

"No offense, Mr. Phillips, but I'd like to see your wife," Sam said, looking past Shane at the kitchen door.

"She's pretty embarrassed right now. I don't think she'd want to see you." Shane maneuvered his body between the officer and the door. "I'll have her call and talk to you later." As he finished the sentence, the click of the door latch caught the attention of both men. Shane whirled around, as if he expected an attack from the rear. The door swung open but stopped halfway. Linda peered out, half of her face exposed, looking like a housewife greeting a traveling vacuum cleaner salesman.

"I told you I'd take care of it, Linda. Now close the door," he said, his effort to disguise the harshness a dismal failure.

Sam stepped around Shane. "Mrs. Phillips, I need to know that you're okay. May I come in for just a minute?" Linda's eyes skipped contact with his but went directly to Shane.

"There's really no need, Officer. I'm really fine. As Shane probably told you, it was something I let get out of hand. I never should have called but I thought he might hurt Junior." She stopped as a slight gasp was covered by her hand flying to her mouth. "I mean, really, we're fine here now. I made a huge mistake." She gently closed the door.

Sam stared at the closed door for a moment. Shane stood behind him, waiting for his decision. When none was immediately forthcoming, he spoke.

"See, it was just like I said, Officer, uh…Officer…" Sam had turned to him in time for Shane to catch his nametag. "…Officer Olden. A little spat happens all the time, nothing to get excited about. You're married, right? You know what I mean."

"Actually, I'm not married, but I know about little spats. Somehow, this seems to have a little more to it than that, but I've got no choice but to honor what your wife said."

Shane smiled broadly, but the smile disappeared as Sam continued. "At least, I'll honor it this time. That's what we're trained to do." He brushed past Shane, got to the steps, and turned around. "Next time might be different, so maybe you don't want there to be a next time." He left the porch and almost jogged down the driveway to his cruiser. He yanked the door open and reached for his radio.

"Olden, here," he said immediately after clicking the radio open. "Leaving the Phillips household and returning to headquarters."

"Roger that, Sam. Are you okay? Sounds like you're pretty tense, like even your hair is clenched."

"Thanks but I'm good," he answered, clicking the radio off. He flipped the visor down and looked in the mirror, then glanced down at his shaking hands. The dispatcher's observation was right. "That woman is really afraid," he whispered, "and that guy is the reason."

"YOU'RE GODDAMNED RIGHT YOU made a huge mistake." Shane had waited until he watched Sam Olden pull away before reentering the house. Linda's back was to him at first but she turned as soon as the door slammed. "You are never going to humiliate me like that again."

Linda gestured toward the kitchen table. "Shane, can we please just sit down and talk about this? You scare me to death when you're so angry. That's why I called; I was afraid you'd really hurt me, or even Junior." Shane just stared at her, dazed, as though coming down off an adrenalin high. He plopped down into one of the kitchen chairs and put his face in his hands, his fingers massaging his forehead.

"Where is Junior, anyway?" he asked.

"He's slept through the whole thing, amazingly enough. I thought we'd be able to talk better about this with him up for his nap. That's why I waited to tell you." She had sat down in the chair next to him. "Talk to me, please. I know another child wasn't in the plans but sometimes these things just happen."

Shane dropped his hands from his face and folded them on the table in front of him, a position that made it seem as if he was praying. "That's what bugs me, Linda. How these things just happen. How in the hell did it happen? I've been careful every time, especially with you reminding me." Linda pushed her chair closer as Shane's anger dissipated even further. She reached out and covered his hands with hers.

"There was that one time, and the timing is perfect. You remember that, about Valentine's Day?" She kept her hands on top of his, watching his expression.

"Yeah, I guess I do. It just seems so unlikely, I mean, the one time I don't use a rubber and you get pregnant. What fucking luck!" A slit of a smile formed on his lips. "Oops, there I go again with that f-word. Sorry." He pulled his hands out from under hers, and reached over, draping one arm over her shoulders. "I heard an old joke for the umpteenth time on this trip, about the couple who just made love and the wife asks the husband what they would name a baby if they had one. The guy slips off his condom and says, 'If he gets out of here, we'll call him Houdini.'" He laughed. "Now, if you promise not to call the cops on me anymore, I'll take you upstairs and show you a good time."

"You are incorrigible, Shane Phillips. That sounds like a good idea, but we'd better be quick before Junior decides to interrupt us."

DETECTIVE PARKER HAVENOT WAS in the breakroom, getting his afternoon fix with leftover morning coffee that was both steaming hot and muddy with age. Sam Olden walked in, still carrying a leftover frown from his Code 53 call.

"Hey, Sam, what's up with the long face?" Parker asked. While not close friends, the two had worked on several cases together and bonded, both respecting the other's unique skills.

"Just got back from a domestic dispute call. What jerks guys can be sometimes, you know? I just don't understand why some husbands have to control their wives with fear and intimidation." Sam shook his head as he drew a cup of the dreadful brew. "Wow, this has been here a while," he said, chuckling.

Parker matched his laughter. "Ego," he said. "It's all about ego. The husbands, I mean, not the coffee."

"I'd bet my career that we'll be back to that house again. These things have a tendency to escalate over time." Sam's frown returned as he said it.

"Probably right," Parker agreed. "Just a matter of time in most of those cases."

# Fourteen

## *Twins*

DR. STEVE CAPALDI SUSPECTED the twins at the eight-week mark of Linda's pregnancy but kept his suspicion to himself. The strong heartbeat, a surprise at that early stage, seemed to have a slight extra sound, almost an echo.

"Everything is going along fine, Mrs. Phillips, right on schedule. We've started doing ultrasounds with every patient now around the twelfth week so we'll be doing that for you next time."

Linda smiled up at him from her awkward position in the stirrups. "We don't want to know what it is, if you can tell. We'd rather be surprised."

"That's true of most people," Sheila Murphy chimed in, her role as guardian of the reputations of both patient and doctor relegating her to occasional instrument supplier and spectator in the examination room. "It's kind of like wanting and not wanting to know what you're getting for Christmas. The suspense is the best part."

"I'd have to say that I disagree," Linda replied as she dismounted from the table. "Having Shane Jr. around the house is the best part, and this one's just going to add to the fun."

Capaldi and his nurse left the room to allow her to get dressed. The doctor pulled the door closed and they stood together for a moment in the hallway. Sheila had been with him for eleven years. She smiled at him. "You saw something in there, didn't you? I could tell from your expression."

"Nice to have a mind reader as a nurse, Mrs. Murphy." He lowered his voice to a conspiratorial whisper. "I believe she's going to be really surprised when we do that ultrasound next month. I think her little boy is going to have two siblings to contend with." He continued down the hallway, stopped at the door to his office, and motioned for his nurse to come in.

"Is everything all right, Doctor? What is it?" she asked just as she walked through the door.

"When she first came to us this time, you told me you were worried about her. She seems to be okay to me."

"I agree, but I wonder how her husband will react if you're right about the twins?"

SHANE HAD TWO TEN-DAY trips during the month before the ultrasound. Linda noticed the change almost immediately after the visit from the sheriff's department. The conscious effort to control his temper was obvious, although, like a caldron might release a bubble of heat intermittently, the tension remained, even if submerged beneath the surface. Now, the call from Dr. Capaldi confirmed what he said he suspected as he looked at the ultrasound.

"I had another doctor look at the film of the test, Mrs. Phillips. We both are convinced that you are carrying twins. I've been around long enough to know that this is generally a shock for folks, so please be aware that we can schedule an appointment to talk with you and your husband if you want. Everything is fine physically, and we want the same to be true emotionally."

After Linda hung up, she began giggling. "Oh, my God! This is going to be so cool." She dialed the phone. Loretta James picked up after two rings.

"It's twins! Can you believe it?" Linda shouted into the phone.

Loretta James let loose with a shout of her own from the other end of the line. "Yahoo! That is so neat." Then there was silence followed by a tentative, "Are you okay with this?"

"Could you just come over for a few minutes?" Linda asked, quickly adding an unnecessary addendum. "Of course, bring the kids," she said, as if Loretta had an option immediately available.

"I'll have a glass of Chardonnay waiting for you and, of course, nothing but a cranberry cocktail for me. I think I could use a little advice."

Ten minutes later, Loretta rang the doorbell. As soon as coats and hats and mittens were all hung on the racks in the mudroom and boots kicked off, the two friends were dancing around the kitchen, holding hands, exclaiming, "Twins, twins, twins!" over and over again. Loretta's two children stood on the edge of the excitement, clueless spectators no doubt wondering if the adults in the room had lost their minds. The burst of exuberance eventually wound down, as it always did, leaving both of the women gasping for breath. Relieved that things seemed to be back to normal, the children edged out of the room, off to find the stash of toys that always awaited them in the small playroom.

"I'll bring Shane in when he wakes up. He'll be excited to see you." Linda then went directly to the refrigerator and retrieved the large glass of promised Chardonnay. "Let's go sit in the living room, and I'll give you the whole scoop," she said. The broad smile that had greeted Loretta at the door remained in place.

"A whole lot of cat images are coming to mind," Loretta said as she sat in Shane's recliner. "Like the Cheshire cat, or Garfield after playing a joke on Odie, or maybe best of all, the cat who swallowed the canary. Seriously, I don't think I've ever seen you so happy. You already had that pregnancy glow but it seems like it's doubled." They both caught the significance of what she had said at the same time and laughed out loud.

"Yep, you could say that, but I guess I'm glad it's not tripled." Linda excused herself and returned a moment later with a large glass of a rose-tinted drink. "My drink of choice for the next six or seven months," she said. The sound of a rattling of crib bars drifted down the stairs, followed by the unmistakable stomp of a toddler jumping up and down on a plastic mattress liner. As if on cue, Kim James, the younger of Loretta's two daughters, appeared in the doorway.

"I think I hear Shane waking up. Can I go up to see him?" The two women exchanged shrugs, and before Linda's nod was completed, Kim was bounding up the steps.

"We're about to get interrupted but I did want to ask you something, real quick. Shane wasn't too happy about this pregnancy, but I think he's gotten used to it, and I just know that he's going to be excited about the twins. I mean, three kids, that'll really make us a family, right? My question is do you think I should tell him when he calls in or should I wait and give him the good news in person?" The thumping from upstairs had ceased, signaling the arrival of Kim at Shane's crib. Muffled voice sounds indicated that a serious kid-style conversation was taking place.

Loretta considered the question for longer than Linda expected, and her response came in the form of a question. "I didn't know he wasn't happy. Why wouldn't he be?"

A slight blush colored Linda's cheeks. "He's just a little possessive, and being away so much, he wondered at first how it could have happened, you know, with protection and all that, but he's fine with it now."

"He thought you might have been fooling around, the lady who wouldn't even dance with another guy at the Grille?" Loretta laughed. "That is ludicrous!"

Jessica, her older daughter, called to her from the bottom of the steps. "Can I go up and see Shane, or is he going to come down when you stop talking?"

"You'd better go get him before these girls get upset with you," Loretta said, smiling. "To answer your question, I say this news is better told face to face."

LINDA FOLLOWED HER FRIEND'S advice and waited for the full week until Shane's latest road trip was over, resisting the impulse to tell him about the twins during his two phone calls home. His first day back assumed the normal pattern. As soon as Linda put Shane Jr. down for his afternoon nap, they showered together and spent the nap time in bed. As usual, their lovemaking was furious the first time, expending the pent-up sexual energy of two weeks in an almost violent connection. The gentle second time resulted in the mellow glow that Linda happily anticipated. Afterward, they fell asleep briefly in each other's arms, but Linda awakened instantly to Junior's hollering from his nursery. She slipped from the bed and threw on the clothes she had draped over the single chair in their bedroom before their shower. Junior began to stir before she left the room. By the time she had changed his diaper and made her way downstairs, the second part of the pattern was falling into place. Shane already was mixing his drink.

The first martini always had the same effect, and halfway through it, the mellow mood begun in the bedroom escalated into a cheerful high. Junior sat on the floor playing with a set of wooden blocks, stacking them until the pile would fall over. A scream of laughter followed, then he would start the process all over again. Linda, sipping her cranberry juice, and Shane, sipping instead of gulping his martini, watched, mesmerized by the sight of a child entertaining himself. After a few minutes of observation Shane called his boy over to him, lifted him onto his lap and began bouncing him up and down and jiggling him from side to side, producing hysterical giggling from Junior. Both parents chuckled as Shane made the movements more boisterous and the squeals reached ear-piercing levels. After an exhausting few minutes, Shane slid Junior from his lap and reached for his drink, draining it in a single swallow. He stood up and started for the kitchen. Linda, buoyed by his apparent jovial mood, caught his hand as he went by.

"Could you just wait a minute for that? I have something to tell you."

He looked down at her, saw that she was smiling, and went back to his chair. "Whenever you say that, with that tone of voice, I feel like it's best if I'm sitting down." His tight-lipped grin effectively concealed his mental state. "So, let's have it," he said.

The practiced speech came out just as she had rehearsed it. She spoke quickly, running sentences together, successfully preventing any interruption until the entire story was out.

"Dr. Capaldi says there is a slight chance they may be wrong, but it really wasn't worth mentioning." Linda, flushed with excitement from giving Shane the momentous news, finished her story while staring at him from across the room. "So, we're soon going to be a family of five, just like that. Isn't this about the coolest thing you've ever heard?"

Shane rose from his chair and grabbed his glass in a single motion. "I'll be right back," he said as he headed for the kitchen.

Junior had returned to his game of piling up the blocks and seemed unaware of his father's flight from the room. Linda went over and sat down on the carpeted floor beside him where she could watch Shane mixing his drink through the doorway. She recognized no evidence of rigidity or tension as he placed a few ice cubes gently into the glass, and slowly poured his usual copious amount of gin topped off by a quick hit of vermouth. She remained on the floor, distracting her worry about Shane's return by absently creating her own tower of blocks. Junior waited until she placed the last block needed for her structure to be higher than his, then he reached over and pulled the bottom block out. The resulting crash took down his handiwork as well, and both of them rolled onto their backs, giggling. The laughter continued until Linda's eyes blurred with tears. She didn't hear Shane come back into the room until she felt his presence next to her. She wiped the moisture away and looked up. He was staring down at her, her vulnerability enhanced by his intimidating, hands-on-hips posture looming over her. When one hand came off his hip and he reached out to her, she flinched, misinterpreting his gesture as a threat. Instead, he just said, "Come on, I'll help you up." Then he took both of her hands into his and gently pulled her to her feet.

Speechless at the uncharacteristic show of concern, Linda finally managed a mumbled "thank you" and hugged him.

"Let me get my drink and we'll talk about the twins. I guess I do think it's kind of cool too." He started for the kitchen, his back to Linda's dumbfounded expression. When he returned, he sat in his recliner and pulled up on the release lever, snapping the footrest into place. After he swigged the first sip of his martini, Linda wondered if he was going to fall asleep, he presented such a picture of total relaxation. The opening of the conversation surprised her, even though Shane asked the question in a soft voice.

"Are there twins in your family?" Shane asked.

"No, not that I know of. Why do you ask?" Linda was still standing, a puzzled look on her face.

"I don't know of any in my family, either. I'm just trying to figure out where these two came from." The softness remained in his voice but Linda saw where this conversation was going.

"Oh, Shane, please don't ruin this." She crossed over to him and knelt by his chair, staring directly into his eyes. "I never even thought of that until now when you mentioned it. Genes for twins can skip many generations, but I'm not even going to talk about this part." She turned and crawled over to Junior, whose attention was divided between the seemingly endless game with his blocks and a little boy's concern over the conversation between his mother and father. He had seen enough of these calm discussions deteriorate that he edged closer to Linda as she sat next to him on the floor.

"Hey, Linda, come on. I'm just making conversation here. We probably both have twins somewhere way back in our family history." Shane smiled and took another larger gulp of his drink. The smile morphed into a distinct leer. "Anyway, I sure like what the twins are doing to your shape. You must have added at least one cup size already."

The comment brought Linda up off the floor like a jack-in-the-box. She snatched one of the soft pillows from the sofa on the way over and thumped him lightly on the head with it. "Like I always tell you, Shane, you are just incorrigible." She raised the pillow again but he grabbed her arm in midair, foiled the good-natured attack, and pulled her down onto his lap. The tussle brought Junior running to join them, but he hung back until the two of them began to laugh, a clear signal that it was safe to approach. "Climb on board," Linda said as she hoisted him up.

From under the tangle of his wife and son, Shane managed to get his arms loose and wrap them around Linda's waist, then made his familiar move, slipping his hands higher.

"Maybe a cup and a half," he said. Junior joined in with the welcome laughter of his parents. It was to be the best and happiest day of this particular break between Shane's trips. Two days later, the pattern returned. As Shane's next long haul loomed, his morose attitude brought on the gloom, and Linda assumed her usual walking-on-eggshells attitude, staying out of his way and keeping Junior tightly controlled.

"I'm still wondering where the hell those twins came from," Shane said as he was leaving for yet another two-week trip across the country. Linda ignored the implication, just as she had each time he mentioned it since that first conversation when he seemed so happy and satisfied.

Shane had his hand on the doorknob when he paused and looked back at her. "Ask that special doctor of yours about the likelihood of twins coming out of nowhere."

"Jesus, Shane. Every time you're ready to leave, you want to start something. You're being irrational here. I mean, do you want me to get a damn paternity test or something?" Linda moved far enough out of reach that he couldn't touch her without making a real effort to cross the room and placed herself squarely in front of Junior.

"Maybe that wouldn't be a bad idea," Shane shouted as he ripped the door open. After the inevitable house-rattling slam, the little boy moved out from behind his mother and looked up at her.

"Daddy's mad, Mommy," he said.

"Yeah, it seems like it, but he'll be fine after his trip. He just doesn't like to leave us, that's all." She walked over to the window in time to see the tractor disappear down the street. Her shoulders sagged as if she had been holding her breath. After pouring herself a steaming cup of coffee, she sat down at the kitchen table.

"Two weeks of peace and quiet," she whispered, so softly that Shane Jr. did not even hear her.

JAQUELINE AND TONYA CHOSE to upset the schedule much as their brother had almost two years before. Once again, Shane scheduled his vacation for the second and third weeks of November based on the projected due date, and his mid-October trip through Texas and on to San Diego had him almost as far away from Hampton Village as he could possibly be. His itinerary contained four major stops, with days in between each one, the longest stretch coming between San Antonio and San Diego. For three days, he would be out of touch unless he called home, which he was doing less and less frequently. Loretta James had no choice but to leave her urgent message at the last stop and pray that he would call in before that.

He didn't, and when he finally did call her, she gave him the news that he was a father again, this time to beautiful twin girls. When Linda asked how he took the news, she could only be honest with the woman who was fast becoming her best friend.

"He just kind of grunted and said, 'Girls, huh?' like he was disappointed." Loretta hesitated, then seemed to make a decision. "Is everything okay with you two?" she asked.

Linda tried to push herself up straighter in the hospital bed. "I'm getting real tired of being in here and it's only been two days." Loretta jumped up and cranked the back of the bed up.

"How long did Dr. Capaldi want you to stay in? They're usually pushing 'em out as quick as they can." While the twins were only slightly premature, Steven Capaldi wanted mother and babies in the hospital for at least two extra days.

"A couple more days, at least," she answered. "But, back to your first question. Why'd you ask if things were okay with me and Shane?"

"It's really nothing, but you seem a lot more relaxed when he's away than when he's home. And he's like a Jekyll and Hyde, charming one day and thoroughly pissed off at the world the next."

Linda laughed. "That's Shane, all right. But he's my husband and that's the way it is. We have our great days and our not so great days. Nothing new there in the world of marriage in the eighties, right?" With a deft segue, she moved the conversation to safer ground. "So, how's Yvonne and her mom making out with Shane Jr.? It's not always easy having an extra kid around."

"You're going to have a hard time getting him back. They love him. Speaking of which, I'd better go rescue her. She's got my girls as well so I could visit." Loretta bent over and gave Linda an awkward hug, the only kind hospital beds allowed. "You take care and behave yourself, like you could do anything else. One of us will come visit again tomorrow." She grabbed her winter coat from the extra chair in the room. "Only October and it's already freezing out there," she said as she left.

The automatic closer pulled the door shut, leaving Linda in the unusual silence of a hospital room with no machines or equipment running. She reached for the Stephen King book on her nightstand, wanting to read some of it before her dinner came. *Cujo* was not a book conducive to producing a good night's sleep and was best read before dark, if possible. After two pages with constant look backs, she gave in to the distraction and placed it open on her lap. She stared at the closed door, which seemed to echo with Loretta's words.

"Yes, Shane, girls, like it or not," she said as if he were standing next her.

Another layer of blocks fell into place on her wall.

# Fifteen

## The Hunting Trip

LINDA AND THE TWINS spent five days in the hospital, one day more than Stephen Capaldi originally indicated, although he had hinted that he might keep them that extra day.

"Everything is fine, Mrs. Phillips," the doctor said when he came to tell her about staying in the hospital another day, explaining that his general policy with twins was to give the mother an extra day of rest if there were other children at home. "You're going to have your hands full, you know," he said with a wide smile. "Better enlist the aid of your husband early on."

Linda looked out the window and framed a cautious answer. "My husband won't be home for another few days, at least, but I've got some good friends who'll be helping out."

THE SIX DAYS IT took for Shane to cross the country represented the longest period he had been on the road with an empty rig. When he called Linda on her first day at home with all three children, he blamed his delay in getting home in a more timely fashion on having some mechanical issues with his truck.

"I don't want to push my luck so I'm taking it easy. I'll have plenty of time when I get back to have it looked at during my vacation time. I've built up enough comp time to give me almost three straight weeks at home." Shane then asked to say hello to Junior, who babbled a bubbly "Hi, Daddy," and then listened for a moment. Linda heard the click and realized Shane had hung up.

"Daddy says bye." Junior handed the phone back to his mother who gaped at it in disbelief.

"IT'LL JUST BE FOR six days," Shane said. "I really don't see what the problem is. Will and Johnny have this guide lined up and they've invited me along. I've never been able to do this before with my schedule." The first lengthy conversation after Shane finally arrived home had taken a surprising turn, one that to Linda assumed a surreal quality.

"So the twins did you two favors—they increased my bust size, which you know is only temporary by the way, and now they're going to send you on a hunting trip since you planned your vacation around their birth. No wonder you've been in such a good mood lately. And instead of having my husband around to help with our three kids, he's taking off to be with the boys for almost a week." Linda increased the sarcastic pressure but her efforts clearly were being ignored. "You're gone most of the time anyway, so not to worry, I'll handle everything."

"Look, Linda, I'll be home for a full week before and after. I think that's way more than my share." Shane immediately reached for a rationale for an outrageous statement. "I mean, I'll be home full time for those two weeks; I mean, add up the hours and…" His voice trailed off as Linda held up her hands, palms outward, and began the universal symbol of "no more," crisscrossing her arms back and forth in front of her.

"I get it, Shane. Really, I do. You work hard and deserve a break on your vacation. Any time you can spend with us will be a plus. Now why don't you call your hunting buddies and let them know you'll be coming with them?"

Shane broke into a wide grin. "You are the best, you know that? Now, I have a little surprise for you." As he began to explain, the telltale whimpering of hungry babies drifted in from the twin bassinets in the living room.

"I'd better get them before they really let go with full-fledged crying. Then we'll have our hands full." The emphasis on the "we'll" was as subtle as a slap in the face and Shane responded as any husband who had just been given permission to go on an extended hunting trip would.

"I'm right behind you. I'll take Jackie and you've got Tonie, if we can tell them apart." He laughed and Linda joined in. Within minutes, they sat in their favorite chairs, each with a cooing and content infant sucking on a warm bottle of formula in the crook of an arm.

"Look at us, Shane. Aren't we just the picture of domestic tranquility?" Linda looked over at him. "Why was it always so hard to get you to do this with Junior?" she asked.

Shane did not answer her question, which had a faint edge lurking beneath the surface. Instead, he returned to his surprise.

"We're going out for dinner this Saturday. I've already asked Yvonne and her mom if they could come over for an hour or so while we escaped, just the two of us. What do you think?"

Linda started to protest, hesitated, and finally agreed. "That's really thoughtful of you to arrange this. How could I refuse?"

LINDA PLANNED THE TIMING for her rare dinner out with Shane carefully, with Junior already in bed, sound asleep, and the girls with full stomachs and likely to be napping most of the time. They arrived at the Village Grille in the transition period between the early-bird special diners and the more fashionable, late arrivers. The crowd of drinkers, mostly single, who came for food, especially on fish fry night but mostly the music and the chance to connect with a partner for the evening, were beginning to filter in when Shane and Linda arrived at just after seven o'clock.

The Village Grille on a Saturday night could equal the energy of any night club in any big city. Linda had experienced that energy during her night out with her friends, but she focused her attention on her husband from the time they left the house. The opportunities for the two of them to be out together since Shane Jr. was born could be counted on two fingers, including this one. Their table was just one row removed from the dance floor and had an unobstructed view of the disc jockey as he set up his equipment.

"What time does he start to play?" Shane asked the waitress. Before she could respond, Linda answered, and instantly regretted it.

"At seven thirty," she said, "right on the dot." Her hand flew up to her mouth, as if to push the words back in. Shane's reaction was instantaneous.

"Oh, yeah, I forgot you've been here dancing before when I was away," he growled. The harshness caught the attention of the hovering waitress, who made a valiant effort to change the direction of the conversation.

"Are you folks celebrating anything special tonight? A birthday? Anniversary? We give away a great free dessert if you are." Her interruption provided Linda with a perfect chance to join in the deflection of a predictably severe follow-up comment from Shane.

"Actually, we are. We're celebrating our first out-to-dinner since our twins were born a couple of weeks ago. Plus I'm celebrating a chance to be out with my great husband and have him to myself for a little while." She was looking up at the waitress but watching Shane out of the corner of her eye. When she saw the tension drain from him, she reached across the table in an obvious gesture, asking him to take her hand.

"Twins!" the waitress exclaimed. "Now that is cause for celebration. You just won yourself two desserts. Now what can I get you to drink?"

"Now you're talking, sweetheart," Shane said at the same time as he took Linda's hand. "My wife and I will both have a Beefeater martini, straight up, and easy on the vermouth." After sending a quick wink in Linda's direction, the waitress scurried off.

"A martini? You know we can't do anything for a month, right? I mean, the first drink I have in over nine months is a martini. You must really want to have your way with me." Linda squeezed his hand and smiled. "Maybe I'll be able to think of something to hold you over."

"Oh, we'll figure out something," Shane said.

The dining room held only the soft murmur of individual conversations until about fifteen minutes after the DJ began to play. The younger crowd, which earlier was filtering in, began to arrive in earnest, raising the noise level with each passing moment and forcing the DJ to ramp up the volume of his music as well. By the time the complimentary dessert arrived, any conversation between Linda and Shane had ceased under the onslaught of loud bantering, louder music, and the clatter of tables being bussed of glass and silverware. They enjoyed the apple pie à la mode with an occasional glance at each other, then the exit, a silent signal that they both were likely thinking the same thing. "Let's get out of here."

Linda was just savoring the last bite when she noticed Shane look over her shoulder at the same time as she felt the presence of someone standing behind her. He abruptly stood up, a wide grin on his face.

"Hey, Tommy, thought you'd be out in the woods tying our deer to a tree. You've only got a few days before you lead us on the guaranteed success trip." He reached across the table to shake Tommy Iverson's hand, an attempt that led to an awkward forward lean on Tommy's part and put him in solid contact with Linda's back. She tried to pull her chair in further to avoid the pressure, but Shane released his grip, and his hunting guide backed off but took his time extricating himself from the lean into Linda. Shane seemed not to notice.

"This must be Mrs. Phillips," Tommy said when he finally was standing straight up again. "It's a pleasure to meet you."

Linda, still with her back to Iverson, mumbled a "Yeah, same here" without making an effort to turn around. The slight blush which began forming as soon as she heard the voice and the name dissipated with the realization that he had no intention of letting Shane know they had met previously.

"This is the guide I told you about, Linda. Guarantees us at least two deer for the three of us. Can't beat that for the price."

Iverson moved around the table one place, pulled out a chair and wedged himself between Linda and Shane, his right knee gently pressing against hers. Keeping the contact, she looked directly at him.

"Two deer, guaranteed, huh? How can you do that? I mean, are you able to call them in or something?" She continued to gaze at him but moved her knee back. Tommy turned his attention to

Shane while spreading his legs apart just far enough to maintain his contact with Linda. She sat up straighter but could not avoid him without the obvious move of pushing her chair back.

"I never reveal my secrets, but it probably has to do with my good looks and charming personality, right, Shane?" he said, flashing a wide grin and winking. He looked at Linda. "That, plus I'm very light on my feet. It keeps me from spooking them. You should see me dance." The pressure on Linda's knee increased but she held firm.

"Well, just see that my husband gets one of those two. We've got a bigger family to feed now." She pushed her chair back. "Speaking of which, we'd better get home to them. Why don't you go find our waitress and pay the bill, Shane?"

All three of them stood in unison and Shane went in search of the waitress. Tommy held out his hand. "Surely was a pleasure to meet you, Mrs. Phillips." She shook his hand and met his eyes. She tried to pull away but he squeezed firmly. "I'll do my best to help bring that deer home. And you really should see me dance sometime. Like I said, I never give away my secrets." His wide smile evolved first into a smirk then into a disconcerting leer.

"You'd better be careful, Mr. Iverson," she said, drawing out the mister into two long, sarcastic syllables. "Husbands aren't usually too happy about their wives being hit on."

"Just being friendly, Mrs. Phillips, just making conversation," he said, holding his hands out in a 'who, me?' gesture.

Shane returned and took Linda by the arm. "See ya in a few days, Tommy," he said. He ushered her through the crowded dining room, the approving looks of many of the men in the room following Linda as she glided toward the exit. Tommy stared after her, running his tongue in a lazy circle around his lips, then wiped the moisture away with the back of his hand.

THE HUNTING TRIP PROVED more successful than Shane had hoped. On the first morning, two of the three buddies had their deer, thanks to Tommy Iverson's expertise. After an hour and half on a pre-dawn stand with no results, Tommy met the hunters at a prearranged spot, poured everyone a cup of steaming hot coffee from his huge thermos and laid out his plan. They listened closely, nodding with anticipation. The coffee disappeared in direct proportion to the increasing excitement. A fifteen-minute, silent creep through the forest brought them to a ridge line with good visibility in every direction.

"Watch to the south, shoot to the south," he whispered when they arrive at the destination. "You go east or west and you'll be shooting each other. And don't leave the fucking stand until I come to get you. If it works out and you shoot something, I'll hear it and come running. Don't you guys go off tracking. That's what you hired me for." He looked each man straight in the eye and, in turn, asked the same two-word, mumbled question.

"You understand?" The response from all three was the same—a reluctant yet affirmative grunt.

The area contained a substantial herd, and Tommy set the men up about a hundred yards apart, then headed east for close to a half mile, a trek consuming twenty minutes as he picked his way among the leaves and downed branches, well aware that a careless crunch could alert the quarry and send them bounding off in unintended directions. Another fifteen-minute trip to the south and he was ready to begin the drive. Circling downwind, he began walking a long, looping, back and forth pattern, ranging over one hundred yards in each direction. He paused every twenty feet and scanned the area in front of him. As he expected, on his third pass, he spotted six deer feeding on the bounteous fall acorn crop in a beautiful stand of tall oak trees. As usual, one of them was watching upwind, confident that any predator approaching from the south could be detected with their keen olfactory senses. As if on cue, the five deer not on watch picked up their heads and stared right at him. One raised its right front paw in alarm but Tommy froze in place. Poor eyesight prevented any of the animals from distinguishing the danger, and they soon resumed feeding. He waited until he saw the tails swishing back and forth, a sure indication that they had relaxed, then made his move. A noisy approach was all that was needed to send the deer sprinting away, directly toward Shane and his friends on stand. He crouched behind the trunk of a large oak and waited as the thumps of the bounding deer gradually faded. It wasn't more than a minute later that he heard the shots. He waited five minutes then made his way toward what he hoped would be at least one happy hunter.

Only one deer was down, Shane Phillips kneeling next to it and Johnny Stanton standing behind him, looking over his shoulder. Just as Tommy arrived at the scene, the buck made a pathetic effort to rise, then shuddered as if going into a seizure and lay back down. Its final breath was nothing but a heavy gasp.

Tommy whistled in admiration when he noticed the bullet hole just behind the shoulder of the animal. "Great shot, Shane," he said. "You put it right where it belongs." He looked around.

"Where's Will?"

"He thought he hit one and went after it. I doubt that he's far away," Johnny said.

"Shit and bejesus!" Tommy exclaimed. "You're supposed to give the fucking deer a chance to lie down and die before you go chasing it. A wounded one could be in the next county if you keep it moving." He finished sputtering just as Will came into sight over a small rise. Even at a distance, his body language gave away his state of mind. He was practically jumping up and down.

"Down here!" he shouted. "Come on and help me, Tommy. I got a good one."

THE FOUR MEN SAT on the porch of Tommy's hunting lodge, gazing out at the two bucks, now hanging upside down on what Tommy called his gallows.

"Not a bad day's work," Iverson said. "Now if we can just get Johnny's this afternoon, we could set a speed record for the shortest six-day hunt in history." He laughed. "I'll be getting you back to your wives and girlfriends a lot sooner than they expected."

Johnny and Will glanced at each other, then looked over at Shane and nodded.

"I guess I'm the spokesmen for the group," he said. "We actually talked about this possibility on the way up here. Not exactly sure how to say this, but we decided that since we paid for the six days, even if we got our deer, we wanted to enjoy the getaway, at least spend five of the days." He stopped when he saw the incredulous expression on Tommy Iverson's face. "Come on, Tommy, you know how it is. This is a guys' escape. We've gotten the time off from work. I mean, what would we do if we went home, anyway?"

Iverson glanced from one to the other and smiled. "I suppose you'd want me to supply some companionship for you, right?"

"Well, maybe just once. We could spend the other nights at that local strip joint in town," Will said, his contagious grin spreading to the others.

"I can't deny the logic. You guys did pay for a six-day hunt and if you all have your deer, we switch over to small game during the day. What you do at night is up to you." He looked over at Shane. "I haven't met Will and Johnny's wives, or significant others, or whatever the hell you call 'em, but I'd sure be anxious to get home to Linda if I were you."

"Not much happening there, not with her just having the twins, but we'll make up for it when she's back in shape. In the meantime, I'm not opposed to something else, if the occasion should arise, so to speak." His comment was met with a round of nervous laughter and raising of their beer bottles in a mock toast. Any humor in his voice drained as he added, "And don't you go getting any ideas about Linda, Iverson."

THE AFTERNOON HUNT CONSISTED of Johnny Stanton on stand and the other three men pushing through the woods trying to drive a deer toward him. Despite several drives from a variety of directions, the hunt was unsuccessful as the deer scattered, and none passed close enough to Johnny's perch for a shot.

Shane's call home early that evening before the hunters headed out for dinner and a marathon evening of drinking was brief.

"No luck today. Saw some deer but always too far away for a good shot. Give the kids a kiss for me, okay?"

Linda's response was cool. "That's too bad," she said. "I was hoping that maybe you'd get one right away and be able to come home sooner."

"That's not how it works, Linda. We help each other out

until everybody is successful. You know that. But who knows, tomorrow could be a good day for all three of us. I'll come home as soon as I possibly can." He hung up, cutting her "Okay. I love you" off in mid sentence.

# Sixteen

*Tommy*

JOHNNY STANTON SHOT A ten-point buck early on Wednesday morning, the third day of the hunt. Tommy Iverson helped him track it. After field dressing it, they registered it with the local fish and game check station, and had it hanging from Tommy's gallows before Will and Shane were even awake. A long night of poker and drinking had left them both with hangovers that forced them to sleep in, despite promises to be up early to assist in Johnny's quest for what he kept calling "the big one," a fantasy buck of mythical proportions in size and number of points.

Even with the truck horn blaring all the way in the long drive to Tommy's hunting lodge, the two friends remained sound asleep, leaving the task of hoisting the 210-pound deer into its position on the gallows to Tommy and Johnny. The unseasonably cool weather allowed for Will and Shane's deer to continue to hang and season, and when Johnny's trophy joined the other two, there was no doubt which was the largest. Will and Shane stumbled out the door just as the raising was complete.

"Tell us all about it over coffee, John," Shane said, eyeing the huge buck. "What did Tommy do, have a salt lick hidden out there somewhere, then put you in a tree right near it?"

"Go fuck yourself, Shane. You're just jealous."

Iverson broke in, despite enjoying the friendly tension between them.

"Here's the deal, guys. As much as I love to spend time with you, I've done my job. You all have good-sized bucks, I've cooked three breakfasts and a couple of lunches for you, and there's everything you need in the fridge if you're going to stay. I'm going to head back. One of you can let me know when you leave and I'll come back and clean up for the next crew. It's cool enough so the deer'll be okay hanging, even if you do stay the whole six days. Just load them up and bring them back to Scotty's. I'll tell him you're coming and he'll be ready to butcher them for you."

The three men stared at him, then mumbled a hesitant agreement. "We'll be fine," Shane said. "Thanks a lot for the guiding. I know I'll be hiring you next year for sure." Will and Johnny nodded.

"You can count on us too," they said together, voices echoing off each other.

Tommy entered the lodge, went right to his room, and threw a few clothes in his backpack. By lunchtime, he was back in Hampton Village, showered, changed, and sitting at the bar in the Village Grille.

THE CALL FROM YVONNE DiMartini disappointed but didn't surprise Linda. Shane had lied to her before. The longer they were married, the more it seemed to be an integral part of his personality. When Loretta James hesitantly remarked one day that Shane fit well into the definition of a narcissist, she was puzzled until Loretta explained that she was just learning about various personality types in her adult evening school psychology class.

"Self-love," Loretta had said. "The world revolves around him. He sure doesn't seem to take your needs into consideration unless it suits him." Fearing that she had said too much, Loretta tried to change the subject, but Linda wanted to know more of the traits. As her friend began reciting her memorized list, Linda stopped her when she came to the need to always be right, even resorting to almost pathological lying to cover mistakes or make excuses.

"That's Shane, all right," she had said. "But it's not dangerous, is it?"

"Depends if the person perceives that his personal well-being, especially emotionally, is threatened." Loretta had just shrugged, as if dismissing her friend's concern. "There's nothing to worry about, honest."

Now, with Yvonne's harmless phone call, she thought of the conversation with Loretta, but grasped for other explanations why Tommy Iverson would be back in town if the hunt was still on in the northwestern part of the state. Wouldn't being a guide mean you stayed with the hunters until either they were successful or time ran out? Yvonne was certain she saw Tommy sitting at the bar eating lunch at the Grille.

"I figured if Tommy was back, the boys must have all gotten their deer. How big were they?" Yvonne asked, even though she had only a peripheral interest in hunting, with just enough knowledge to ask the right questions and impress her male hunter friends.

"Oh, no, none of the guys are back that I know of. Last I heard, they were still trying to get the first one."

"That's a little strange. Oh, well, maybe Tommy just took the afternoon off or something. It's only an hour or so drive up there, right?" Yvonne's voice lapsed into set-your-friend's-mind-at-ease mode. "I'm sure there's a logical explanation. Shane will probably call in tonight. Just ask him. There're all kinds of reasons for Tommy to be back in town."

"You're right. I'll just wait to hear from him." Linda disconnected and reached for the phone book. Tommy Iverson, to her surprise, had his number listed in the yellow pages under Hunting Trips, Guided. His tiny ad mentioned "Success guaranteed" right after his name. "I thought his business was all word of mouth," she said to herself. She dialed the number, expecting a robotic answering machine voice to respond with a canned answer. She almost hung up when she heard his husky "Hello, this is Tommy," and realized that it was not a machine.

"You probably don't remember me," she said, faltering. "This is Linda Phillips, Shane's wife."

"You are kidding me, right? Not remember you!" He laughed. "I've met you twice in person and almost nightly in my dreams ever since. What can I do for you, Mrs. Phillips?" A silence stretched into a long, uncomfortable pause. "Mrs. Phillips? Are you still there? Is everything all right?"

Tommy's questions finally forced Linda to respond. "This is a mistake. I shouldn't have called. I'm sorry to have bothered you."

"Wait a minute, please. Don't hang up. You obviously wanted something. I was just joking about the dream thing. I really didn't mean to offend you. So, come on, what's on your mind?"

"A friend of mine saw you at the Grille around lunch time and called me to see what had happened to the hunting trip." Linda was stammering. She struggled to make her explanation sound plausible. "I guess I just figured if you were back, maybe the boys would be coming back today as well, but I haven't heard anything from Shane about coming home early." She could almost feel Tommy shrug through the phone when he answered.

"Look, Linda, ah… Mrs. Phillips, I'm home because I did my job, and when I left, the boys, as you called them, were pretty happy with me. I'm going to let it go at that. They're grown men making their own decisions. I have no idea when they'll head home, but I'm sure they'll have more than their share of war stories about the trip."

Once again, a long silence followed, but this time Tommy waited for Linda to be the one to break it. "Thanks, Mr. Iverson, you've been a great help," Linda said. "And I am sorry to have bothered you. It was silly of me." She hung up and didn't hear Tommy's unusual response.

"Wish you luck, Mrs. Phillips," he said to the dial tone.

# Seventeen

## *Watershed*

LATE FRIDAY AFTERNOON, WILL Comfort's truck pulled into Shane's driveway. The tailgate was down so the three carcasses tied in the bed of the pickup were in plain sight. Shane jumped out of the passenger side, took the steps two at a time and hurtled through the kitchen door, hollering all the way.

"Come on out, Linda! You've got to see this." He slammed the door behind him and looked around. Linda came rushing into the kitchen, leaving Junior making funny faces at the twins in the living room, a valiant attempt to coax the first full-blown smiles out of them.

"What is it? What's wrong?" Shane's unexpected appearance had her befuddled. Her confusion faded with her realization that the hunting trip was apparently over, one day early. Shane grabbed her by the hand and pulled her out into the yard. Will and Johnny had exited the truck and were leaning over the side of the pickup, admiring the fruits of their five days in the woods.

Shane continued to drag Linda toward the truck, his boyish excitement becoming contagious. He took her around to the rear of the truck. "Mine's the one on the left, but get a load of the one in the middle that Johnny got. That could challenge for the season record, at least for the county."

Linda had seen more than her share of dead deer but three such magnificent bucks taken in one trip caused her to pay more than just a desultory attention. "You guys sure did yourselves proud," she said with clear admiration. "That must have been quite a trip. When did you all get them?" Her question hung in the air as the three men exchanged quick glances. "Well, Shane'll tell me all about it, I'm sure, but I'd better get back to the little ones. Congratulations again to all of you." She turned and started back to the house. Shane reached out and gripped her arm.

"Can't the hunter home from the hill at least have a welcome back kiss?" he asked. Linda leaned in for a passing peck on his lips then pulled her arm loose. "Are you coming in, and why didn't you let me know you'd be home? I'd have planned something special."

"Sorry about that—just got busy packing up and so on . . . I'll be back right after we drop these off at Scotty's. He'll butcher them up for us and we'll be having a venison roast on Sunday night. It shouldn't take long." The three hunters watched her walk back to the house.

Johnny Stanton was the first to speak after they were back in the truck. "Bet you're anxious for the waiting period to be over, Shane, even with the tension reliever the other night at the camp. You are one lucky dude to have her." He started the truck and backed down the driveway.

Shane glared at him until they were on the road, then his face relaxed into a grin. "I think the waiting period is over. What difference could a few days make, anyway? And that lady the other night did help, but there's nothing like home cooking, right?"

They shared a chuckle before Will chimed in.

"She just had twins, Shane. Maybe you should go easy on her, at least for a little longer." The answer to his observation was dead silence. No one spoke again until they reached Scotty's Butcher Shop, and even then, Linda's name was not part of the conversation.

DURING THE HALF HOUR when the hunters were dropping off the deer at the butcher shop, Linda searched for something quick and easy to serve for dinner, finally settling on spaghetti. Shane seemed to be just as happy with a Chef Boyardee jarred sauce as he was when she made her homemade.

"This'll just have to do," she said to Junior, who watched her scurrying around the kitchen from the doorway. "He could've at least called ahead, right?" He looked at her, uncomprehending, but nodded in agreement anyway.

She opened the jar and had just dumped the contents into a saucepan when the cooing sounds from the living room grew into more insistent whines, threatening to become howls. Junior disappeared from the doorway, and a moment later, she heard him babbling at the girls in their bassinets. Their fussing diminished, causing Linda to smile. "Thanks, Junior," she called out as she used the reprieve to wrestle a large kettle out from a cabinet under the counter. After filling it halfway with water, she set it on the stove, flipped the burner on high, then snapped it off again. "He's sure to want a couple of drinks before dinner," she said to herself.

Junior's magic in the next room began to wear off, and the twins once again were fussing. Linda hollered to them as if they could understand her. "Putting your bottle on now. Just be a few minutes." She went to the refrigerator and grabbed two bottles, already prepared with formula. After filling another saucepan with water and placing it on a burner next to the sauce, she turned the heat to high and went into the living room to get the twins.

"What's for dinner?" Shane asked before the door slammed behind him.

Shane Jr. heard him and came running to greet him in the kitchen. "Daddy!" he exclaimed, wrapping his arms tightly around Shane's leg.

"Hey, boy, how're you doing? Where's your mom?" Junior relaxed his grip and tugged on Shane's pants leg, pulling him toward the living room. Linda sat in her chair, Tonie in the crook of her left arm while she held the bottle in her right. Jackie was stretched out between her legs looking up at her mother as she gently swayed back and forth. Other than the occasional sucking sound coming from Tonie, the room was silent.

"Looks like you've got your hands full," Shane said, chuckling as he entered the room. "Let me get a drink then I'll take one of them." He reached down and pushed Junior's hand away from his trousers. "Be right back." He disappeared into the kitchen before Linda could answer but was back in an instant. "Sorry! Can I get you anything?"

"Not until I'm finished here. It's a little hard juggling two babies and a drink at the same time. I'll wait for now but maybe later after the kids are in bed..." Her voice trailed off when she realized she was speaking to Shane's back as he left the room.

Just as Shane returned from mixing his pitcher of martinis and pouring a double into a tumbler, a loud burp escaped from Tonie, who was now draped over Linda's shoulder. "You can take her. She's finished eating and apparently is finished her burping, judging by the sound of that." Junior was still giggling from his little sister's noisy indication of satisfaction. Shane set his drink on the end table by his chair and lifted Tonie into his arms. No sooner had he sat down with her and placed her between his legs, duplicating the rocking method Linda used with Jackie, than Linda opened the conversation.

"I'd really like to hear all about the hunting trip. On a day-to-day basis, you know, like how the hunt went, where you ate, what you did in the evenings, that sort of thing." Her interest seemed genuine and betrayed no hidden agenda. She also had been around hunters enough to know that they shared much in common with fishermen, with the strongest mutual thread being a desire to enhance the drama of man against nature. The retelling of a successful hunting story held as much an attraction for hunters home from the hill as the "the one that got away" cliché was irresistible to fishermen. Shane would not be able to resist recounting such a successful hunt.

"First of all, it was great that we all got deer. I mean, how often does that happen? That Iverson guy really knows what he's doing." The excitement of reliving the adrenalin rush of killing a wild animal had Shane's rocking motion increasing almost by the word. The effect caused an abrupt interruption from Linda.

"Look, both girls are just about asleep. Why don't we put them down and then you can use all the dramatic gestures you want?" She stood up, walked softly toward the matching bassinets, and laid Jackie down on her back. Shane remained rooted in his chair;

she returned to him and took Tonie, repeating the same moves. Both babies made gurgling sounds, then, typical of infants, fell asleep as fast as a puppy upon returning from a long walk.

"Junior is into his toys. He can entertain himself for what seems like hours so you've got the floor and my complete attention. Let's hear those war stories!" her exclamation a curious mix of enthusiasm and probing. "Let's start with day one."

Shane drained his tumbler and, with a slight stumble, made his way into the kitchen for a refill. He started to talk before he even sat down on his return. Linda, as her friends always told her, paid attention when someone was speaking. "I love talking to you," Loretta James remarked one day. "You are such a good listener." She put that skill to good use as Shane spun his version of the five-day hunt. She listened without interruption as he regaled her with the details of being on stand for hours at a time, "always thinking about you, of course" he inserted at proper times in his narrative. When he finally reached the description of Wednesday morning, the day when he said both he and Will killed their bucks, Linda waited until he finished then asked her innocent question.

"Doesn't a hunting guide usually stay with the group until the hunt is over?" she asked, gazing across the room at him.

"Oh, sure. Tommy would never leave. That's why he stayed until today. Didn't leave until we had Johnny's deer all packed up." Shane's attention seemed centered on a painting behind Linda's chair, a focal point for his eyes to keep from looking directly at her.

Linda abruptly stood up. "I think I will have a glass of wine after all," she said. "I'll be right back." She left Shane fidgeting in his chair. In the kitchen, she went directly to the liquor cabinet and grabbed a plugged bottle of Cabernet. "Wonder how old this is?" she mumbled as she pulled the stopper out, releasing a pop reminiscent of Cold Duck on New Year's Eve. Before pouring a full glass, she placed both hands on the counter and drew in several deep breaths to steady her shaking hands. A moment later, she was back.

"Well," she began, lifting her glass toward Shane, "cheers to a successful hunt. We'll be enjoying venison for this whole year." Shane, caught off-guard, fumbled with his glass, finally raising it in an awkward response. Linda took a small sip of her wine at first, then gulped a fortifying swallow. She set the glass down and stared at him until he had to meet her eyes.

"Why are you lying to me, Shane?" Her voice quivered as she asked the short question.

Shane's response was instantaneous, full of righteous but phony indignation. "What the fuck are you talking about?" he shouted, his voice carrying into the playroom. Junior peeked his head out but immediately withdrew back into the room. He'd watched enough of these scenes to know he didn't want to be in the middle of it.

Linda was out of her chair. "I'll tell you what I'm talking about. And I won't have to use the f-word, either." Her voiced cracked a second before she continued. "Your precious hunt was over on Wednesday; for all I know it could have been sooner. All I know is that your great guide was back in town for lunch on Wednesday, so unless he left you and your friends in the lurch, which you say he wouldn't dare, then you could have come home at least two days sooner. Why, Shane, just tell me why you would lie about something like this?"

As stunned as he was by Linda's vehement questioning, Shane refused to lose control of the situation. He stayed seated, allowing Linda to retain the dominant physical position in the argument; but his clenched fists thumping on the arm of his chair were his only response. She inched backward in the silence, as if expecting some sort of retaliation. When none was forthcoming, she went on the offensive again.

"Don't you like to be home?" she asked, the hurt in her voice showing through despite a valiant attempt to conceal it. "We've got three kids, now, Shane. Like you said, we're a real family now." The words ran together in a nervous staccato. "I could have used the help if the hunt had been finished earlier."

The silence that followed as she waited for a response produced a shiver in Linda's spine that caused her to take another step backward.

"We're going upstairs." The words were not out of Shane's

mouth before Linda began a stumble backwards lasting for three more steps.

"You've got to be kidding me," she said, swallowing her outrage. "The doctor said we should give the stitches a chance to heal, especially with the twins and all."

"Yeah, and those stitches are supposed to make you as good as new, and, I've heard, might make you even better, so I say we try it out."

Linda's jaw went slack as the realization of what he said penetrated her mind.

"What about the kids? The twins might wake up and need something, or Junior will get tired of playing. We can do something later, Shane. Come on. I'll make a drink for you and we'll—" Her plea was interrupted as Shane came out of the chair.

"We're going upstairs, right now!" He rose from his chair and grabbed Linda's wrist. "It's been a long time and I'm not going to settle for anything less than the real thing."

As Shane pulled her up the steps, Linda listened for any sound from the twins. None! Junior was so immersed with working on his Legos project that he didn't notice his mother being led, more like dragged, up the stairs.

LINDA AWAKENED AT TWO in the morning to Shane's snoring. She padded out of the room, having heard nothing from the three children since putting them to bed after Shane's vicious marital rape, not her first and likely not her last. A quick peek informed her that all three children slept soundly in their bed and cribs. Although not a nightly ritual, she visited the bathroom before returning to bed. The bright red blood smear she found as she gently wiped herself produced a fluttering in her stomach and sent an involuntary shiver rippling through her body.

"Shane, could you please come in here?" she called in a quiet voice, tinged with desperation. A moment's wait told her that no assistance was coming. Becoming more anxious with each passing second, she called out again, this time turning up the volume

slightly. "Shane, I'm bleeding!" With no indication that Shane
heard her, and worrying about waking the children if she shouted
any louder, she stood up, folded several layers of toilet paper into
a makeshift pad and held it between her legs as she struggled awk-
wardly to make her way to the bedroom.

"Shane, wake up," she said as she shook his one bare shoulder
peeking out from under the blankets. When a few tentative jiggles
failed to awakened him, she pulled the covers down, revealing
most of his upper torso. "Shane, you've got to wake up," she hissed
in his ear as she used the free hand not holding her homemade pad
to shake him more vigorously. Finally, he reacted, sitting up in the
bed.

"What the hell…?" he muttered, trying to clear away the
effects of a deep, alcohol-induced sleep.

"You've got to get up, Shane. Something's wrong. I'd better go
to the emergency room."

The content of her plea combined with the anxiety in her
voice brought him to full attention.

"I'll call Yvonne. Her mom lives with them. She'll be able to
come over and stay with the kids." Linda's composure returned as
she assumed charge of the situation, but Shane remained befuddled.

"What do you mean, something's wrong? The emergency
room? What in the hell are you talking about?" He had managed
to swing his feet off the bed and sat on the edge, rubbing his eyes.

"I'm bleeding, Shane, now get dressed. I need you to get with
it!"

Still shaking the grogginess clouding his vision and his mind,
he mumbled an almost inaudible "okay" and stumbled toward the
chair where his clothes lay strewn in a wrinkling heap.

A HALF HOUR LATER, they drove up to the emergency room
entrance at West Covington Medical Center where, less than two
weeks before, the twins had been born. Only a few patients were
scattered around the waiting room. None looked to be in dire
need of attention as they dozed or sat staring blankly at outdated
magazines.

Shane approached the registration desk, where a young nurse looked up to him with a unspoken question on her face. He took her cue and stammered out an answer.

"My wife, she, uh, uh, she's bleeding, from uh, um...She just had twins a couple of weeks ago." At the word "bleeding," the nurse was on her feet, already reaching for a wheelchair that waited behind her.

"Come on, we'll take care of the paperwork later." After getting Linda in the chair, she pushed past the triage room and went directly to ER 3. Shane followed, looking sheepishly like a chastised puppy trailing after its master. "I'm Kathy, and you are?" she asked as she closed the door.

"Linda. Linda Phillips."

"So, what's going on, Linda?" Kathy asked.

"I just had twins and I think maybe some of the stitches have let loose. It's not like I'm hemorrhaging or anything. I made a pad but I think it's still bleeding some." She glanced across the room at Shane, who seemed to be trying to make himself invisible among the intimidating machines ringing the perimeter of the room.

"Who's your doctor?" the nurse asked.

"Steven Capaldi. But you don't have to call him, do you? It's the middle of the night." Linda's voice drained of its earlier confidence and quivered slightly.

"I know Dr. Capaldi, and believe me, if we didn't notify him of this, we'd all be hearing about for the next ten years." Kathy turned to Shane.

"Help her get undressed and then put the johnny on. I'll be right back with the doctor. Then I'll call Dr. Capaldi." The nurse's straightforward directions left no room for discussion.

AN HOUR LATER, STEVEN Capaldi opened the door to the waiting room. Of the five people remaining, four immediately looked up from either the magazine they were reading or the intricately tiled floor. Only Shane failed to react, his face buried in a *Sports Illustrated* magazine featuring a gorgeous girl clad in a skimpy bathing suit on the cover. When the doctor tapped him on the shoulder, he flinched like a dog accustomed to being rapped with a newspaper.

"Come with me, Mr. Phillips," he ordered, then turned and headed back toward the door. Shane threw the magazine on the chair with enough force to send it sliding onto the floor. Once the door closed behind them, Capaldi escorted him back into ER 3.

"Have a seat. This will only take a minute." Shane looked around for a chair but stopped when he saw that the hospital bed was empty.

"Where's Linda?" he asked, a nervous bitterness creeping into his voice. The doctor nodded toward the only available seat in the room, a rickety, card-table-type chair. Shane sat down heavily and Capaldi leaned on the empty bed, facing him.

"Linda's been taken up for surgery prep. I'll have to go in and repair some of the stitches from the births. She tells me that she did some heavy lifting today, a laundry basket and some pots and pans. She thinks that's what caused this issue. Is that how you see it, Mr. Phillips?"

Shane shifted in the chair, which groaned and creaked as if about to collapse. He looked in the direction of Capaldi, but focused on a blood pressure device hanging on the wall over the doctor's shoulder. When he finally answered, the hesitancy between words revealed his struggle with exactly what to say.

"I, uh...just got back from a hunting trip late today. She was pretty pissed off that I wasn't around to help with the kids and other stuff. So, uh, yeah, she did do some heavy stuff today, I guess. She'll be okay, right?"

The doctor slipped off the edge of the bed and stood straight up, his cold stare so unnerving that Shane continued with his explanation but with little pause and more determination. "I screwed up. I should never have gone in the first place but she insisted she'd be all right. I don't get that much time to have any fun. I work my ass off for her and the kids. And you still haven't told me if she'll be okay."

Capaldi paced back and forth as he answered. "She'll be fine, but it will set back her total healing period a couple of weeks. I don't want her to do anything, especially things like laundry." He stopped pacing and glared at Shane. "And all the same postpartum restrictions apply to any other activities, as well. I trust you know what I mean."

"Yeah, I know what you mean, Doctor. I'm back to work in a week anyway, then I'll be away, so no worries in that department." Shane smiled. "I can wait if she can."

The doctor took a step toward him, his mouth drawn into a tight slit. "I'm going up to help your wife now, Mr. Phillips. I'll probably be able to discharge her by tomorrow afternoon, but I'll have the nurse call you with a time." He started toward the door, then turned around. "Just so you're aware, I believe I know what caused the stitches to tear, but Linda was so insistent that I didn't contradict her. She must love you very much." Anything in the room that wasn't bolted down rattled when he closed the door behind him.

"Or else she's scared to death of you," he whispered once outside the room.

"THEY'RE GOING TO KEEP her until tomorrow afternoon." Shane's voice broke as he finished his brief explanation. "I'm not sure what I'm supposed to do. I don't know how to take care of kids. Shit!" He appeared to be in as emotional a state as Yvonne had ever seen him.

"Don't worry about it. My mom has it covered at my house and I'll take a personal day tomorrow. We can do this." Yvonne moved the open book from her lap to the table next to Linda's recliner and stood up. She crossed over to Shane. "You need a hug," she said, and put her arms around him. Shane clung to her, burying his face into her shoulder. She patted his back and moved away. "I'll just sleep in the recliner—it's comfortable, and it's only a few hours until the twins will be waking up."

"You're a special friend, Yvonne. I really appreciate this." Shane smiled and reached out for her hand. His smile turned into a leering grin. "If you decide you want to be more comfortable, you could always come upstairs."

Yvonne shook loose of his hand and took a step backward. "What did the doctor say caused Linda's problem?" she asked, ignoring the implications of what Shane had just said.

Shane summarized what Linda and the doctor blamed for the bleeding. Yvonne nodded in apparent agreement. "That would do it, for sure. Look, I'm really tired. We'd better get some sleep to prepare us for those kiddos. They've got us outnumbered three to two, you know."

Without another word, Shane turned to go upstairs, Yvonne's not-so-subtle rebuff of his proposal clear. "I was only kidding, you know, about coming upstairs. Just a bad joke. Sorry."

"Of course, I knew that. What kind of guy would hit on one of his wife's best friends while she's in the hospital?" She laughed and he joined in.

"Yeah, what kind of a guy?...Good night, Yvonne, and thanks again for everything."

After she heard him finish in the bathroom and close the bedroom door, she crept up the stairs to use the bathroom herself. After washing her face and hands, she replaced the guest towel on the rack above the hamper. "What the heck...?" she muttered as she noticed the unclosed lid of the hamper. It was filled to over-flowing with at least two days of laundry.

"What happened to you, Linda?" she whispered as she tried to force the lid back down. "More work for tomorrow."

# Eighteen

## Capaldi and Havenot

DR. STEVE CAPALDI AND Detective Parker Havenot had met under unusual circumstances, but over the years, their friendship had moved through the "friends for a reason" to "friends for a season" phases, finally coming to rest on the sought-after "friends for a lifetime" stage. When one called the other, either the doctor's secretary or the police dispatcher knew to put them right through without the usual screening. After making his daily rounds at the hospital, which included a visit to Linda Phillips and arranging for her discharge in early afternoon, Dr. Capaldi returned to his practice. The decision to have office hours on Saturdays came after lengthy discussions with his nurse, Sheila Murphy, who felt they needed to accept the fact that many women were working full time.

"Just makes sense to make it easier for them to schedule appointments," Dr. Capaldi had said. His nurse agreed with an enthusiastic compliment about how thoughtful he was, which the doctor dismissed with a shrug.

As he passed Sheila's desk, his concern must have been obvious. He hadn't even finished hanging up his coat when she knocked on the partially opened door of his office.

"Is everything all right, Doctor?" she asked. "I don't mean to pry, but you really seem distracted today."

Capaldi laughed. "My gosh, Sheila, what are you, clairvoyant or something? You scare me sometimes with your perceptions. Sit down for a minute and I'll tell you all about it. Maybe I should lie down on the couch, and you could psychoanalyze me."

It was Sheila's turn to laugh, which she did as color filled her cheeks. "You give me too much credit, Doctor. Anyway, what is it that you want to share?"

The doctor provided an abridged version of the early morning call to the hospital and the repairs performed on Linda Phillips's stitches. Sheila listened in rapt attention without interruption. When he finished, she rose from her chair. "I'd better get back out front. Office hours start in just fifteen minutes." After a hesitation, she continued. "You don't believe she did it herself, do you?"

"There you go again, reading my mind!" Capaldi grinned, then instructed her to try to get Detective Havenot on the phone as soon as she had a chance.

THEIR CONVERSATION BEGAN IN the usual fashion.

"How's my friend who spends his entire workday in places men dream about most of their waking moments?" Parker quickly apologized. "I know, I know, it's just a job but I like giving you a hard time about it. Sorry."

Steve Capaldi was used to the ribbing from most of his male friends and had a standard comeback. "I do regret not studying to be a podiatrist. That would have been fun too," he said.

"Okay, we've got the preliminaries over with. What's going on? You probably want to treat me to lunch at that new expensive restaurant that just opened, right?" Parker and Steve Capaldi met for lunch at least once a month with much good-natured joking of which one was the most frugal.

"Actually, I do have a favor to ask but I'm not exactly sure of the ethics involved. I mean, are you allowed to tell me if any official domestic violence complaints have been filed with the police or sheriffs' departments?"

"Of course not, unless they make it to the courts, where they're listed in the paper anyway. You know how it is—usually we respond and wind up in the middle with both parties beating on us as a mutual enemy." Parker heard chuckling coming from the other end of the line. "So, why are you asking, anyway?"

"I've got a patient that I'm worried about. She hasn't said anything but I have my suspicions that she covering up, you know, protecting someone."

"Happens all the time, Steve. Usually because a wife or girl-friend is afraid of the repercussions—reporting someone often makes things worse. Now, you asked me about official complaints, right?" Parker waited.

"Yeah, I guess so. What other kind of complaints are there?"

"I can't tell you about official complaints without permission to reveal them, but if you give me a name, I could maybe find out something unofficial. Naturally, I'd have to ask for your discretion should anything show up. So, what's the name?" Parker already had his pocket notebook out. "I'm ready anytime."

"That's the other issue, Parker, and I know I can be right up front with you about this because we've talked about it before. I've some serious reservations about sharing the name for the same ethical reasons, but I frankly don't know what to do about it. I'm afraid this woman is going to get hurt. I had to treat her last night at the hospital for an injury that I'm not at all sure could have happened the way she insists it did." Capaldi hesitated, waiting for some sort of reassurance before continuing.

"Look, Steve, we go back a long way. If you think someone's in danger, you're going to have to trust me to handle it appropriately, just like I'd trust you."

"I'm afraid I'm going to have Hippocrates haunting me tonight in my sleep. I'll just tell him I'm concentrating on the part of the oath about remembering that I'm a member of society, with special obligations to all my fellow human beings. Anyway here it goes. Her name is Linda Phillips. Husband's name is Shane." The doctor's voice sounded relieved and stressed at the same time.

"I'm impressed. When did you take that oath—yesterday?" Parker smiled to himself. "Just kidding. That name already rings a bell. Let me get back to you on that. Maybe I could supply some information over lunch at the Green Briar Country Club, your treat, of course. I heard that the hot dogs only start at twelve bucks. And, by the way, I'd be honored to have such a concerned doctor, but I guess that's out of the question, right?"

Steve Capaldi laughed. "I'd say so, Parker. Anyway, what you're suggesting is shameless bribery, but sure, we can do that. And thanks a lot, Parker. I do appreciate it."

"I really was only kidding, about the bribe, that is. I hate it when guys are beating up women. Talk to you later." After disconnecting, Parker picked up the intercom and dialed the deputies' break room. A moment later, he had Sam Olden on the phone.

"Hey, Sam, sorry to bother you in the middle of a cream-filled chocolate donut, but do you remember that domestic call that upset you so much a while back?" he asked. "I know you've had quite a few since then, but..." He stopped speaking when Sam interrupted.

"Yeah, I remember because we talked about it, agreed it probably wasn't the end of it. I'd have to look up his first name but the family was named Phillips. I think her name was Linda."

"Yeah, that's the one. I'm just checking an anonymous tip that just came in. Thanks, Sam. Go on back to your donut. You've been a big help."


YVONNE DIMARTINI HAD DONE almost three loads of laundry and cleaned the entire downstairs of the house during the morning nap time for the twins. She assigned Shane to watch Junior, who was taking morning naps only on an irregular schedule now. The call from Dr. Capaldi's office came in the morning but informed them that Linda could not be discharged until three in the afternoon. After feeding the twins in the late morning and giving Junior his favorite lunch of dry Cheerios in a bowl, which he promptly dumped on the tray of his highchair, Yvonne and Shane managed to get all three children down for naps. Both were exhausted and Yvonne heated two cans of Campbell's Chicken Noodle soup, which they ate as they sat at the kitchen table. With the children out of the picture, an uneasy silence prevailed until Shane broke it.

"You've been a life saver today. The poor kids would have been suffering if you hadn't stepped up."

"That's what friends are for. Besides, you sell yourself short. It's amazing what people can do when there's no one else around to do it. You'd have been fine." She smiled. "You're the daddy, you know.

You'll just keep getting better at it." The silence returned, broken only by the occasional slurping sounds of soup being consumed.

As soon as Shane finished, he got up and took his bowl to the sink. When he went into the mudroom to get his coat, Yvonne called to him. "Hey, where are you going? It's only one o'clock and she can't be picked up until three."

"Well, the kids are all asleep so that'll be no problem. You'll have couple of hours of peace and quiet all to yourself. I thought I might stop in at the Grille and see some of the boys; you know, brag about the hunt, tell lies, you know how that goes." He looked at her as she stood up. The boys he was going to see often talked about her, especially what she was like when she was in a teasing mood. "I could stay home, if you'd rather, in case the kids do wake up. You might need some help. Or maybe I could help relieve your stress in other ways, if you'd like."

"You'd better head on down to the Grille, before you get in trouble." She smiled. "Or before both of us get into trouble."

"You're absolutely right," he said, and a moment later he was backing down the driveway.

LINDA COULD HAVE WALKED out, but the hospital protocol, designed to make certain that patients made it off the property safely, and more importantly, reduce the risk of liability claims, required a wheelchair exit.

"Hey, great, you're all ready," Shane called across the room as he peeked in the doorway. He approached her and pecked her on the cheek. "I'll go get the car and meet you at the entrance." Linda recoiled as his breath drifted under her nose. She flashed a fierce glare but remained quiet. Shane glanced at the nurse, who was tucking in a blanket around Linda's lap, asking the question with his eyes.

"That'll be fine, Mr. Phillips. I'll have her out there in a few minutes."

After he left, the nurse finished getting Linda ready, then rolled her out of the room but stopped suddenly once they reached the hallway. She came around to the front of the wheelchair.

"Look, Mrs. Phillips, this is none of my business, but are you okay going in the car with your husband? He seems to have been drinking." She blushed, then apologized as Linda just gazed up at her. "I'm sorry, it really isn't my place, but I was just concerned."

"No need to apologize, Maggie," she said, reading the nurse's name tag for the first time. "But I'm fine. He probably just had a beer with his lunch." She smiled, easing the nurse's mind considerably. "Just a short ride, anyway. Besides, I've seen him a lot worse."

The two were silent until they arrived at the curbside, where Shane was waiting. With the nurse guiding her, she slid into the passenger seat.

"Don't forget, Mrs. Phillips, the doctor was pretty specific about no strenuous activities, especially no lifting for at least a week. Give those new stitches time to heal." Maggie squeezed her hand then backed away and closed the car door.

Shane started the car. Before he could slip the gearshift into drive, Linda released the first salvo of her attack.

"You've been drinking! You have been freaking drinking!" Her outrage spilled over as she undid her seatbelt and turned to face Shane, continuing to shout at him. "It's only three in the afternoon! Couldn't you have waited until I got home, at least?"

Shane, taken by surprise, had automatically continued to drop the shift and the car began to roll down the street. He glanced in the rearview mirror to make certain no other cars were coming before pulling into the traffic lane. Nurse Maggie stared after the car, one hand on her hip and the other holding the wheelchair.

"Put your seat belt back on, Linda. Right now, before I pull this goddamned car over and do it for you!" Shane recovered enough to regain control. He waited until he heard the click of the seat belt engaging and glanced over at Linda, who was staring out the passenger side window. "Now, that's more like my girl and the responsible mother of my children. Now you can just listen," he said, his attention back on the road.

Linda did not give him a chance to continue. She swiveled in her seat, pulling the seat belt so tight that it locked into place and kept her from leaning closer to him. "What do you want me to say, Shane?" she hissed. "That I'm sorry you put me in the hospital? That it's my fault you have to keep me right under your thumb?

That I should be grateful that you're such a great provider and a wonderful husband and lover?" Linda paused to catch her breath, a hesitation that gave Shane his opening.

"That's pretty much exactly it, Linda. All but the part about the hospital. I didn't know that was going to happen. But, yeah, you're my wife, and I do need to keep you under my thumb, as you put it so well. Otherwise who knows what you might be doing when I'm out of town. And you are lucky to have me. I bailed you out, remember? Now, we've got three kids and a picture perfect family to the outside world." Shane reached across the seat and grabbed her wrist. "Look at me, Linda." She kept her head turned away. "I'm telling you to look at me." She tried to pull her arm free but he squeezed tighter until she relented and turned to stare at him. "And I plan on keeping it that way." He let go and she let her hand fall into her lap.

The remainder of the trip home was quiet, except for an occasional sniffle coming from Linda as she gazed through the windshield, noiseless tears staining her cheeks.

PARKER HAVENOT AND STEVE Capaldi scheduled their lunch for Tuesday. The Green Briar, a popular lunch establishment for the local businessmen clientele, was crowded, but the hostess glanced over the glasses resting on the end of her nose at the reservation book. Not finding Capaldi's name, she ran her finger down the list, then looked up. "Oh, here it is" she said, after making an exaggerated pointing gesture to something in the book. A minute later, they were seated at a prime window table overlooking the expansive practice area of the golf course.

"I'm impressed," Parker remarked. "You didn't really think ahead enough to make a reservation, did you?" He smiled warmly at his friend. "This is just a wild guess, but she's not by any chance a patient of yours, is she?"

Steve Capaldi laughed. "What can I say? My patients all love me." He steered the conversation into a less personal area. "So, how are things in law enforcement? You folks keeping all those bad guys under control?"

"Just the opposite with us—the bad guys all hate us." Parker picked up the "Today's Luncheon Specials" flyer and scanned at the offerings. "Yikes! I'm sure glad it's your turn to treat."

"Actually, it isn't my turn, but our deal was a meal in exchange for information. So, why don't we decide what we want to eat, then you can tell me what you found out about Shane Phillips." Capaldi's demeanor turned serious, not a trace of any smile lines crinkling his face. He reached for the second flyer and the two men studied the possibilities in silence. A minute later, their waitress arrived with water glasses topped with generous slices of lemon. Parker was the first to order.

"I'll have the French dip roast beef, since my friend here is paying. And, if you wouldn't mind, could you put a little rush on it? I need to get back to work fairly quickly."

"And for you, Doctor?" the young girl asked, tilting her head and leaning forward as if he might share some intimate bit of information. "Sally, the, uh, uh, the hostess, told me you're her doctor. That's how I knew." Her eyes sparkled as she smiled despite the slight stutter.

"I'll have the same," Steve Capaldi said, taking the flyer from Parker and handing both of them to the waitress, who seemed reluctant to leave. When she finally turned away from their table he directed his attention to Havenot. "Well...?"

Parker preceded his report with a mini-lecture on the need for discretion, to which Steve Capaldi rolled his eyes.

"I'm a doctor, Detective Havenot. I know all about discretion. This conversation seems like déjà vu all over again, as Yogi Berra would say." A bit of the seriousness of a moment before left his face. "So, what do I get for this spectacular lunch?"

"We responded to the Phillips's residence for a Code 53, just one time. It was a while back, but less than a year. The wife said it was all a mistake on her part, but my deputy had a really bad feeling about it, like there probably was something to it. He said..."

Steve Capaldi interrupted. "I should know this, but what exactly is a Code 53—some sort of domestic violence or something?" he asked.

"Could be violence but it's a general category; domestic dispute, but not always violence. Most of our people would rather respond to anything but a Code 53. More often than not, they get put in the middle." Parker stopped speaking as the perky waitress flitted to their table, inquiring if everything was all right, even though their food had not yet arrived. He waited while she hovered over Steve's shoulder until he nodded. After she left, he had to ask. "Do you always get this much attention?"

Capaldi shrugged. "Not usually, not unless they know I'm a gynecologist. That seems to put them at ease, like I'm not a threat because I spend all day with women. As I've said only to my best and most trustworthy friends, it's a tough job but someone has to do it." He chuckled while Parker laughed out loud.

"Back to the topic at hand," Parker said when he caught his breath. "What happened with Mrs. Phillips that made you call me?"

"I had to repair some work I did when she had her twins. She said she overexerted herself and tore some stitches. I think her husband..." The doctor glanced around the room. No one seemed to paying any attention to them. He lowered his voice. "I think he forced her to have sex with him, even though they should have waited another week or so, at least."

Parker rested his chin on his thumb, assuming the posture of the Thinker, his right elbow propped on the table. "Just for a second, Steve, bear with me on this. I'll be the devil's advocate. What if she didn't object, was a willing partner? She's also been without for a long time."

"I'm not buying that, Parker. I've been around for a while. Women in her situation aren't quite ready that soon. For one thing, I'll guarantee that it was painful and would have brought her up short. For another, having twins does a number on the system. Nah, she wasn't a willing partner, if that's what happened."

Parker hadn't moved from his pose. "Exactly. It's the 'if it happened' part that's a hang-up here. Linda Phillips says she hurt herself. If she refuses to tell the truth, then we can't do a damn thing about it. We probably couldn't anyway. They're husband and wife, for goodness sakes." He straightened up, realizing that the volume of his voice had risen a notch.

"Look, I'll tell you what I'll do." Capaldi leaned forward but retreated as their meals arrived.

The cute young waitress carried the doctor's plate while a busboy delivered Parker's.

"I hope you enjoy your meal, Doctor. She bent closer, almost whispering in his ear. "And if there is anything else I can do for you, just give me the high sign," she said, somehow expanding the 'anything else' into seven or eight syllables.

Meanwhile, the busboy set down Parker's plate and was already on his way back to the kitchen, having not uttered a word. As their waitress sashayed to another table, Parker started to chuckle.

"I was going to tell you what I'd do, Steve, but it sounds like she'll take care of anything you might need. I know for sure that I'm not going to whisper it in your ear, at least not in public." Capaldi's mouth curled into an impish grin as Parker continued to chuckle.

"What can I say? My charisma just overflows beyond my control." His grin evolved into a laugh. "Eat your heart out. Now, what was it you were going to do?" he asked as he dipped his first bite of sandwich into the au jus.

"All I can do is have our boys pay attention. This is a small town, as you know, although it's getting bigger all the time. Most of the guys live here and they hear the gossip just like normal people, even if they are cops to the suspicious general population." He paused as he took his first bite of the dripping roast beef roll, holding his napkin under his chin. "It's about all I can do for now," he said after swallowing. "Hey, this is really good. We should come here any time it's your turn to pay."

WHEN PARKER RETURNED TO the Sheriff's Department headquarters, he summoned Sam Olden, his favorite deputy, to his office. Sam listened as he explained the basic content of his conversation with Dr. Steve Capaldi over lunch. The puzzled look on the deputy's face when he finished told him he needed some further explanation.

"I'd just like you and the rest of the boys to kind of keep an ear out, you know, for any kind of gossip about the Phillips family. I know it sounds like an unusual request but the tip came from a pretty reliable source. It's actually someone Josie knows pretty well, a good friend and a real compassionate guy. You were worried about Mrs. Phillips yourself, right?"

"Yeah, actually I was, but I thought my visit might have sent a message. From what you're saying, maybe it didn't work as well as I thought."

"Nothing obvious, Sam. I don't want our locals to think we are harassing them. Just be aware and let the boys know through the grapevine to be aware as well." Parker smiled at him. "It'll give you guys something to do in your free time."

"Right." Sam's reply was coated in sarcasm. "Half of the city of Hartford is moving in on us and we've got nothing else to do." Then he smiled as well. "Not to worry, Parker. We'll be listening."

It would be a while before they heard anything.

YVONNE DIMARTINI GREETED LINDA and Shane at the door with Jackie in one arm and Tonie in the other. Junior came running from the playroom when he heard the door open and wrapped his arms around Linda's legs so tightly that she almost lost her balance. He looked up at her.

"Mommy okay?" he asked, his plaintive expression of concern bringing tears to her eyes.

Shane reached down, broke Junior's grip, then picked him up. "Mommy's fine. A few days of rest and she'll be as good as new," he said, as much for Yvonne's benefit as for his son's.

Linda reached out to take one of the twins but Yvonne backed away. "Oh, no, you don't. You're not going to be lifting anything for quite a while," she said, directing a meaningful gaze at Shane, who had made his way into the kitchen. Both he and Linda caught the unsubtle hint that he'd better be doing his part.

"The kids have been great, Linda. I'd take these little girls home with me in a heartbeat. Both slept all night, ate everything I gave them, and didn't even cry any time I changed their diapers." She walked in to the living room where the bassinets were and deftly placed first Tonie then Jackie into their beds. When she stood up and turned around, Linda was right behind. During a crushing bear hug, a second round of tears filled her eyes.

"You are a great friend. I just don't know what I would have done without you," she said, watching Shane over Yvonne's shoulder. He had put Junior down in the playroom but was not successful in keeping him there.

"So, what did the doctor say when he said you could be discharged?" Yvonne asked. Before Linda could react, Shane answered for her.

"The usual crap about no undue exertion, no lifting more than five pounds, that sort of stuff," he said, then added more information that caused Linda to turn a lovely shade of red. "Plus, can you believe this, he warned me to stay away from her. You know, physically, which I'm pretty accustomed to doing by now."

Yvonne had no choice but to ignore the obvious tension between them and tried to lighten the mood with an innocuous comment about them really looking like a family, as Junior clung to his mother's slacks while she stood between the bassinets with the now sleeping twins.

"Yeah, that's exactly what I was telling Linda on the way home. We're a family, and I aim to keep it that way, whatever it takes." Shane's pronouncement garnered a questioning glance from Yvonne, who suddenly seemed to want to get going.

"Look, Linda, I'll be taking off but please call me if you need anything. My mom can control things at my house and I can be here in five minutes." She hurried out the door, sidestepping Shane's futile attempt to step in front of her and give her a hug of his own.

"Thanks a lot for your help, Yvonne," he called after her as the door closed. He turned his attention to Linda, who had found her way to the recliner and plopped down.

"So, what can I do for you?" he asked. Her cool reply did not appear to surprise him.

"Nothing, right at the moment, but I'm sure now that we're home, you're going to mix yourself a drink, even with your head start from the Grille this afternoon."

"You're damn right I am. Do you have a problem with that?" The harshness of his response sent Junior scurrying up into his mother's lap.

"Would it matter if I did?" she asked. His disappearance into the kitchen was his answer.

# Nineteen

## *A Social Life*

Just over one year after the procedure, as Dr. Capaldi referred to it, Linda Phillips sat visiting in her living room with her two best friends, Loretta James and Yvonne DiMartini. As their older children became more capable of entertaining themselves, and Linda's three younger children took regular two-hour afternoon naps, their original high teas evolved into a sharing of their favorite wines, leading to a gentle buzz which in turn led to deep conversation and open sharing of their personal lives.

Their get-togethers never happened when Shane was home but his increasing workload kept him on the road more than ever. On this particular weekend, Shane wasn't due home from the second annual hunting trip with Tommy Iverson as his guide until late Sunday afternoon, but Linda expressed her nervousness that he might come home early.

The solid overcast with just a dim sun peeking through on the cold November day gave every indication that the local WFSB weatherman might actually be correct with his doom-and-gloom forecast. The sky threatened to let loose with a heavy snowfall at any moment.

"I can't believe they'd stay up there hunting with the weather closing in like this. Maybe you girls better head out." Yvonne and Loretta placed their wine glasses on the table in unison.

"Hey, if you want to get rid of us, don't sugar coat it. We've both been thrown out of better places," Yvonne said, sending all three women into paroxysms of boisterous laughter.

"You know it's not that," Linda replied. "It's just that Shane thinks you two are a bad influence on me. If he comes home and finds us drinking wine in the afternoon, he'll..." She paused and searched for just the right words but Loretta finished her sentence for her.

"...be totally pissed off, right?" Once again, all three laughed loudly.

"Yeah, I guess that about says it all," Linda said.

"And our bad influence does what to you? I mean, just because we took you out one night to the Village Grille for dinner, and you didn't dance, we're not good for you." Yvonne put on a hilarious pouting face. "He doesn't like us, Loretta. We are sinful and unclean. Shane and the Bible tell us so."

Linda and Loretta were laughing so hard that neither could catch her breath. Loretta was the first to recover.

"I've got a great idea. What if the snow holds off like they said it might until late tonight? We put all the kids to bed first, then invite Yvonne's mom over to be here for a couple of hours while we go out to the Grille for a late dinner."

Yvonne smiled. "That truly is one great idea, just the latest in a long line. The only hitch is Shane. Wouldn't he just be Mr. Happy Husband if he came home early and found his wife out with the girls again?"

"Too bad!" Linda shouted as her two friends stared at her with mouths open. "Yeah, it's too bad. He can be the boss when he's here but he's not here. Let's do it, as long as it's not snowing by then. If he comes home in the meantime, I'll call you."

Loretta asked the obvious question. "You sure this isn't the wine talking?"

"If it is, then I'll have another glass. And he won't come home anyway; he'll stay away as long as he can."

"I KNOW YOU DON'T like to spend the money but I think we should get out more when you're home." Linda broached the subject while Shane was still in the euphoric state of mind that goes along with bagging your deer on the final day of the trip, a success made easier by the unexpectedly light overnight snowfall that telegraphed the movements of the buck he was after. With fifteen minutes until the ABC Sunday Night Movie would start, Linda decided that the time was right to introduce a subject that bothered her more and more, especially with the memories of such a pleasant evening out with her friends the night before. With the children down for the night and the mellow buzz of the cocktail hour lingering, there wouldn't be a better time before he left on his next trip.

"You're probably going to be upset with me, but Loretta and Yvonne asked me to go with them to the Grille last night for dinner, and when the snow hadn't materialized, I thought I would." She saw that he was listening and already forming an answer in his mind. "Now, please let me finish before you answer, because this is important." With some hesitation, she left her chair and crossed the room, sitting on the sofa right next to his recliner. His reaction, or lack of one, surprised her. He just nodded, as if asking her to continue.

"During the dinner, I realized how nice it would have been if I had my husband with me for the conversation. I wished you were there, Shane. It would have been nice for you to get to know my friends a little better."

"Why do I doubt that they would have been happy for me to be there? It would have put a crimp in your girl talk, for sure." His calm expression brought a smile to Linda's face.

"So, you're not upset that I went out with them? The last time you weren't too happy." She moved off the edge of her seat and settled back into the soft cushions.

"Why would I be upset, Linda? Things are good. And I agree that we should be looking for a little more social life, and getting to know Yvonne and Loretta better would be a good start. Maybe we could just start with an hors d'oeuvres night or something if we could figure out what to do with the kids." He smiled at her. "Now why don't you come on over and sit on Daddy's lap and we'll discuss anything that comes up." The familiar leer appeared on his face, and his voice turned husky. Linda pushed herself off the couch and went to him.

"I'll admit to being surprised. I thought you'd have a totally different reaction to all of this, especially my going out with them last night." She sat on his lap and leaned into him.

"I'm full of surprises, Linda. You should know that by now. Now, what time of the month is it for you?" he asked as he slid his hands under her blouse. "Safe enough for some bareback riding?"

"Probably," she said, "but I'm not sure we should take the chance, not unless you want a bigger family."

"I say we just be a little wild," he said as he extracted one hand from under her blouse and began unbuttoning it while unsnapping her bra with other. "A little spontaneity never hurt anyone, right?"

Over an hour later, they made their way upstairs with clothes in hand after an exhaustive session on the couch. The question that Shane called out from the bathroom had an innocent ring to it but still sent an involuntary shiver down Linda's spine.

"What did you wear for your night out on the town?" he asked through the partially closed door. "I'd just like to know how good you looked." She finished putting on her pajamas and when she heard him start to brush his teeth, she went to the closet. Fingering the red, clingy, V-neck jersey she had worn, she hesitated for a minute. Then she pushed it aside and selected a bulky, knit, cable-stitch black sweater. The faucet in the bathroom had stopped running. She quickly selected a matching pair of comfort-cut black slacks instead of the form-fitting jeans from the night before. The outfit was spread out on the bed when Shane came out of the bathroom.

"Pretty conservative, don't you think?" Linda's wide smile covered a nervous twitch at the corner of her mouth. "It was pretty cold last night and that sweater was just the ticket."

"Yeah, pretty conservative is right." Shane grinned at her. "Not what I expected at all." His grin shifted into a pleased smile. "I think you're getting it, Linda. That's why I wasn't upset that you went out. You're catching on that you're the wife and I'm the boss." He looked at her and laughed. "Those flannel pajamas don't do you justice."

WITH HIS NEXT TRIP coming up on Tuesday, Shane drove to the

parking lot to check on his truck on Monday morning. As he usually did, he swung by Yvonne DiMartini's house, always with the hope she might be coming or going and he'd have a chance to flirt with her. Since the provocative interplay between them when Linda was in the hospital, she had been cool and distant whenever they came into contact, but that hadn't stopped him from trying to get closer to her.

As he passed by, he saw the garage door going up, and he made a quick U-turn, stopping in front of her house. He was out of his car before she got the end of the driveway. She waited until he stood at the driver's side window before lowering it.

"What's up, Shane?" she asked. "It's a pretty cold morning for us to be having a conversation out here."

"I was just passing by and saw you leaving. Just stopped to say hello, you know, trying to be friendly." Shane had turned up the collar on his coat against the fierce wind blowing the feathery light snow around the yard.

"Well, hello, now you'd better get back in your car before you catch cold." She started to raise the window but Shane put his hand on it and she stopped.

"Heard you had a nice time on Saturday night. I know Linda enjoyed herself. Thanks for getting her out of the house for a while." He continued to hold on to the half-raised window. "But no dancing, right?"

"No dancing, Shane, although she sure would have had the chance. You've got a great woman there. I hope you appreciate her." Yvonne moved her hand toward the window button. "I really have got to go, now."

Shane began to back away. "I know I'm a lucky guy. Hey, by the way, she showed me what she wore the other night. Nice outfit."

"Sure was. I could see the guys drooling over that red jersey." Yvonne sucked in her breath as she realized what she had said. "You know you really are a lucky guy, to use your words," she said, in a vain attempt to make him forget about the drooling guys. She closed the window and left Shane standing there, stunned. He watched as she drove away, then slowly made his way back to his car.

SHANE CROSSED THROUGH THE kitchen as if on a mission. He mumbled something unintelligible as he passed by Linda sitting at the kitchen table with Junior, who was working on mastering his balancing act on a new booster seat. Linda didn't have a chance to say anything before he bounded up the steps to their bedroom, taking them two at a time. She just shrugged as Junior shot her a questioning glance. Not more than a minute later, Shane thumped down the steps and came into the kitchen. He was shaking the red jersey Linda had worn out to dinner in his clenched right hand.

Linda stood and approached him as Junior clambered down from his chair and skittered off toward his play room. "What are you doing with that, Shane?" Greeted with only a grunt and more violent shaking, she insisted. "Give it to me; that's one of my favorite things."

"Not anymore," he hissed. He held the piece of clothing out in front of him, found a seam, and with a vicious yank, ripped the jersey almost in half.

LESS THAN TWO MONTHS later, Shane shared his news with his hunting guide turned good friend, Tommy Iverson, at the bar in the Village Grille.

"That's really tough, Shane. I mean, I can't imagine what the hell it must be like losing a kid and all that stuff." He wasn't prepared for the vigorous response from Shane.

"Fuck that," Shane said. "We already got three and in this day and age, who the hell needs a fourth." Shane gulped down the rest of his second martini of the evening. "Besides that, it wasn't a kid yet anyway. Just a bunch of blood swirling down the toilet, at least that's how Linda said it. Like she'd just had her period or something."

"How's she taking it? I guess for a woman it's pretty tough. And she always seems like a really great lady."

The creased frown on Shane's face couldn't have said it plainer. *Shut up!* it screamed.

"No offense, Shane, but it just seems like Linda's had her share of shit..." Shane's frown became a mask of silent fury and Tommy did as the frown instructed. He shut up and shifted his attention to his frosted glass of Budweiser on the bar.

"Probably wasn't my kid anyway," Shane said after he called for his check. He slid off his stool but used a hand to steady himself. The statement snapped Tommy's head around, his rapt visual involvement with his Budweiser suspended instantly.

"What the hell do you mean by that?" he asked as he spun the barstool so he had direct eye contact with Shane.

"Pretty much what I said, Tommy. I'm gone a lot of the time and she's a good looking woman with needs of her own. Sure is a distinct possibility the way I see it," Shane answered in a much calmer voice than expected, considering the content of what he said.

"You really must be kidding me. I know most people in this town and I get around a lot, but I ain't never heard anything like that about Linda. Christ, she wouldn't even dance with me that one time. Gave me the best and fastest brushoff I've ever had. You've got a great woman there."

"Yeah, so I've been told." He grinned at Tommy. "So you asked her to dance, huh?"

"Sure. And I'd do it again. Don't see no harm in jumping around the floor with a friend's wife. Dances today, you can't even tell who's dancing with who anyway. You guys ought to come down here on a Friday or Saturday night. Get a sitter and have some fun."

"We've been thinking about it, especially as the kids get older." The bartender came with the check. Shane glanced at it, threw his usual ten-dollar bill down on the bar and set his glass on top of it. He flashed Tommy a crooked smile. "And you can ask Linda to dance, if we do come down, but I'll be watching. You might not want to get too friendly. But those times I'm not around, I expect that you'll keep an eye out for her, right? And not just around here. Just call it another kind of scouting trip."

PARKER HAVENOT AND DOCTOR Steven Capaldi were halfway through their lunch when Parker inquired in passing about Linda Phillips.

"I haven't heard anything since that incident after she had the twins, so I guess all is well in the Philips household. That was what, over a year ago?"

"You are a nice person, detective, and very thoughtful. I don't know many cops who would remember something like that. What, you don't have enough bad guys to chase?" Steve laughed. "Only funning you, you know that. Anyway, Linda Phillips actually did have a problem recently."

"Really? Sorry to hear that but it's probably doctor-patient privilege. Is everything all right? Nothing illegal, I hope." The concern showed on Parker's face to such an extent that Steve felt he had to answer.

"It's really not that big a deal but it was to her. She had a miscarriage," the doctor said, adding quickly that there were no signs of any kind of mistreatment. "She just lost the baby; happens more frequently that you'd think. Some women lose babies before they really know they were pregnant in the first place."

"That's really too bad but maybe it's for the best. That husband didn't seem to be the most patient guy in the world. Our deputies kind of kept an eye out for a while but time has a way of eroding your interest, if you know what I mean. But, nothing else has happened that I know of."

"What's it been—twelve, thirteen years since you had that so-called accident, the one where we first met each other?" Parker's question caught Steve by surprise and it took him a minute to respond.

"Probably more, but where in the world did that come from?" Steve waited for an answer but clearly Parker meant for him to sort it out for himself. "Oh, yeah, I get it. You always thought it was an angry patient or an irate husband that caused that. Don't worry, I'll look out for Shane Phillips, but by all that is rational, he couldn't possibly blame me for this."

"Right, by all that's rational. By the way, I'm still convinced that somebody deliberately sabotaged your car. I'm still working on it." He looked over at Steve, who had begun to laugh.

"Listen, don't rush into solving that, will you. Maybe you could make the solution a present for my retirement, in, say, about two or three or decades." The doctor laughed harder as Parker joined in.

"THEN I THINK YOU need to get a vasectomy. You obviously don't want any more children. Dr. Capaldi says he can't guarantee that I wouldn't have another miscarriage, so it seems that we need to do something." The discussion had started with Linda's announcement that she wanted to do something more permanent and foolproof about birth control. All three children were sound asleep, probably for at least a two-hour afternoon nap, although Junior was beginning to protest his daily naps. "You don't want me to take birth control pills, you don't want me to get my tubes tied, I guess I don't see any other solution, Shane. You don't like using condoms. The doctor says that we should use a diaphragm with condoms if we really want to be sure."

Shane listened to Linda's logic, nodding in agreement. "All right," he said. "But can you let me think about it during my trip? I leave tomorrow and won't be back for ten days, if all goes well. When I get home, I'll have made a decision. How's that sound?"

Linda, unaccustomed to having a discussion that didn't end up in a power struggle, let out a long sigh. "Thanks, Shane. I really do appreciate it. I wasn't looking forward to this discussion but you've made it much easier." She crossed the living room, bent over, and kissed him. His response was typical. He slid his hand under her blouse and squeezed her right breast.

"Too bad," he said, without a smile. "These things seem to be shrinking. Having kids sure helped out in that area." He withdrew his hand. "Only kidding." Linda looked down at him. His expression spoke as clearly as any words could have. He wasn't kidding.

# Twenty

## *Two Dramatic Surprises*

"YOU SHOULD DO IT." Alex Prohl's answer was so unequivocal that Shane asked for further explanation. The two men originally met at a bar outside of San Diego, and the acquaintance evolved into a friendship. On the road, their trips often had them making deliveries in the same area, and they made it a point to meet as regularly as scheduling allowed. The rapport between them came primarily from like philosophies like conservative politics, easy and available women, and the fallacy of religious beliefs. As they sat at lunch in a Love's Truck Stop on I-8 outside of Casa Grande in Arizona, the conversation turned to Shane's current dilemma—his potential vasectomy.

"Seriously, you should do it and here's why. You getting fixed will give you all kinds of freedom. Her getting fixed would do the same for her. It's a no-brainer. You have the freedom, and she has to worry about getting pregnant. To me, it's as good a way as any to control your old lady while you're gone. Plus, it won't even hurt." He smiled. "Just do it, Shane, okay?"

"What you're saying makes sense, Alex. Thanks a lot." The waitress appeared with the bill and Shane grabbed it from her hand. "I'll get this. Least I can do for your advice."

They walked out to their rigs, reaching Shane's first. Alex touched his arm and Shane turned to him.

"Look, Shane, I'm going to take a chance here, but I think I've gotten to know you pretty well, and I'm sure I can trust you."

Shane was nodding but his quizzical look said he didn't know at all where this was headed.

Alex reached into his shirt pocket, took out a business card, and handed it to him. "Keep this card. It's got a number on the back that I check all the time. If you're ever in a jam and need something or even someone taken care of, give me a call. I kind of have a business on the side to supplement my real job." His eyes locked onto Shane's. There was no doubt what he meant.

"I'M GOING TO DO it. I've thought of nothing else for the last week, and I've decided that I'm going to do it." The unmistakable sounds of a rowdy bar mingled with Shane's slightly garbled words, but Linda paid little attention to where the call originated; only the content mattered. She squeezed the receiver and tapped it against her chest, as if saying a silent prayer or a mea culpa. When she raised it back to her ear, tears had already formed and begun a slow trek down her cheeks.

"Thank you, Shane. This really means more to me than you know." Her voice quivered at first, but she recovered quickly from the surprise call and asked the predictable questions. "How's the trip going? When can we expect you home? Junior keeps asking for his daddy."

Shane drew in a deep breath, an audible sigh that Linda recognized as an effort to modulate his voice and control any slurring of his speech. "That's great, Linda, but listen, I'd really better go now. Could you do me a favor and call Dr. Fisher for me? Tell him what it's about. He does these things himself and I've heard he's good at it."

"He's your G.P. Don't you think you'd want a specialist to do it?" a question which produced another heavy sigh on the other end of the line.

"Just do what I told you, okay? This is fucking hard enough. Now, I've got to go." The line went dead.

"Okay, Shane, sure I will," Linda said, knowing that he was already gone.

THREE MONTHS AFTER SHANE "got himself fixed," as he called it when talking to her about the procedure, Linda made a decision. After observing how much at ease Shane seemed to be, even entertaining their friends with hilarious descriptions of his adventure into the intimate realm of male birth control, she settled on a surprise for his twenty-seventh birthday. As if he needed a boost, the vasectomy increased his interest in sex to a degree that even took her by surprise. With that in mind, Linda was certain he would like his present. On a warm, early spring Monday as Junior watched morning cartoons and the twins napped, she made the phone call.

"DR. STEVEN CAPALDI'S OFFICE. This is Sheila." Sheila Murphy answered with her unique combination of warmth and professionalism. She recognized the voice immediately. "What can I do for you, Mrs. Phillips?"

After a long hesitation, Linda spoke up. "I wondered if I could come in and talk to you for a few minutes some day soon?"

Puzzled and confused by the unusual request, Sheila asked for clarification. "Did you mean you wanted an appointment with the doctor?"

"Actually, I wanted to speak with you. It really wouldn't take long. It's just kind of personal, and I know I could trust you to keep it in confidence. You've been so good to me in the past."

"Couldn't you just ask me over the phone?" Sheila asked, already guessing the answer. Her aroused curiosity was getting the better of her.

"No, I'd be much more comfortable in person." Linda's voice had gone from firm to pleading in a matter of minutes.

"Okay. I'll see you but I will have to inform Doctor Capaldi that I met with you. He's very strict about the professional ethics in this office, as you can well understand. Now, when did you have in mind? After regular office hours would be best for me. It's always so busy here during the day."

"I could try to get a sitter, but that's not always easy at that time of the day. I was hoping…" Linda hesitated just long enough for Sheila to realize the problem.

"Look, I have an idea. I've been by your house a few times and it's not far out of my way. How about if I just stop by later today for a few minutes? I don't want to interrupt family dinner but you said it wouldn't take long, right?"

"That'd be great! Shane left early this morning on his next trip so it'll just be me and the kiddos. Might be a little hectic but I think we can manage that."

SHEILA MURPHY TRIED TO mask her shock but without much success. "I would have thought this would be something you'd like to talk over with Dr. Capaldi." Suddenly the previously muted voice of Captain Kangaroo blared into the kitchen from the living room, and Linda was on her feet in a second.

"Sorry. Junior loves to turn up the sound. I'll be right back." She left the room and a few seconds later the volume returned to its muted state. "I'll be done in a minute, then we'll get dinner together," Linda said in a soft voice as she left the room. The attention of the three children apparently had already returned to the antics of the Captain.

"I'll admit to being a little embarrassed, actually a lot embarrassed, but I just thought it would be easier to talk to you. You know, with you being a nurse and a woman, you'd understand. I can't imagine talking with Dr. Capaldi about it." A tinge of color rose in Linda's cheeks. "I'm sorry to get you involved."

Sheila shook her head. "Look, Mrs. Phillips, it's becoming more common all the time so there really is no need to be embarrassed. I'll call you from the office tomorrow and give you the contact information for a couple of plastic surgeons that I know Dr. Capaldi recommends to his patients. I don't see any harm in that. It's really your decision."

Linda chewed on her bottom lip for a moment, then looked directly into Sheila's eyes. "It's just that, um...well...Shane liked the way I looked right after the twins were born. I was quite a bit more buxom, if you know what I mean. I think he'd like it if I was that way all the time."

Sheila response was a frown that could only be interpreted as disapproval. "I really need to be going." Abruptly, she pushed her chair away from the kitchen table and stood. "I'll call you with those names. Their work is about half reconstructive and

half cosmetic, mostly augmentation like you're talking about."
She headed for the door just as Captain Kangaroo's volume was
boosted again from the living room. "I hope this works out for you
the way you think it will."

   "So do I," she said, "so do I."

# Twenty-One

*Linda's Surprise*

"THE RECOVERY PERIOD IS usually two weeks, Mrs. Phillips. And I have to tell you that we have always included the husband in this decision. It is, after all, surgery, and there are inherent risks." Dr. Samuel L. Weers issued the warning in such solemn tones that Linda eyed the door as if she were ready to bolt. The doctor, trained in just such reactions and perceptive enough to see the trepidation, quickly added his usual addendum to the speech about the risks.

"However, we have a 99 percent success rate with the type of implant we'll use for you. The risk I mentioned is truly minimal." He pushed his rolling desk chair back from the huge wooden desk that might have served as a fortress if he ever needed one. "I want to show you a few photos that illustrate quite well how natural this augmentation surgery looks." He bent over, disappearing briefly as he slid open the bottom drawer, then emerging with a three-ring binder, which he passed over to Linda. She automatically began thumbing through the pictures of women of all ages naked from the waist up. The before and after poses were so dramatic that she gasped with each turn of a page. After seven or eight, she closed the book and looked across the expanse of the top of the desk.

"Wow is about all I can say, Doctor. These are pretty impressive." She reopened the binder and peeked at a few of the photos again. "Yep, wow's about it," she said, handing the book back.

"Now, tell me why you are doing this without your husband's knowledge. It's highly unusual. Most often, it's the husband's idea." He hadn't finished speaking before Linda was blushing, turning darker shades of red by the second.

"I wanted to…um…surprise him," she said, stammering. "You must get other women who want to do this for their husbands."

A blank look crossed Dr. Weers' face, then he smiled. "Truth be told, Mrs. Phillips, you're the first I know of who wants to do it as a surprise, but with the way things are going in our society, I have a feeling you won't be the last. Now, how soon would you like to schedule it?"

"I'll have to get back to you on that. It'll depend on my husband's travel schedule."

Dr. Weers moved out from behind his desk and extended his hand. "It's been a pleasure meeting you, Mrs. Phillips. Just give us a call when you have a schedule. And please don't worry if you change your mind. A lot of women do, as they think about it. I hope this all works out for you."

Linda accepted the proffered hand and shook it. "Thanks, Doctor, and I'll be in touch." She exited the glossy office and closed the door gently behind her. "Seems to me I've heard that song before," she hummed as she passed the receptionist.

ON SEPTEMBER 1, 1985, Shane entered the offices of Riggins Trucking Company. After spending his requisite several minutes flirting with Janie Bosworth at the receptionist's desk, he went into the executive meeting room where the master schedule for November had just been posted. As he expected, his last trip in October had carried over into the first two weeks of November. The seventeen-day trek would be the longest of his career, with multiple legs for extra contracted work beyond his commitment to Riggins clients. It was a win-win situation with Shane receiving double time pay and Riggins picking up a 10 percent fee for use of their equipment and driver, a fee that was found money and didn't cost the company a penny. He sat down at one end of the long, mahogany meeting room table and pulled a folded calendar from his pocket. With the calendar flattened out before him, he checked the dates.

"Hot damn," he exclaimed. He rushed from the room and went directly to Janie's desk.

"Do you mind?' he asked as he grabbed the phone from her desk and began dialing a number.

She moved out of his way, smiling at him. "No problem, Shane," she said. "Anytime."

Two rings later, Tommy Iverson answered.

"My schedule fits perfect for that week I told you to hold for us. I'll only be home for less than a day between, but that won't be a problem. I'll let the other guys know, but you can lock us in." He was breathless when he disconnected. "Thanks a lot, Janie!" he said, his pat on her back turning into an unwanted massage. She pulled away and watched Shane hurry out the door.

"DAMN COMPANY KEEPS THE screws on," Shane said as Linda delivered his favorite sandwich to him at the kitchen table. He immediately ripped off a huge bite of the BLT and was unable to answer her question about what he meant. After swallowing, he explained his schedule.

"So, with the hunting trip, you'll be gone, what, twenty-three or four days?"

"Yeah, that's how it looks. I'd change the hunt but I already committed to that. Iverson's pretty hardnosed when it comes to cancelling, and he's got the deposit already." Shane chomped on his sandwich again, negating any possibility of a quick answer should more questions be forthcoming.

"We'll manage here, Shane. You work so hard—you deserve to have some down time after a trip like that." Linda smiled as she watched his eyes widen in surprise at her response.

"IS THE 28TH OF October available?" Linda asked. The receptionist asked her to hold as she transferred her to the scheduling department. Ten minutes later, she was on the phone to Loretta James. "I've done it. I'll have at least three weeks to recover while Shane is gone. This is going to work out perfectly. They scheduled the procedure for the morning of the 28th of October. I'll really need help for just a couple of days." Ten minutes after that, she delivered the message to Yvonne at work. Her one sentence low-key response told Linda that other people were nearby her desk.

"That's great but I still can't believe you're doing this." Then she hung up.

# Twenty-Two

## *The Hell Years*

SHANE ARRIVED HOME FROM his extended road trip one day later than expected, delayed by an unpredicted snowstorm that stranded truckers all across the high country of Interstate 80 in New York. His fierce and angry call to Linda warned her to be ready for anything when he returned home early on the morning of November 14, 1985, the very day he was scheduled to leave for his now annual deer hunt with Will Comfort, Will Stanton, and, of course, their can-do-no-wrong guide, Tommy Iverson.

"I want you to call the guys and Tommy. Tell them what happened but I'll be ready to leave by noon tomorrow and they damn well better not leave without me," Shane told Linda. "That means I'll just be home for a couple of hours at the most and I'll have to pack my gear so you and the kids will have to wait for a real homecoming after I get my deer."

"Drive safely, please, and don't worry about us. We'll be fine, but we'll really celebrate when you get home after the hunt. It'll be a wonderful Thanksgiving holiday with you home for quite a while." When she hung up the phone, she let out a long sigh. "Another few days for these things to heal," she said to herself.

True to his promise, Shane managed to get home just after ten the next morning after a relatively sleepless night in a rest area in Eastern New York. Also, as Linda expected, he breezed in with barely a word of greeting and spent the next two hours bustling

175

around the house, swearing occasionally when he couldn't find something. With minutes to spare before his friends were to pick him up, he was ready. Only then did he take the time to visit with the children, who had stayed well out of his way during his packing.

"Look, Linda, I am sorry about rushing off like this, but I couldn't help the goddamned snowstorm—stupid weathermen can't predict anything—a damned drain on the taxpayers' money. I'll make it up to you when I get back. We've got some catching up to do, right?"

Linda, who wore a loose-fitting smock and a large apron, reassured him. "Just go get that deer again. We're all getting spoiled with you providing venison for us every year."

A car horn blared outside. "I gotta go. I'll let you know how we're doing as the week progresses." He grabbed his duffle bag and started for the door. "Bye, kids," he called out to the playroom. "Daddy'll be back soon."

Linda watched him gather his hunting gear from the mudroom. "Hey, Shane, here's something for you to think about while you're on your deer stand." He stopped and looked back at her. "I'll have a nice surprise for you when you get home." She flashed a wide smile and tilted her hips in her most provocative pose. "If you know what I mean."

Shane returned her smile. "That's really not fair. What am I supposed to do with this in the meantime?" He glanced down at his crotch and laughed. Then he was out the door.

Linda reached her right hand up and under her breasts, absently searching with her fingers for the disappearing small scars through several layers of fabric.

"I hope you like them, Shane," she said aloud.

PREDICTABLY, SHANE'S HUNTING EXPEDITION stretched out to late Tuesday afternoon, the last scheduled day of the hunt. Once again, Johnny Stanton was the last member of the party to get his deer, a young buck weighing in at just over 127 pounds. With the cloudy weather and temperatures in the thirties, the three friends decided to let the successes be proclaimed to their neighborhoods through Thanksgiving, scheduling the butchering for the Friday after the holiday. To most people in the rural environment of Covington County, a deer hanging in your front yard was a badge of honor and the men helped each other hoist the animals onto their own handmade gallows, as Tommy Iverson so eloquently called his seasoning apparatus.

"We were all successful yet again, thanks to that amazing Tommy. He's like magic in the forest," Shane exclaimed as he came through the door, sucking a frosty draft in with him.

Linda had his martini chilling, and her homemade spaghetti sauce simmering on the stove sent waves of delicious aroma wafting through the kitchen. "That is so great, Shane! Isn't it kind of unusual for that kind of success rate?" she asked, then added an irresistible dig of someone wondering about the concept of hunting. "I've got to admit that it's always been kind of funny to me that hunting is the only sport where the words success and killing are synonymous."

"We're doing the deer a favor; half of them would starve to death if the herd wasn't thinned out some." Before he could expand on his argument, Junior came running from the playroom, the twins on his heels. The three children formed a tight group hug around his legs. "Well, well, look at this welcome!" He looked across the room at Linda, who smiled and then quickly joined in. "One big happy family, right?" Shane said as he knelt down and kissed the girls while tousling Junior's hair. "Let me go get changed and I'll tell you all about it. You can make me a drink while you're waiting. That is, if you don't mind."

"Already done and in the refrigerator. I'll have it waiting for you."

"I'm more anxious to see the surprise you mentioned when I left," Shane said, smirking at her. "Spent a lot of hours in my stand thinking about that."

Linda turned away, blushing ever so slightly. "I kept the kids up from naps today so they'll be ready for bed early. It's been a long time."

THEIR FIRST LOVEMAKING SESSION in almost a month went as expected, with both of them so aroused that it was over in minutes.

After a brief spell spent catching their breath, Shane propped himself up on his right elbow. With his left hand, he traced lazy circles across her breasts and Linda started to giggle. "Do you like the surprise?" she asked.

Shane stopped caressing her and stared into her eyes. "What are you talking about?" His gaze drifted down and stopped at her chest. "What the hell...?" he muttered as he finally noticed the difference. "You can't be pregnant. At least, you'd damn well better not be. What's going on, Linda?"

"I did it for you. You always liked my figure when I was pregnant, so I decided to make it that way all the time." Linda rolled out of the bed, stood up, and placed her hands under her breasts, imitating the stimulating pose of a gentlemen's club lap dancer. Shane watched, transfixed as she walked around to his side of the bed and knelt on the bed beside him. He reached out to touch her and she put her hand on top of his, pressing it hard against her. "These are all for you," was all she said before he pulled her down on top of him.

Afterward, they both fell sound asleep, not another word passing between them.

LINDA WHISTLED SOFTLY AS she prepared breakfast. She glanced out the kitchen window, and the sight of Shane's buck hanging from the makeshift seasoning rack reminded her of how well the night had gone with him. With a long Thanksgiving weekend, by far her favorite holiday, approaching, everything was looking up for the Phillips family. She hadn't mentioned the invitation to Yvonne and her daughter and mother to join them for the holiday dinner, but Shane seemed to like Yvonne so that should be a non-issue. This would be a busy day of preparations, but with a husband around to help with the children, things should go smoothly. She had awakened early and slipped out of bed without bothering Shane, whose snores echoed off the walls of the bedroom.

For a half hour, Linda puttered around the kitchen, only occasionally sitting down to enjoy the quiet and her first cup of coffee. Junior was the first to awaken, jumping down the stairs two at a time with the exuberance of a little boy looking forward to yet another day in a new and exciting world. Not long after, the twins began to stir, and he went bounding up the steps in much the same way as he came down. A minute later, the girls' laughter came tumbling down the stairs as Junior played his usual game of peek-a-boo, popping out from behind doors and under beds. This was going to be a great weekend.

THE CHILDREN HAD JUST finished their favorite breakfast of hard-boiled eggs, toast, and chocolate milk when Linda heard the toilet flush upstairs. "Daddy's up. Why don't you go up and get him down here for breakfast?" she said to Junior. The boy looked up at her with questioning eyes, an "are you sure?" unspoken but clear.

"Daddy'll be in a good mood this morning for certain. Now, go ahead and tell him breakfast is ready whenever he is." Junior climbed down from the table and started for the stairs. He glanced back and Linda sent the universal motherly signal for 'go on,' shooing him along with a dismissive flip of her wrists.

Linda listened as his footsteps came to the top of stairs and padded down the hall to the bedroom. Junior's plaintive little boy's voice was barely audible but his father's was not.

"Tell her I'll be down when I'm ready," Shane bellowed. Linda could hear Junior retreating from their room before Shane finished the sentence. "You go down and tell her that, right now," he called out as Junior stumbled down the stairs and arrived breathless in the kitchen, Jackie and Tonie staring at him in childish concern.

Linda turned down the heat under the frying pan she was going to use for Shane's eggs. She knelt down and hugged a shaken Junior. "It's okay, honey. Daddy's just waking up."

Moments later, Shane came clumping down the steps. The three children watched wide-eyed as he entered the kitchen and went directly to Linda, who stood at the stove with her back to him.

"Two eggs or three?" she asked, without turning around. Shane slid his arms around her waist and let his right hand stray just high enough to nudge her breast.

"How much did these things cost, anyway?" he whispered into her ear. "And who's going to pay for them?" He backed away and turned to the girls. "Good morning, ladies. And sorry I raised my voice up there, Shane. You just startled me."

Junior immediately ran to his father, who scooped him up into his arms. "Let's go look at my deer, Shane." He turned to Linda. "Hold my breakfast for a few minutes. And I'll just have two eggs. We have to cut back a bit, right, Linda? What with your medical issues and all?"

Linda stared at him, her eyes locked on his.

"Eight hundred dollars each," she said. Then, with another figurative slap to his face, added, "and none of it's covered by insurance. Cosmetic surgery, you know. Might have been cheaper to keep me pregnant but it's kind of too late for that."

Shane glowered at her for an instant, then grabbed Junior's hand and yanked him out the door. Linda went to the window, watching Junior's first close-up introduction to a dead deer. Shane must have decided that he was now old enough to be indoctrinated into the hunting fraternity. She couldn't hear the conversation, but the body language was clear as the young boy tried without success to pull free and back away from the carcass hanging upside down with its body cavity propped open to the air with two sticks. Linda raised the window a few inches. The loose fitting, old-fashioned storm sash allowed the conversation to drift through.

"Ugh! Gross, Daddy!" Junior complained as his father pivoted the deer so the field-dressed side faced him.

"What?" Shane acted genuinely surprised by his son's reaction. "What do you think is so gross?" He released Junior's hand and spun the deer around 180 degrees then reached down and grabbed the antlers. "Look at this rack, son. Come on. Count the points," he said, holding the head up to his son's eye level. The dull-gray dead eyes staring back at him and the extruding colorless tongue appearing to tease him proved too much for the boy. He turned and ran into the house. Shane put his hands on his hips and stared after him, shaking his head.

Several minutes later, he finally followed Junior back into the house. As he hung his coat on the rack in the mudroom, he tossed a disgusted look at his son, who was sipping from a cup of hot chocolate at the kitchen table.

"Got a fucking wimp for a son," Shane hissed at Linda as he passed her on his way to the stairs. After she heard him close the bathroom door, she turned to Junior. "I'll be right down. Could you just entertain the girls for a second?" Then she raced up the steps and threw the bathroom door open without knocking, then slammed it behind her. Shane had his back to her, just zipping his fly.

"Don't you dare ever call him that again!" she screamed. "Like you're a big macho man with a dead deer hanging in your backyard. He's just a little boy." She stopped short when Shane turned to her, his reddening face contorted in rage. She never saw the slap coming and it sent her reeling against the door with a sickening thud.

"You're spoiling him and I'm not going to have it. Now get that through your head. When I'm home, I'm the master of this household. Now get the hell out of here and go take care of your kids."

Linda was rubbing her burning cheek furiously with one hand, and she reached for the doorknob with the other. "I don't even know you half the time," she stammered before stumbling down the stairs.

"Mommy, are you okay?" Junior asked as Linda went directly to the sink in the kitchen.

"Mommy's fine. Just ran into the doorjamb," she said, splashing cold water on her face.

THANKSGIVING DAWNED COLD AND overcast with a forecast for a few snow flurries. With Yvonne and her family scheduled to come over in midafternoon, Linda was up early preparing for the huge meal she had planned. Before even getting out of bed, she informed Shane that she would need his help with the children, at least for a couple of hours in the morning, the intense atmosphere of the day before pushed aside but not forgotten.

Shane's profuse apologies for his behavior sounded, as usual, sincere, and, also as usual, Linda relented.

"My dad used to knock me around all the time, Linda. It was his way of letting off steam and I guess I got his genes or something. It's just that when I get pissed off, I react." His promise to try harder to "keep his cool," as he phrased it, softened her determination to keep the silent treatment going through the entire day. She didn't even object to his remark about her breasts when they made love that night, taking it as a bit of a backhanded compliment, but a compliment nonetheless.

"Eight hundred a piece, huh?" he had said as he buried his face between them. "Worth every penny."

He spent the morning in the playroom with the children, mostly as an observer but occasionally interacting with some of their games. About an hour before lunch, he started asking how the preparations were progressing, his patience beginning to wane. Linda had her dinner well under control by noon, much to Shane's relief, and she took over while Shane plopped down in front of the television to watch the annual Detroit Lions Thanksgiving Day football game.

Yvonne and her family arrived amid the snow flurries, which had already accumulated an inch on the ground, at two o'clock. Yvonne's daughter disappeared into the playroom, first with Junior, then with Jackie and Tonie when they awakened from their naps, allowing the adults the luxury of spending the afternoon sipping wine and visiting. Even with Shane's switch to martinis, which resulted in subsequent flirtations with Yvonne, the entire day fit perfectly into Linda's favorite-holiday-status until the two women found themselves alone in the kitchen with the cleanup duties.

"Okay—two quick questions. First of all, what happened to your cheek? That's not just a wine blush there." Yvonne continued to scrub her way through the stack of pots and pans that only a Thanksgiving dinner can produce as she waited for an answer.

"What do you mean?" Linda asked. She bent over to put the turkey roaster under a counter, giving her a chance to think. When she straightened up, her left hand, dish towel and all, was unconsciously touching her face. "Oh, this. I walked into a door this morning. Stupid, klutzy me, you know? Now, what was your second question?"

"I'll accept that, but just for now. Not going to let you off that easily. Now, the second question: How did Shane like your new attraction?"

Linda kept the towel against her cheek but a full-fledged blush lit up her face.

"Guess that answers that question. And you do look spectacular, Linda." Yvonne returned to scouring and Linda to drying, both lost in private thoughts until the chores were completed.

# Twenty-Three

## *Escalation*

THE REMAINDER OF THE Thanksgiving weekend evaporated in a mist, the blur of time that families with young children experience on a regular basis. Linda's decision to have the augmentation surgery appeared to be a good one. Shane couldn't seem to walk past her without slipping his arms around her, always just high enough to touch her breasts. He was more affectionate than he had been in a long time during the day and wanted to make love every night, a request she was happy to oblige. The euphoria lasted until Monday morning when it was time for Shane to return to the road for a long trip, likely lasting at least ten days. Linda recognized the signs immediately as she served him her special hungry-man breakfast, a feast designed to send a long distant trucker off with enough food to last him through the day without a lunch stop. "A truck that's not moving is not making money," he repeated like a personal mantra to her on numerous occasions.

His order to sit down set the tone for the upcoming conversation.

"Sit down while I go over some rules" he said as she set the plate overflowing with three pancakes, two eggs, four slices of bacon, and two pieces of buttered toast in front of him.

"Let me check the kids first," she said, but he grabbed her by the wrist.

"Sit down, I said. They'll be fine for a few minutes, and they'd whine anyway if they needed you." He pulled her arm with just enough pressure to make her sit in the chair next to him.

Between swallows of his meal, he laid out his expectations. As if he had timed it, he finished both his lecture and his breakfast at the same time. "You're my wife, and I expect you not to embarrass me." Abruptly, he stood up and summarized his instructions. "Remember, no clothing that shows off your new assets, no Village Grille on DJ nights, and no girls' nights out unless I know where you're going and what you're doing in advance."

Linda sat at the table, stunned into silence just long enough to allow Shane to pick up his duffle bag in the mudroom. Then she reacted. "I'm not a possession you can order around, Shane," she shouted to him. "You really can't control me." Shane dropped his bag and came toward her.

"That's where you're wrong, Linda. You're my wife, and you damned well better do what I tell you unless you want to get hurt." He stood close enough that she inhaled his stale coffee breath. "I mean that and you know it."

Linda backed away. "Sometimes I wonder why you married me, Shane." She closed her eyes as though expecting another slap, but his response was verbal.

"Because I loved you and wanted you. That part hasn't changed, and I'm not going to let it change. You made a vow: till death do us part.' Well, guess what? Like it or not, you're going to keep that vow." He hoisted his bag again and headed for the door, then hesitated as if just remembering something. "Say goodbye to the kids for me," he said over his shoulder. Then he was gone.

"I WANT TO SEE your new bras, Linda. All of them." Shane's demand came on the night of his fifth day at home after the lengthy road trip. The established pattern of several days of relative normalcy was followed by increasing agitation as the next trip loomed, this one scheduled to have him possibly away from home for the Christmas holiday.

"Why, Shane? I had to get new ones because of the procedure. You know that." Linda's determination did nothing to dissuade him. His persistence prevailed and she finally relented.

"Okay, but I still don't know what you're looking for." She got out of bed, her legs wobbly from the just-completed intense lovemaking session, and went to her dresser. Four of the five bras, all white, passed his cursory inspection as she held them up while standing naked in front of him. The fifth brought him to a sitting position in the bed.

"Put it on," he commanded.

"What the hell...?" Her response was cut short.

"I said, put the goddamned thing on!"

Linda complied, his sudden harshness draining any resistance from her. She slipped the straps of the sheer black undergarment over her shoulders and turned her back to him while she hooked the front clasp. When she turned to face him, his reaction was instantaneous.

"That one goes back or else it gets thrown away," he hissed, staring at the revealing cleavage the bra provided.

The emerging pattern of clothing inspections allowed Shane yet another method for controlling Linda's behavior, or so he imagined.

"IT'S THE CHRISTMAS SEASON and you deserve a break. You know my mom loves your kids and she'll be excited to have a chance to be with them for an evening." Yvonne DiMartini dropped the invitation during an unexpected drop-in visit a few days after Shane left. She then cajoled Linda with her most convincing argument of all. "If you wanted to, we could even go out of town where no one would recognize us."

"No," Linda replied. "We'll go the Grille. I just have to let Shane know that I'm going out with you girls." When she noticed Yvonne staring at her, she launched into an explanation. "I mean, he doesn't like me going out unless he knows about it. I'll just tell him when he calls in. It's really no problem. It's just an understanding we've come to while he's away."

"Okay, the Grille it is. I'll set it up and let you know the details." She hesitated. "You really have to tell Shane where you are all the time?" The disbelief in her voice was unmistakable.

Linda looked away, composing herself. Finally, she responded.

"Husbands worry, that's all. He really is concerned about me when he's gone. With three kids, by myself, you know, it's worrisome to him. He just wants to be sure I'm all right. I think it's endearing."

"Oh yeah, it's endearing," Yvonne said, sarcasm seeping into her voice. "But I sure wouldn't want any part of it. Some women might see that as a way to control them." She watched for any reaction but Linda's face remained impassive and expressionless. "Okay, I'll get back to you. Maybe this Saturday night; it's the fish fry again, if you don't mind." She grabbed her coat off the back of her chair. "Talk to you later," she called out over her shoulder.

Linda mumbled a "thanks for the invitation" to the already closed door. "Wonder how Shane will take this?" she whispered as she walked into the playroom to check on the children, who had been unusually quiet all during Yvonne's visit. She was relieved to find them on the floor engaged in putting together a jigsaw puzzle, a large-piece mural composed of African animals. All three looked up at her but only Junior spoke.

"You look worried, Mommy," he observed, then went back to the puzzle.

LINDA HAD SHOWERED AHEAD of time and was in her robe when Yvonne and her mother arrived. "It'll just take me a minute to get dressed," she said as she hurried up the steps. She had two outfits spread out on the bed, both of them approved by Shane for public wear. Dropping her robe on the chair, she turned to the full length mirror. "Hell with it," she said aloud and went into her closet.

Moments later, Yvonne reacted with a predictable shout as Linda came into the kitchen. "Wow! You look spectacular! Are you going to carry a club to beat off the guys tonight?" She laughed as Linda performed a perfect pirouette, the short, kilt-type skirt lifting as she twirled around. She had selected a Shane-approved blouse, loose-fitting but still unable to conceal her voluptuous figure. The top three buttons were undone, revealing a tantalizing peek of the black bra underneath. "So, did you get the necessary permissions?" Yvonne asked, expecting an affirmative answer.

"Actually, what you said about control got me to thinking. I felt like being my own person tonight so I just told Shane when he called that we were going out for dinner. I did do a little of the mental reservation trick, not lying, of course, when he asked what I was wearing." She smiled. "I told him I was wearing this blouse, but he probably thinks it's buttoned up to my neck."

Yvonne had begun to giggle at the mental reservation comment and burst into outright laughter when Linda finished. "Well, then, let's go have a good time!" she exclaimed.

TOMMY IVERSON HAD ALREADY downed several beers before Shane joined him at the bar. As most businesses in the area closed at noon the day before Christmas Eve, giving their workers an extended holiday, the lunch crowd at the Village Grille was exceptionally raucous. The noise from several holiday parties already in progress spilled out of the private rooms off the main dining area, and the bar filled with people happy to be done working for at least a few days. With a light snow falling, the Christmas spirit could not be denied, its festive soul permeating the atmosphere.

After the usual cordialities, Shane glanced at Tillie and soon had his patented martini sitting in front of him. "We sure are enjoying that venison," Shane said. "Even planning on having one of the roasts tomorrow night—special Christmas Eve dinner." The conversation hung on hunting for a few minutes, during which Tommy downed most of yet another sixteen-ounce Budweiser draft.

Tommy wiped his lips with the back of his sleeve. "Yeah, Linda told me you guys were liking this deer better than any you've had before," he said. His comment captured Shane's closer attention.

"When was that? She hasn't mentioned seeing you." He set his glass down and rotated the bar stool so that he faced Tommy instead of looking in the mirror behind the bar.

"Oh, she probably forgot. I ran into her a couple of Saturday nights ago here. Passed by her table and stopped to say hello. She sure has some good looking friends."

Shane revolved his chair back to its original position. "Yeah, she does. She did tell me she was coming here for dinner. If her friends got your attention, how'd she look?" He was now looking at Tommy's reflection in the mirror and had his drink back in hand.

"Never saw Linda look so good. Like I've told you before, you are one lucky SOB. And, also like I said before, why you go sniffing around on your hunting trips is beyond me when you've got that at home." Tommy finished off his Bud and motioned to Tillie for a refill.

"Just curious, but when you say "never looked better,' what exactly are you talking about?" Shane continued to stare at the reflection as if wanting the answer to come from an imitation of the real thing.

"First of all, that kilt thing was a killer, but then her blouse was open from here to there, if you know what I mean." It was Tommy's turn to watch a reaction in the mirror, and even from a distance, he saw the red flush of anger spread across Shane's face. "Hey, I didn't mean anything. Shit, she's your wife and I..."

Shane once again swung the stool around and faced Tommy, interrupting. "Not a problem, honest. I'm just happy to know what my wife is up to. Everything's fine." Tommy noticed his balled up fists just as he shoved them into his side jacket pockets. "Now, speaking of Linda, I need to go home to watch the kids so she can do some last-minute shopping. Have a merry Christmas, Tommy, and thanks for the information. Have another beer on me!" Shane pulled out his wallet and threw a twenty-dollar bill on the bar. "And merry Christmas to you too, Tillie," he called over to his favorite bartender. He drained the last of his martini and was still chewing on the olive as he walked out into the snow.

When Linda returned from her shopping trip, the first thing she noticed was a fire in the barbeque pit which doubled as a fire pit in the fall. On occasion, Shane had started the fire on a chilly October evening, and the family pretended they were on a camping trip. She had never seen him do it in the winter. "Maybe a treat for the kids but who knows?" she muttered as she pushed the door open with her hip, balancing packages in both arms. The snow had diminished to just a few flurries, but she still kicked off her boots in the mudroom. The second thing she noticed was a brown paper shopping bag sitting on the kitchen table. Curious, she dropped her packages on the floor and walked over to examine it. She hadn't reached it when the three children came charging into the kitchen. The bundles on the floor caught their attention and interrupted their greeting, but Linda headed them off.

"Hey, you guys, it's getting close to Christmas. No opening bags or packages allowed." She laughed at their halfhearted protest, then asked, "Where's your dad?" They looked at each other, seeming stymied by the question, almost as if they just remembered that he was in the house.

"Probably in the living room, watching TV," Junior said. As if called on cue, Shane appeared in the doorway.

"Did I hear someone call my name?" he asked, smiling. He looked down at the packages. "Looks like you had a successful shopping trip. Christmas is a great time of the year, isn't it, kids?" All three nodded, the childhood sparkle at the thought of Christmas evident in the sheen of their eyes.

Linda moved toward the bag on the table but Shane stepped in front of her. "What's in the bag?" Shane reached for it, grasping it by the handles and pulling them together so that it closed.

"Just some stuff I think we need to get rid of. I would've done it sooner but I thought you should know about it before I throw stuff away." His earlier relaxed smile morphed into one that resembled a plaster cast that could crack at any moment. "I'll show you as we gather around the fire pit. Get your boots and coats, kids. I'll get some marshmallows to roast."

"What the hell is going on, Shane?" He ignored the quizzical look she sent his way.

Preparing three children to go outside in the winter was always a challenge, and almost ten minutes passed before the Phillips family stood around the pit, staring at the mesmerizing flames. Shane was the first one out and had added several dry logs from the stack under a tarpaulin next to the pit, causing the fire to shoot several feet into the air before settling back to a steady roar.

"Before we do the marshmallows, we have some things to get rid of." While the children gazed into the fire, which had the usual hypnotizing effect on them, Linda stood with her arms across her chest, shivering more than she should have been as she watched Shane open the bag. She gasped as the first item came out. It was the skirt she had worn to the Village Grille the last time she was there. Before she could react, the flames devoured the garment. The next thing out of the bag had Linda telling the children to get back into the house. It was the black bra, and its lacy fiber burst into flames before she managed to herd the youngsters away.

"We'll do marshmallows some other time. It's really too cold out here." Linda shot Shane a look but he turned away. By the time she and the children reached the steps leading up to the house, he had thrown the entire bag into the fire, its paper exploding in flame and the contents already disintegrated.

Not a word passed between Linda and Shane until the children were asleep. Despite the temperature in the house hovering just above seventy-two degrees, the atmosphere carried an undeniable chill. When they finally sat down at the kitchen table, it was after nine o'clock. They glared at each other as if daring the other to speak first. Linda broke the silence.

"What in the name of God is wrong with you?" Her eyes began to water, the tears threatening to drizzle down her cheeks. "What you did is sick, you know that? What the hell do you think the kids thought about what you were doing?" She covered her face with her hands.

Shane stood and began to circle around the table, but stopped short when Linda held up one of her hands. "Don't come near me, Shane. I just want an answer."

Shane stood up straighter, throwing his shoulders back. "You want sick, Linda? You really want sick? Here's sick—a married woman going out in public deliberately bringing all kinds of atten-tion to herself. That is sick. We've been through this before. You are my wife. Period, end of story. There will not be a next time where you let the local bar-hounds, drool all over their beer just because you're flashing your new titties. If I hear of it again, I'll beat the living shit out of you. Is that clear enough?

Linda struggled for a comeback but the look in Shane's eyes shut down any possibility of keeping things equal.

"Yeah, Shane, I guess I get that." She started to stride out of the room with confidence but faltered before she got to the door, her attempt at strength vanishing into a meek retreat. It was all Shane needed.

"All you need to remember is who's boss in this household," he shouted. "Now, you go on upstairs and I'll turn out the lights. You'd best be ready for me 'cause we're going to have an early Christmas celebration."

# Twenty-Four

## *Sunrise/Sunset*

THE UNBRIDLED EXCITEMENT OF the twins as the summer of 1989 drew to a close with an unusually dry August countered the recurring hostility in the house whenever Shane was home. The exuberance of Jackie and Tonie at the prospect of going to school for the first time could not be squelched, not even by the tension between their parents. For her part, Linda's enthusiasm for their entry into school increased with the phone call from Steve Chambers announcing that Chambers and Stone Realty was, as he said, "eagerly awaiting the return of the best receptionist they'd ever had."

"It's going to be a new start for me," she told friends Yvonne DiMartini and Loretta James, as they sat on the veranda sipping iced tea on Saturday of Labor Day weekend. "With the girls in school, there'd be no point in me staying at home." Both friends nodded in agreement, but Loretta posed the obvious question.

"What's Shane think of you getting back into the working world?"

Yvonne chimed in. "Yeah, I was kind of thinking the same thing."

Linda stared out at her children, chasing each other around the swing set in the backyard, and took a lazy swallow of her tea, as if she needed to consider her answer. "He's fine with it, especially with the fact I'll be making some money instead of spending it. At least that's what he says right now." She paused briefly, then continued. "I'm hoping maybe this can be a change of direction for us; you know, a fresh start all around."

Her two friends looked at her, expecting further explanation, but none was forthcoming.

SHANE WAS NOT DUE back from his latest trip until the Wednesday after Labor Day, missing the occasion of putting his two daughters on the school bus for their first day of school. Linda had the children to herself for two more days before the changes in the family routine started. Late Sunday morning, a drizzle began to fall, and with it, the temperature dropped as well. "Looks like this will be an inside day, Mommy," Junior observed as they drove home from church. Making an unusual spur-of-the-moment decision, Linda turned into the parking lot of the Village Grille. Before the turn was completed, the twins were clamoring from the backseat. "What are we doing?" they asked in perfect unison.

"Since you girls will be starting school on Tuesday, I thought we'd celebrate with a nice lunch at a restaurant. What do you think of that?" The squeals of glee coming from both the passenger seat and the back seat sent a clear picture of what her three children thought of the idea.

After a lunch of burgers and fries topped off with a double dip chocolate fudge sundae, Linda decided to add one more treat to the day. "How about if we stop at the video store and rent a movie for this afternoon, maybe even two if you want." Once again, the children acted as though they'd been told Christmas would come twice this year.

"Do I get to pick?" Junior asked. "The girls don't know anything about videos."

Linda laughed out loud. "Sure, but don't sell your sisters short. They're going to school, you know!"

As she expected, selecting the movies stretched out to almost an hour with *Oliver and Company* and *Honey, I Shrunk the Kids* finally winning out. They walked toward the checkout counter and passed by the section of musical comedies. In another spur of the moment decision, Linda grabbed her favorite, not certain when or if she would watch it in the two-day checkout period. She could practically recite the dialogue and sing every song from *Fiddler on the Roof*, but she loved the story and could easily watch it once again.

A long afternoon of watching the children's movies coupled with the dreariness of the day precluded any chance of dancing with the fiddler, and soon after putting her children to bed, Linda found herself curled up in bed with *C is for Corpse,* her attempt to keep up with the popular Kinsey Millhone series by Sue Grafton. The adventures of Kinsey kept her awake for less than ten minutes.

The next day, the final day of the last holiday weekend of the summer, all attention was focused on preparations for the first day of school. Junior spent his time making certain his school supplies were in good order, checking on notebooks, pens and pencils, and three-ring binders. The twins wrestled with deciding what they should wear. The day passed quickly and when it came time for bed, the girls showed the familiar signs of nervousness as they faced the new experience: fidgeting, squirming, and jabbering as Linda tucked them in. Shane Jr. put on his blasé face, a veteran of several years of schooling, but he couldn't stop rattling on and on about the unknowns of a new school year. Linda finally had to take a firm stance with him, and by eight thirty, the house was quiet. She went down to the living room and inserted *Fiddler on the Roof* into the video cassette player.

The film, always moving and poignant, held her in its grip despite its familiarity. As the scene of the wedding during which Tevye and Golde sing "Sunrise, Sunset" approached, and she knew it was coming, Linda reached for the remote and placed her finger on the FF button. Every time she watched the movie, she would cry during the scene. Tomorrow, her two little girls would start school and it wasn't difficult to anticipate the effect the lyrics of that song would have as the parents lament the startlingly rapid passage of time.

When the scene began to play, she dropped her hands and the remote along with them into her lap and watched. When the song ended, she searched for the stop button on the remote through blurred eyes, tears streaming down her cheeks.

As though in a daze, she started to recite aloud—"swiftly fly the years, one season following another, laden with happiness and tears..." She sat staring at the television screen, now just a snowstorm of white noise. "When did he get to be so tall..." The tears wouldn't stop coming and she made no effort to stem them. "I don't remember growing older..." She looked around the room, glancing at a photo on the end table of the twins as toddlers, adorable smiles briefly raising her spirits. "Is this the little girl I carried?" Her gaze shifted to a companion photo showing Shane Jr. swinging his first baseball bat. "Is this the little boy at play?" The collar of Linda's blouse was thoroughly dampened and still the tears would not subside.

"Dammit, Shane, we've got to make this work!" She looked around, almost embarrassed as she realized how loud she had shouted.

After rubbing her eyes with her blouse tails, she picked up the phone and dialed Yvonne's number. As soon as Linda identified herself, Louise DiMartini greeted her warmly. "How're those little darlings?" she asked. "All ready for school?"

Linda choked out a shaky yes then asked to speak to Yvonne.

"Could you come over for a few minutes? Everything's okay, but I'd just like to talk to you if you could."

"Be right there," Yvonne said, and ten minutes later she was sitting on the couch next to her friend, listening to an in-depth description of several years' worth of Shane's physical, verbal, and emotional abuse, beginning with the burning of her clothes. Yvonne's eyes widened when Linda told her about calling the police several times, events that somehow had escaped the town gossip mill. When the narrative finally finished, she moved closer to Linda and put her arm around her shoulder.

"Why don't you leave him? You really can't continue like this."

"I can't do that. We're a family. The kids need a dad and most of the time he's pretty good with them." The tears that had dried up reappeared in Linda's eyes. "I'm the one he takes everything out on, and I don't even know why. I've done nothing but try to please him."

"Why did you call me over here, Linda? I mean, you know

what you should do, kids or not. I just don't know what to say."
Yvonne's disappointment in her was obvious and Linda had to
respond.

"I called you over so that someone will know that if I ever
wind up dead, it will be Shane that did it. And you know what?
My worst fear is not that he'll kill me but that he'll get the kids."

THE 1989 VERSION OF the annual hunting trip, guided by Tommy
Iverson, lacked its usual result and Shane Phillips was not a happy
hunter. Will Comfort was the only one of the three friends to
come home with a deer. When Shane complained as they were
packing their gear for the trip home, Tommy was quick to react.

"You missed the fucking first shot I got you, Shane. Don't
blame me for your failure. I guarantee one deer per group, and
you guys got that. You're just a spoiled jackass."

Shane dropped his knapsack and grabbed his rifle from the
back of the truck. Will and Johnny Stanton were on him in
seconds. "Give it up, Shane," Johnny said, yanking the rifle out of
his grip. "Tommy's right. We've all been spoiled. We just had a bad
year. As they say, wait till next year."

Tommy and Shane glared at each for a few seconds, then the
tension evaporated. "Sorry, Tommy, I just hate to be going home
empty-handed. It's like I wasted my time and money, you know?"

"Understand. Lucky for you, you got Linda for a wife. She'll
provide plenty of soothing solace for you, I'd imagine." He smiled
but Shane didn't.

THE CALL CAME TWO weeks later, a day after Shane had left for a
short trip.

"Look, Mrs. Phillips," Tommy said, "I'm sorry to have bothered
you. I thought Shane wasn't leaving until tomorrow. My mistake.
Just let him know I called, please."

"What's this about, Tommy? Maybe I can answer your question
for you." Linda had seen Tommy practically every time she went
out with her group to the Village Grille, and every time he had
been overly polite and cordial, not coming close to what she could
characterize as a hit since the first time. When they were alone, she

actually found him pleasant and easy to talk to. As Yvonne pointed out on numerous occasions, he also was handsome, "when he's cleaned up," she said once, causing the other women to explode in laughter.

"Well, I guess I could tell you," Tommy said, clearly reluctant. "It probably slipped his mind, but he never gave me the second payment for the trip and, I was hoping to catch him 'cause I could use the money right about now."

"How much?" Linda asked without hesitation.

"You know how much the trip was, right? I mean, being his wife and all. Well, it's half of that."

Linda giggled. "Am I on *Candid Camera* here? Why don't you just tell me so I don't have to look it up."

"Three hundred and fifty, but I'll wait till he gets back. Thanks for passing along the message, Mrs. Phillips."

"Oh, for God's sake, Tommy. You call me Linda at the Grille. What's with the formality? Just stop over and I'll give you a check. You shouldn't have to wait for your money. I'm not going anywhere tonight. Just get here before the kids go to bed, okay? Like, before seven thirty."

"Thanks a lot, Linda. I really do appreciate this. I keep telling Shane how lucky he is. I sure hope he knows it. I'll see you in a little bit."

Without answering, Linda hung up, then muttered under her breath. "Oh, shit—how am I going to explain this to Shane?"

Ten minutes later, Tommy rang the doorbell at the front door, a rarely used entrance. The sound of the chimes startled Linda and brought the three children running into the kitchen. She went to the door and pulled aside the closed curtains, sending a tiny dust cloud drifting to the floor. After a quick glance around the bare and unused foyer, she motioned through the glass for him to come around to the back of the house.

Linda introduced him and Junior immediately announced to his sisters that "this is the man who helps daddy kill the deer," a declaration that resulted in cold stares from the twins. Linda excused herself to go upstairs to her desk to get her checkbook, and upon her return was stunned to see Tommy and her children sitting at the kitchen table having what appeared to be a serious discussion.

"I just asked them how school was going. I've been listening ever since." Tommy laughed and Junior joined him, his joke lost on the younger girls.

"Well, I've got a blank check. You said three fifty, right?"

Tommy nodded. "Make it out to Iverson's Guide Service, if you would, please. I need to make it look like my business makes money once in a while for the IRS, you know."

As Linda wrote out the check, the conversation about school continued around the table. "Here you go, Mr. Iverson," she said when she finished. Tommy took the check, folded it, and put it in his pocket.

"Guess I'll be going, kids," he said as he stood up. "Thanks a lot for telling me about your school. I enjoyed hearing about it." He started for the door but was stopped by Jackie, who had jumped from her chair and was tugging on his pants leg.

"Will you come back sometime to see us?" she asked, tilting her head back as far as she could to look up at him.

In a single motion, he swept her up into her arms, causing a spontaneous giggle. "That'd be up to your mom and dad," he said as he gently put her down. He caught Linda's eye, a wide grin crossing his face. "But I'd like that. You kids could be a lot of fun."

Tommy held out his hand to Linda, who responded in kind and shook it. "Thanks for the check. I hope this doesn't cause any problem with Shane."

"Heavens no, why would it? He owes you so I'm paying you. So, what's with you and the kids? It looked like instant rapport. You don't have kids of your own, do you?" Linda asked as they moved toward the door.

Tommy reached for the knob, then turned around. "None that I know of." His impish grin returned. "I've always gotten along well with kids. Kids and dogs all love me. Adults, not so much." He entered the mudroom. "Next time I'll know to come to the back door," he said as he left.

LINDA WAITED TO TELL Shane about Tommy Iverson's visit until he had been back for a full day, the reconnect day, as she called it. She always planned to work just a half day, giving them most of the afternoon before school dismissed. "I love matinees," Shane said many times. Although this trip had been shorter than most, Shane's libido raged as powerful as it had ever been when he was away for twice as long, its effect producing a long and sensual afternoon which lasted right up to the time the children were due home from school.

"You've worn me out and the kids'll be home any minute," Linda said, looking at the clock on the nightstand. They were barely dressed when the familiar sound of the diesel engine slowing down signaled that the school bus was stopped out front.

The first day was always the best. Shane developed a reservoir of patience while on the road and he spent the remainder of the afternoon in the playroom with the children. Linda busied herself with preparation for a special first-night-home dinner, a habit that had become part of the pattern of their lives, as ingrained as making love the first afternoon or Shane finding something to argue about by the second day.

At dinner, after the requisite three-martini cocktail hour placed Shane in the happy place that allows the troubles of the world to vanish, he directed the clichéd questions to his three children.

"So, how's school going and what's new since I saw you last?"

Junior's answer to his father's question sent the special dinner plan spiraling out of control.

"School's great, Daddy, and Mr. Iverson came over for a visit. He's a really nice man."

Shane's reaction was swift and, to Linda, predictable. She watched the fuzzy world of alcohol-induced contentment empty from him as surely as water swirls down an open drain when a plug is pulled.

"He came here to the house? When I'm not home? What the hell did he want?" Each question brought more color into his cheeks. All three children pushed their chairs away from the table, allowing enough room to bolt to the playroom if the occasion called for it.

Linda glared at him. "First of all, there's no need to swear in front of the children. Second, you owed the guy money and he needed it. I don't blame him for calling. He was really very polite about it. Why didn't you pay him?" Her calm demeanor managed to keep Junior in his seat, but the two girls climbed down and came over to her, snuggling up on each side.

Shane tried to match her gaze with a scowl of his own but was the first to break eye contact. "It really isn't any of your business, but I'll tell you anyway. I was thinking of reducing what I paid him. I didn't get a deer, and if someone doesn't do the job, they shouldn't get the same pay."

"But you agreed to the fee, right? Seems to me that it's kind of like a contract even if nothing is written down. When were you going to tell him?" Linda stopped, her logical argument placing Shane on the defensive.

"How come you're on his side in this? His charm win you over or something?" Shane started to push back harder with a comment about Tommy having a schoolboy crush on her, but it backfired as Linda came right out of her chair, brushing Jackie and Tonie to the side.

"He's your friend, or maybe not after you were going to stiff him, but all I did was pay a bill for you. Tommy stayed a few minutes, even was nice to the kids, then left. So don't you go getting stupid ideas in your head."

Without saying a word, Shane picked up his plate. As soon as he stood, the three children hurried from the room, Junior in the lead. He took one giant step to the sink, and scraped off his entire dinner. "Here's what stupid thinks of your special dinner," he hissed as he flipped the garbage disposal on, the sink vibrating violently as the machine struggled to grind up the chicken bones.

"I'm going to check on the kids," Linda said, but she had not gone two steps before Shane caught up with her and grabbed her right arm, twisting it until she yelped in pain.

"Don't you ever call me stupid again!" he shouted, bending her arm further behind her back. "Now, I'm going out for a while, and I expect the house to be quiet when I come home—everybody in bed and that includes you." His fingers dug into her arm. "Is that understood?"

Instead of a verbal answer, she just nodded, her teeth grinding together from the pain.

When the door slammed behind him, Junior came running into the kitchen. Linda was rubbing her arm while forcing back tears. "Are you okay, Mommy?" he asked, his innocent look of concern choking her.

"I'm fine, dear. Now why don't you get the girls and we'll finish our dinner. Your daddy had to go out for a bit, and he probably won't get back before you all go to bed."

Halfway through the meal, the phone rang, and Linda hesitated to answer it but finally picked it up, surprised to hear Tommy Iverson's voice.

"Hey, Linda," he said before she even answered. "This is Tommy. I just wanted to make sure everything was all right with Shane when he found out you had paid me. I know he can be pretty tough sometimes."

"Things are just fine. Yeah, things are just fine and dandy." She hung up.

# Twenty-Five

*Christmas, 1989*

SHANE PROMISED LINDA THAT he would be home for Christmas. His schedule called for him to make his last delivery in Northern California by December 20 at the latest, allowing one day for possible weather delays. The legal limit of eleven hours of driving time would be sufficient to get him back to Connecticut late Christmas Eve if he encountered no weather problems across the country. As he always did, he would push the legal limit and fudge his log so he could get home earlier. He called Linda as soon as his last shipment was unloaded, telling her that he would not be home until at least noon of Christmas Day.

THE LIGHT AND FLUFFY snowfall in Hampton Village early on Christmas Eve morning converted the village green into a traditional Currier and Ives scene. Linda dropped her three children at Loretta James's house with the promise to pick them up after the luncheon party Steve Chambers arranged for his staff and some special clients of Chambers and Stone Realty.

"Have a glass of wine for me," Loretta joked as she said goodbye. "And don't stay too long at the Village. You know how that place gets later in the day."

"Not to worry, although I might be tempted with Shane not due back until tomorrow afternoon. Plus it's Christmas Eve. The usual crowd won't be hanging around, or at least I wouldn't think so." Linda thanked her for watching the children and headed out into the romantic snowstorm.

The morning at the office passed slowly, as the phones were as silent as the snow drifting past her window. At eleven thirty, Steve came out of his office to announce that as of that minute, they were closing and heading for the Village Grille to get an early start on the celebration.

"You can ride with us, Linda. We'll come back this way to get your car later," he said.

She started to protest but a glance out the window changed her mind as the intensity of the snow seemed to increase. "Okay. Thanks." Ten minutes later, they were ordering their first drinks of the day at the Village Grille, which was already crowded with early partiers. The picturesque snowstorm only enhanced the prevalent Christmas spirit, and when Linda idly wondered aloud if she should be drinking before noon, she was roundly kidded by her companions.

"It's afternoon someplace," one reveler shouted over the increasing din in the bar.

SHANE TRAILED THE SNOWSTORM as it moved eastward, delaying his arrival only slightly as the warmth of the major highways melted the snow as it fell. At two thirty in the afternoon, he dropped his empty trailer off at the company lot. A cold front streamed in behind the storm, freezing the snow and slush mixture on the roads into crusty ruts. He navigated through the rural roads into Hampton Village to his house, which showed no signs of life. He backed his tractor up the driveway and parked between the barn and his car, noticing that Linda's car was missing from its usual place in the garage.

"Where the hell are they?" he whispered, remembering that her office was only going to be open until noon.

The cold wind had blown most of the three or four inches of fluffy snow off the paved surface, relieving him of snow removal duties. The frosted window of the kitchen door told him to anticipate a welcome blast of warm air when he opened it, and he was not disappointed. His first move as he entered the house was toward the liquor cabinet, tossing his heavy mackinaw jacket onto the empty wooden bench by the door. The hooks that usually held an array of winter coats were empty, and the boots he insisted always be in a perfect line along the floor were missing as well. He grabbed an eight-ounce tumbler from a cabinet over the sink and filled it with a solid three fingers of scotch. The first toss, undiluted by ice, burned his throat and brought tears to his eyes. The airtight woodstove still was emitting an ample supply of warmth, but he set his drink on the kitchen table and picked up a log from the bin. Using his foot, he unlatched the stove door and watched as the fire sucked in the fresh oxygen and leapt into life. The well-dried log instantly burst into flame, and he shut the door, again with his foot. Gathering his scotch, an occasional early afternoon substitute for his usual martini, he moved into the living room and sat down heavily in the impractical, decorative rocking chair, which emitted rebellious creaks and groans from his weight.

An hour and two more generous helpings of Dewar's later, his family still was not home. He downed the last swallow of his drink and stood up, swaying from side to side as he focused his attention on the doorway leading to the kitchen. Walking a straight line from his chair to the door proved a daunting challenge and the collision between the doorjamb and his right shoulder spun him into the kitchen with such force that he almost fell. After recovering his balance, he picked up the phone and dialed Yvonne DiMartini's number.

"Where the hell are they?" he bellowed before "Hello" was out of Yvonne's mouth. "Here I get home early from a fucking exhausting two-week road trip on Christmas Eve and my wife can't even be here to greet me."

Yvonne tried to calm Shane, but her attempts seemed to infuriate him even further. "She thought you weren't getting in until tomorrow, Shane; at least, that's what she told me."

"Well, I got here today and that's what counts. A man's family is supposed to be home on Christmas Eve. Do you know where she is or not?" As Shane became more agitated, the words ran together in a slurred blur.

"No, I don't, but…" Shane interrupted her with another thundered outburst.

"Forget it," he shouted, "I'll find her!" He slammed the phone down and headed out into the stinging cold without picking up his coat.

Shane arrived at his car, a Ford Escort that was dwarfed by his truck parked next to it. He brushed the snow off the windshield, not bothering to clear the rear window. Only after he plunked down in the seat did he realize that the keys were still hanging on the key hook by the kitchen door.

"Son of a bitch," he swore. His trip back to the house through the biting wind allowed time enough for a semblance of common sense to take control. The large oak log he had placed in the wood-stove burned at full strength, filling the kitchen with such inviting warmth that he didn't even reach for the keys. Instead, he grabbed his glass from the sink and the Dewar's from the counter. After pouring yet another generous measure into the glass, this time diluting it with several ice cubes, he made his way to the rocker, sat down, and stared out at the driveway, waiting, his eyes watering from his effort to focus on the beautiful winter scene outside the window.


YVONNE'S CALL TO LORETTA James had the unmistakable edge of panic in it.

"Is Linda there with you?" she asked, her voice shaking. When Loretta confirmed that she and Linda had been enjoying a Christmas Eve afternoon glass of wine while the kids played games in the basement, Yvonne's voice assumed a somber seriousness. She mentioned the call from Shane and the fact that he had come home a full day ahead of time, then told Loretta of her real concern.

"He's been drinking and he's really pissed off. One of us better go home with her."

"I'll go with her," Loretta said. "Thanks for the heads up and I know Linda will appreciate it. I'll call you later and let you know how things are." She hung up and went to pass on the bad news. Linda's response did not come as a surprise.

"I'll be fine. He'll probably be passed out by the time I get home anyway." Linda worked hard to convince her friend that going home with the three children would be fine. Loretta wasn't buying it.

"You know what he's like when he's drinking. He's bad enough when he's sober." Loretta said, realizing immediately how harsh she sounded. "I'm sorry, Linda, I didn't mean...I mean, he is your husband and all, but I just worry about you sometimes..."

Linda, her eyes filling, sat down heavily on the sofa. "I worry about myself, sometimes," she said. "I don't know how much longer I can stand it. It was all good at the beginning, but now it's mostly bad. It's the Jekyll and Hyde show. Sometimes he scares the living daylights out of me, then he can turn around and be romantic with me and loving with the kids." She wiped her eyes as Loretta sat down next to her.

With her arm draped over Linda's shoulder, Loretta reached over with her other hand and placed it firmly under Linda's chin. Like a mother telling a child to "look me in the eye when I'm talking to you," she turned her friend's face toward her. "Here's the plan," she said. "You can leave the kids here for now; let them play for the rest of the afternoon. You go home and find out what kind of mood Shane's in. You can call me later and we'll arrange something depending on what you find out."

Linda shook her head rapidly from side to side at first, dismissing that possibility out of hand, then saw the concern in Loretta's eyes. Her determination drained from her as she considered the offer. "You're right; it's Christmas Eve and I'd better check things out. I don't want Christmas ruined for them if Shane's in one of his snits." She reached up and patted Loretta's hand. "You're a great friend; I'm not sure what I'd do without you." She stood and went into the recreation room where all the children were deeply involved in a game of Sorry. She gathered her three around her and hugged them. "I'm going home for a bit to see Daddy," she said. "He got home early from his trip so he could be here for Christmas morning. I'll be back to get you a little later, okay?" Linda smiled as they each turned back to their game with a simple nod. A minute later, she waved goodbye to Linda and headed for home, a kaleidoscope of butterflies flitting around in her stomach as she wondered what she would find.

SHANE HEARD THE CAR come up the drive but did not get up. When the kitchen door opened, he waited for the expected bois- terous shout from Shane Jr. calling out to him but there was no sound other than Linda moving about as she shed her coat and her boots in the mudroom. The realization that the kids were not with her brought him out of the rocker.

"Whoa," he whispered as his world spun for a few seconds before he steadied himself by reaching backward to the arms of the chair. He crossed the room toward the same doorway that had jumped into his way earlier. Linda arrived at the entrance to the living room at the same time as Shane did, and they wound up face to face.

"Where's the kids and where you been?" Shane slurred the questions, his forced effort to appear sober failing. As if surprised at seeing Linda, he backed up a few steps and stared at her, his glance traveling from her head to her toes and back again, pausing briefly at her chest level each time.

"The fuck you dressed like that?" The question came as no surprise to Linda.

Linda, defensive under his withering stare and faced with answering several questions at once, also backtracked a few steps, but Shane followed her, quickly filling the gap between them.

"This is just one of my dressier work outfits. We had the party today, if you remember. The children are playing over at Loretta's. I thought I'd come home to see you first, then go get them later." The tension building in the situation sent a shiver through her entire body.

"How'd you know I got home early?" As he asked yet another question, he again scanned her body, but this time a troublesome leer crossed his face as his gaze lingered on her chest.

As she realized the effect it was having on her husband, Linda was regretting her choice of a bright red, formfitting dress to wear to the company party. She involuntarily reached up to close the neck tighter in the face of Shane's lascivious stare.

"Yvonne called over to Loretta's," she stammered. "I was sur- prised to hear that you made it a whole day early."

"Well, then, here we are, no kids to think about. I feel like celebrating." He reached out and grabbed her hand. "Come on, Linda. It's Christmas Eve." He pulled her through the doorway into the living room and pushed her down on the sofa. She started to get up but he pinned her down, all the while pushing her dress up to her thighs.

"Why don't we wait until later, Shane? After the kids are in bed." She tried to get up again but he shoved her deeper into the cushions.

"I've been gone for two goddamned weeks and you want me to wait!" He was pulling on her pantyhose and the whiffs of Dewars coming from his ragged breath almost made her gag.

"There you are dressed like a fucking hooker for your party today and I'm your husband. You damn well better not try to say no to me."

She didn't dare.

"When I get back, you can answer the rest of my questions." Shane climbed off her and weaved his way to the downstairs powder room. Linda pulled her dress down over her torn panties, not even bothering to pick up the pantyhose from the floor. She sat rigid on the sofa and waited, knowing from past experience what to expect when Shane had been drinking.

He came out of the bathroom, his pants still unzipped, and stood over her with his hands on his hips. "So, the kids are at Loretta's, and I'm just as glad you didn't bring them home with you." He smirked down at her. "We wouldn't have had the chance to get reacquainted, right?"

Linda looked up at him, her face blank.

"Now, I want to know where in the hell you were all afternoon. The party was for lunch and you didn't get home until after four. So, who else was enjoying the view of you in that dress?"

"Shane, I'm not going to put up with the third degree from you yet again. You do this all the time when you've got no cause." She started to stand and move around him, but his fierce slap caught her hard on the left cheek, and she sat down hard on the sofa.

"Here's what we're going to do. You call Loretta and tell her I'm coming to get the kids. We're going to have Chinese take-out tonight like we always have on Christmas Eve. We're going to decorate the tree that I set up two weeks ago, and then we're going to the early service down at the church. It's going to be a merry little Christmas around here, and we'll be the happy little Phillips family. There's no reason for anything to be any different than it always has been."

Linda glared up at him as she rubbed her cheek, which had already turned a bright pink. "You might find that things are going to be different, Shane. I'm not going to put up with much more from you. And there is no way you're going to get the kids in your condition." She rose from the sofa again, ignoring Shane's balled up fists, and pushed her way past him. "I'm going to change and head over to Loretta's. It'd be nice if you could sober up so you don't ruin Christmas for the kids again." She was halfway up the stairs to their bedroom but still heard his mumbled response.

"Bitch!"

ON THE WAY TO Loretta's house, she passed by the China Buffet Restaurant and stopped to order the family dinner. As she got out of the car, the sharp wind pummeled her and practically ripped the door from her hand. Turning to shield her face, she exposed her cheek. The tenderness of the reddening blotch accentuated the sting, and she pulled up her collar for protection. She glanced in the side view mirror; the abrasion was getting more obvious by the minute.

"Loretta's going to need an explanation," she whispered, and pondered the thought. "Just tell her the truth," she said in a determined voice, loud enough to almost convince her that would be the best course of action.

As usual, the take-out order from the restaurant was inexpensive but would supply them with enough leftovers for several more meals.

"I'll pick it up in about twenty minutes," she said to Amy, the daughter of the owner, after paying in advance.

"Great, Mrs. Phillips," Amy replied, "and I wish you and your family a merry Christmas."

Linda returned the familiar greeting and turned to leave but stopped short when Amy called out to her.

"I hope that rash on your cheek is okay by tomorrow morning," she said with a wide grin, "Wouldn't want Santa to catch anything when he kisses you."

Her good-natured joking only reminded Linda that she would have some explaining to do in the next few days. She left the restaurant with a halfhearted wave, facing a five-minute drive to rehearse the story for Loretta. "Tell her the truth" echoed in her head but she was a firm believer in the white lie. Not everything was black or white. How often did she hear a real estate salesman mention that his sales pitch had a degree of truth in it, which clearly indicated that there must also be a degree of untruth as well. There was nothing wrong with a small amount of mental reservation, of holding back for the sake of protecting someone from worry or hurt. It wouldn't be the first time and likely not the last. She arrived at Loretta's house, her decision made.

THE THREE CHILDREN SAW the car pull into the James's driveway first. "Mom's here," Tonie and Jackie called out simultaneously. Loretta hurried to the back door and greeted her friend with a warm hug.

"I've been worried about you, and the kids have been at the window waiting for an hour. What the heck kept you so long?" Loretta broke off the hug, took one step back and put one hand on each of Linda's shoulders. The small space between them forced Linda to look directly into her eyes. All resolve to allow Loretta to think everything was all right evaporated in the compassionate mist of the friendship the two shared. Linda held herself together for a group hug with her three children, who almost knocked her off her feet as they swept into the kitchen. Shane Jr. spoke first as he looked up at his mother.

"What happened to your face, Mom? It's all red," he asked, the sincere concern coupled with the wonderful naïveté of a young boy evident in his voice.

"It's really cold out, Shane. I was just rubbing my cheeks to get warm as I was coming in. Now you guys gather all your stuff and we'll head out. It's Christmas Eve, you know, and we've got a

Chinese dinner to eat and church later on. And thank Aunt Loretta for having you over this afternoon."

While the children rushed around the house retrieving clothes, books, games, and other paraphernalia, Loretta nudged Linda into the narrow hallway between the kitchen and the mudroom that overflowed with boots and associated winter gear for the first time since the previous winter.

"Tell me what happened, quickly before the kids get back here," she whispered. "And I know something did." She used the maneuver she had earlier, placing her hands firmly on Linda's shoulders and forcing her to look straight into her eyes.

"He just smacked me one time, you know, with an open hand. He's been drinking much of the afternoon so I kind of expected it." Linda shifted her gaze and tried to make a move into the mudroom. "I'd better get the kids' coats; they're sure going to need 'em. It's really cold outside."

Loretta recognized the diversionary tactic and squeezed her fingers deeper. The pressure made Linda stop, wincing. "That's not all, is it? Come on, you can tell me."

The thumping on the wooden basement stairs signaled that all the children were charging up to the main floor. The irrepressible Christmas Eve excitement spilled over into loud giggling which turned into squeals of laughter as they reached the top of the steps. Jackie and Tonie were the first to find the adults. "They're in here," they shouted, and soon all five of the children crowded into the hallway, each competing for parental attention. Loretta released her grip on Linda's shoulder and backed up a step.

"This discussion isn't over, you know," she said as she contin-ued to try to be in charge of the situation, but a smile curled the corners of her mouth. "You'll tell all if I want you to. I know you too well, Linda Phillips."

Neither mother could ignore the demands. Loretta's two began asking over and over when they were going to eat. Linda's three had dived into the boot bin and were in various stages of getting dressed to go home. The activities eliminated any chance at further conversation. When Linda finally had her Jackie and Tonie dressed for the elements and checked Shane Jr.'s apparel, she shooed them out the door toward the car. "I'll be one second," she called to them.

She turned to Loretta. Her voice broke and her eyes filled when she began to speak. "I'll just say this one time because putting it into words is too frightening." She paused and drew in a deep breath. "I'm scared to death that he's going to hurt me. Like I told Yvonne, if they ever find me dead, Shane will be the one that did it." She hurried down the steps, and in a moment, the car with the Phillips family was gone. Loretta fumbled for the door jamb and leaned against it for support.

"Oh, my God! What in the hell is going on in that house?"

# Twenty-Six

*The Tipping Point*
*Memorial Day Weekend, 1990*

SHANE MADE GOOD ON his promise to be back for Junior's first little league game on Saturday of Memorial Day weekend. He rolled into town on late Friday afternoon, guzzled a few beers at the Grille, and arrived home in the relaxed state that alcohol usually produces.

"I've got dinner ready," Linda said as soon as he came in. She kept her back to him, focusing on the sizzling frying pan in front of her. "You don't have time for a drink, but obviously you've already had a few." Shane approached her and nuzzled at the back of her neck. She tensed, and he backed away.

"What's wrong? I've been away so I couldn't be in any trouble already." He smiled but she couldn't see it. "I'll go get the kids."

"They're not here." She turned from the stove to face him. "You usually aren't interested in seeing them until you've had your stress relieved from the long trip, so I asked Yvonne to have them over. I figured you'd come straight home so we'd have a couple of hours at least." The frizzling hamburger forced her attention back to her cooking. "She'll be bringing them back right after dinner so we don't have time now," she said over her shoulder, adding, "I hope you enjoyed the time at the bar."

Shane grabbed her arm and spun her around, sending the spatula and droplets of grease flying across the room. "So that's

214

why the chilly reception, just because I stopped for a drink, he hissed into her ear. "Well, guess what, we're going to have time."

"No, Shane, not this time. It's not going to happen this time." She unrolled several paper towels and knelt down, wiping up the grease spatters until she came to the spatula. As she picked it up, the click of the burner on the stove being turned off made her look up. Shane stood over her.

"You've been going through the motions ever since last Christmas, Linda," he said as he reached down for her. "You think I don't notice stuff? You got your job, go to parties, and treat me like a fucking stranger in my own house. Well, we're going to keep going through the motions. Now get up. We'll eat whatever the hell that is in the pan later."

"Do you know what a tipping point is, Shane? Do you have any idea?" Linda did not resist as Shane pushed her up the steps in front of him.

"I don't know what the hell you're talking about and don't much care right now." Shane's voice quavered with the huskiness of a man in heat.

"It's close, it's really close," Linda whispered as he slammed her face down onto their bed.

"Isn't anyone else available? I'm beginning to feel like a member of the damn family." Sam Olden knew the answer to his question before even asking but tried anyway.

"You got Sunday and Monday off completely. Don't complain to me. I'm just the messenger. But you'd better get going. The lady said she thinks her kid needs to go to the ER." The dispatcher signed off without hearing Sam's swearing.

"Oh, Christ, now he's hurting the kids. Goddammit!" He hurried to his cruiser, flipped on the flashing lights and headed for the Phillips home.

The scene when he arrived had become a familiar one: Shane Phillips stood on the porch, arms folded grimly across his chest. The house was quiet behind him.

"So, Mr. Phillips, what's happened this time? Your wife said she thought one of your kids might be injured."

"Same old, same old, Officer Olden. Just a family disagreement..." His explanation was interrupted by the kitchen door swinging wide open. He turned around. "Oh, shit. Linda, I told you I'll take care of this."

Linda came out followed by Junior, still in his baseball uniform, his face bright red and streaked with tears. He held a plastic bag filled with ice cubes to the side of his head. "He's bumped his head, Officer. I think it's all right but maybe it should be looked at."

Shane went over to the boy and stood between him and the officer. "It's just a bump. Kids fall on their heads all the time. It's like their sacred duty or something." His stilted laugh fell flat as Sam Olden called Junior over to him.

After a brief examination, Sam made his diagnosis. "I've seen a lot of these. The swelling's a good sign, but stay with the ice. If he gets sleepy or feels nauseous, I'd take him to the ER, but I think, as Mr. Phillips says, kids are forever bumping their heads."

Linda took her son's hand. "I'm taking him in to sit down and watch television, but I'll be right back out. Please don't leave, Officer."

"There's no need, Linda. I'll can tell him what happened," Shane said.

"As I said, Officer, I'll be right back."

She returned a moment later and began her explanation.

"My husband got angry with me and grabbed me. My son was shouting for him to stop hurting me, and he tried to get between us. Shane shoved him aside and he fell. He either hit the edge of the table or one of the legs when he went down." By the time she finished the description, her eyes filled. "He could have been really hurt."

Shane listened without interrupting. "See, it was like I said—an accident. I didn't mean to make him lose his balance. Just a family disagreement, that's all." His crooked smile exuded no charm, just a flat chill.

"I guess we're fine, now, Officer Olden. You really are a patient guy with us. I was mainly concerned about Junior," Linda said with a thin-lipped tight smile.

"If you say so, but you both better be aware that when kids get involved, everything goes to a whole new level." Olden tipped his cap and left Linda and Shane watching him leave.

After the cruiser disappeared down the street, Linda turned and glared at Shane.

"Whether you realize it or not, you just witnessed a tipping point!"

# Twenty-Seven

*Freedom*
*June, 1990*

WITH SCHOOL DUE TO end for the summer vacation the next day, Linda asked her two best friends to join her for lunch with the proviso that she had something serious to share with them. They would have met her anyway, but the solemn tone of the invitation made the decision easy.

The Village Grille offered quality of food and speed of service for the business people in town and the restaurant section was filled with the usual lunch crowd. Every stool in the bar was taken, mostly by salesmen whose jobs allowed them a noontime cocktail or beer. Linda had made the reservations and arrived fifteen minutes early, hovering in the crowded vestibule until her table was ready. She ignored a soft tap on her shoulder, believing it to be an accidental bump, but the second tap was a bit harder and more insistent. She turned around and found herself staring into the face of Tommy Iverson.

"Hey, Linda, haven't seen you around for a while. How are those adorable kids of yours?" he asked with a warm smile.

"Uh, uh, they're just fine Tommy, and thanks for asking. How's everything with you?" Before he could answer, Linda saw Loretta James come through the door. "Excuse me, will you? I'm meeting someone and she just arrived. Good to see you."

She pushed her way through the crowd to greet Loretta, leaving Tommy behind, muttering, "I'm just fine, too."

AFTER THEY ORDERED, LORETTA cleared her throat the way people do when either they are going to say something important or when they want someone else to say something important. The sound effect contained no subtlety and Linda responded.

"I guess you're wondering why I called all of you here today," she began, hoping to relieve some of the tension, but the attempt at humor fell far short. Both Yvonne and Loretta regarded her with intense interest. "I'll just say it and you can react, if you want to. I really don't..."

Yvonne interrupted. "For God's sake, Linda, get on with it, will you!" She laughed, but Linda caught the nervousness behind it.

"I'm asking Shane for a trial separation." She waited while the anticipated gasps from her friends rose and then subsided. "It's just gotten to be impossible. Since last Christmas, we might have one day of relative calm each time he's at home but the rest is nothing but tension. I just can't take it anymore. He's never happy with anything I do; he threatens me all the time, which I can handle, but now it branches out with the kids and that I won't put up with." When she finished, both friends reached across the table and held her hands. Tears spilled over. "I'll tell him it's just for the summer. People do this all the time, right? Then they get stuff straightened out and things are good again."

It was as if a cone of silence right out of the old *Get Smart* television show dropped over the table, shutting out the din of the restaurant. All attention was focused on Linda.

"How do you think he's going to take this? I mean, where will he go? Christ, Linda, this is going to be a horrific scene." Yvonne didn't realize how hard she was squeezing Linda's hand as she spoke until she heard a knuckle crack. "What do you think, Loretta? I think this could even be dangerous."

"I agree, but I figure it really is time to do something. His mother has a big house, plenty of room—maybe he could move in with her for a while."

Linda laughed through the tears dribbling down her cheeks. "I'll let you suggest that to him." Her two friends joined in the laughter with Loretta bringing everything back into perspective.

"This is going to be very interesting," she said. "And, of course, you know we'll be there to do whatever we can to help." Her words had the effect words like that always have when spoken with genuine concern and compassion. All three women reached for their napkins at the same time, dabbing judiciously at the moisture threatening to ruin their eye makeup.

THE CALL TO THE Covington County Sheriff's Department came in on a beautiful Sunday afternoon in June, the kind of day when people should be so happy to be alive that there couldn't possibly be room for any disputes. Deputy Sam Olden knew better. People could be vicious no matter what the weather.

He had responded to calls from the Phillips household on previous occasions, always finding an apologetic wife and a thoroughly pissed-off husband. He had no reason to expect anything else as he approached the porch. He climbed the steps and, as had been the case before, the first person to greet him was Shane Phillips.

"She's throwing me the fuck out and I'm going, but you'd better tell her that I'm coming back. She made a vow and she's gonna keep it." Shane was carrying a huge duffle bag that had him leaning to one side. He set it down when he got to Olden, who was trying to assess the situation.

"What exactly do you mean, sir?" Sam Olden was renowned as an officer who could diffuse the most intense domestic disputes. "Where are you going?" he asked in a low voice.

"Fucked if I know. Just for the summer...what a crock that is. I know how these things work. A few months, then an extension, then next thing you know, you get served with divorce papers. Well, that's not going to happen!"

"Sir," Deputy Olden asked, his concern for the other side of this dispute surfacing. "Where is your wife right now? I'll need to speak to her since she called."

"She's in the house, but she said she didn't need to talk with you if I agreed to go so I'm going, at least for now." Shane dragged his bag down the stairs and across the driveway to his car. "Tell her this isn't over, not by a long shot," he called out as he threw the bag in the back of his car. He was heading down the drive when Linda came to the kitchen door and opened it just a crack.

"I'm fine, Officer. I really am. I'm going to go pick up the kids and bring them home. Their daddy's out of the house now, and that's a good thing…" She paused, and Olden, peeking through the small opening, saw her raise a white towel, obviously doubling as an ice bag, to her face. "I'm really fine," she repeated in a muffled voice. "Now I need to get ready to get my kids. Thanks a lot for coming over. Another wasted trip for you but he finally agreed after I called." She shut the door, leaving Sam Olden with nothing to do but file yet another report on the Phillips household.

THE RESTRAINING ORDER CAME four months later, after Linda told Shane that she wanted the trial separation extended for at least another six months.

"That's bullshit," he said over the phone. "I'm coming over and we can discuss it. You can't keep me away from my own house."

"No, Shane. I swear to God if you come over here now, I'll call the cops again and they won't be too happy." She was about to slam the phone down, but something stopped her, almost as if she had to hear what he was going to say.

"You better watch your fuckin' back, bitch!" His shout reverberated in her ear. It was the worst of what had been more obscure threats during the initial separation.

Her next call was to a female attorney, Alison Novak, a lawyer who came strongly recommended by two of the female agents at Chambers and Stone. "She's a great advocate," they agreed. "I sure need a great advocate, and a lot of prayers, too," Linda had responded.

She was able to get an appointment within a day, taking an hour off of work during the day with the blessing of Steve Chambers, with whom she had shared a little of her home situation. "You're a great employee, Linda. We're lucky to have you, so go and get this straightened out. You shouldn't have to worry about this."

After effusive thanks to Steve and a hearty "go get him" from her colleagues, she drove to the offices of McNamara and Novak, and an hour after getting there, left with a copy of a one year restraining order request against Shane Phillips. A simple outline of the verbal threats and the unsolicited visits to the house were enough for the attorney to join her side. The three middle-of-the-night intrusions, all including the clear threat inspired by the vow of "till death do us part" sealed the commitment.

"We'll get it done, but we'll go for one year because sometimes the judge will cut it back, especially if you've filed for divorce. Even six months will take you into the spring of 1991, then we can decide from there what to do next," Alison Novak told her. "If we get the whole year, we'll be into September."

"Do you handle divorces as well?" Linda asked. "I'd like to think we'll get back together but I truly kind of doubt that."

"Let's just keep him away from you for now, then we'll deal that issue when it comes up, but, to answer your question, yes, I handle divorces too."

The next day, Alison filed the original order in the Covington County Courthouse, and used her influence to expedite the hearing, a hearing where Shane Phillips did not appear to contest the order. It was filed and official. Shane Phillips was to have no contact with his wife or his children unless specifically permitted by both Linda and the presiding judge for a period of one year.

THE ORDER WAS IN effect for nine months when Linda met again with Alison Novak and asked her to draw up the necessary papers for a divorce. That afternoon in May of 1991, Linda Phillips began her journey to be free of the suffocating presence of Shane in her life.

The wall to seal off the unpleasantness of her past, started so many years before, was closer to becoming a reality.

# Part Three

## A Walk on the Wild Side

# Twenty-Eight

## *Trial Separation*

SHANE PHILLIPS ADMITTED TO his mother during the second week of staying with her that it just was not going to work out.

"I thought that just for the summer, until Linda gets over this, I could handle it, but it's just too weird. I feel like I'm in high school again." His mother just nodded, agreeing that it was weird having a grown son around. "We've got a satellite trucking company down in South Britain, and the boss doesn't have a problem with me using that as a base for the summer. I'm sure I'll be back up here in the fall. I just don't feel like being around if I'm not living there, you know?"

His mother, more sympathetic with Linda's plight than his after having finally kicked his father out after years of physical and verbal abuse, nodded again.

"I understand completely," she said. "Your father and I had some issues also, as you might recall."

"Who could forget?" Shane said, a sardonic grin crossing his face.

Twenty minutes to the south of Covington County, South Britain was within easy reach of Hampton Falls and Shane made the trip on a regular basis, most of the time under cover of darkness. His trips included regular scouting expeditions past his house, and almost always included a stop at the Village Grille for his consistent two-hour stint at the bar. These visits often resulted in his

225

dropping in at the house in a befuddled state and winding up in an argument with Linda. When he was served with the restraining order, he decided not to fight it. Hiring a lawyer was not in his financial interest, and he could stay away easily enough. She was bound to come to her senses sooner or later. It was still a trial separation, he told himself often enough to believe it.

The annual fall hunting trip with Tommy Iverson as guide was another successful adventure, one Tommy insisted he pay for in full and in advance. After Shane killed his deer on Wednesday afternoon, he began celebrating and by late evening when the poker game was just starting, he was ranting about how miserably Linda was treating him.

"First, the fucking trial separation, then the fucking restraining order! I can't believe the judge won't let me see my kids without supervision." His friends were staring at him as his temper clearly was getting the better of him. "She is such a bitch. I can't figure out why I ever married her." He had started knocking on the table with both fists, knocking over stacks of poker chips in the process.

"Come on, Shane, calm down," Tommy begged. "Let's get back to the game."

"The hell with you, Iverson! I've seen the way you look at her—probably can't wait to get me out of the way!" Shane shouted. "But I'll tell you one thing. There's not going to be a divorce. She took a fucking oath, or a vow, or whatever the hell you call it. Till death do us part, right? Well, that's how it's going to be. She's embarrassed me enough." He slammed the table with one final, decisive crash of his fist and stood up, toppling over his chair. "Till death do us part," he snarled once more as he stormed from the room, leaving the other three men gaping after him.

"WE'RE SEPARATED, NOT DIVORCED," Linda kept reminding her friends when they tried to convince her into going out with them during the separation. "We're just trying to figure stuff out." Both Yvonne and Loretta rolled their eyes with no effort to conceal the expression of disbelief. After nine months of denying that the marriage was over, Linda asked them to come to her house for an important announcement. It was nine o'clock before all three women could finish with their commitments. Linda filled the glasses well beyond what was customary for red wine in advance of her friends' arrival and sat in the kitchen waiting for them.

Yvonne and Loretta arrived at virtually the same time and walked up to the house together. The well-lit kitchen revealed Linda sitting at the table, staring into space. They let themselves in and she looked up them and smiled.

"Thanks for coming over," she said as they each chose a seat with a glass in front of it. After a moment of silence, both of her friends leaned forward as if to say, *well?*" Linda lifted her glass and took a sip. "Cheers."

The other women automatically followed her lead. "Cheers back at you," Yvonne said. "Now, what the hell is going on?" she asked without rancor and with a broad smile.

"I'm seeing Alison tomorrow. I'm going to file for divorce. Shane's never going to change, and I just think we'll all be better off without him." The inevitable tears threatened to surface but Linda forced them back. "I thought he'd get better but it's just gotten worse. Even with the damn order, he still comes by occasionally to hassle me about something. And, quite frankly, he scares the devil out of me."

"I don't mean to add to the fire here, but what do you think he'll do when he gets served with the papers?" The creased furrows of worry on Loretta's brow deepened as she spoke.

"I guess we'll find out, won't we?" Linda answered.

ONE WEEK LATER, LINDA was awakened by the sound of heavy footfalls on the stairs. She sat up in bed, wiping the blurriness from her eyes just enough to read the red numbers on her new digital clock. "Four o'clock. What the hell…" Then Shane was shoving her back down into the mattress. He clamped his hand over her mouth.

"Don't say a word when I let you go," he hissed into her ear. "We wouldn't want to wake the children, now, would we?" She nodded against his firm grip and he removed his hand. He reached across her and turned on the nightstand light.

"I want to know what the fuck these things are." He pulled a thick sheaf of papers from his jacket pocket and waved them in her face. "I told you before; you promised in a church and in front of a bunch of people: We don't part until one of us dies. I think that means divorce doesn't enter the picture."

The adrenaline coursing through Linda's veins had her firmly in the fight or flight mode she'd experienced with Shane before. Flight wasn't an option. "Yes, it does, Shane. Divorce is entering the picture, whether you like it or not. Now you better get the hell out of here before I call the police."

Shane threw the papers on the floor, then grabbed her hands and pushed her back down. "Oh, I'll get the hell out, all right, but not before I take advantage of my conjugal rights. Whether you like it or not, we're still married and a wife can't refuse her husband, as I understand it." He reached down and pulled up on her nightgown until it was wrapped around her waist. "Don't fight it, Linda, you know you'll like it. Besides, you don't want me wake up the kids."

"You bastard," she said, as she gave up the fight.

# Twenty-Nine

## *The Village Grille*

After Shane's humiliating visit, an event she determined would be her secret, Linda Phillips adopted the persona of a soon-to-be-divorced woman. Frequent articles in Redbook, her favorite magazine, addressed the dilemmas faced by women in the beginning, middle, and end stages of a divorce, with most of them citing research that lent some credibility to what she was feeling. For over ten years, virtually her entire existence centered on fulfilling the needs of a man who had abused her. Now she could concentrate on her children, and, most importantly, herself.

Instead of Yvonne or Loretta or other of her neighborhood friends inviting her to go out with them, she initiated the idea most of the time. Saturday night at the Village Grille became a permanent fixture on her calendar. Babysitters, including Louise DiMartini, were arranged far in advance so there was no chance of missing the fish fry, but especially the music of the DJ after dinner. Tommy Iverson, no stranger to the Grille, always managed to secure a table near Linda's no matter what time she arrived or who was with her.

"You are really something else," Dolores Freeman remarked one night after Linda had danced with a variety of men, Tommy Iverson most often, but her husband, Paul, also, over the course of the night. Dolores and Paul, social acquaintances when Shane and Linda were a couple, became supportive of her in the divorce and moved into the closer friends' circle. Paul seemed especially interested in helping Linda make the adjustments to her new life.

Technically, as Shane pointed out so vividly that awful night, she was still a married woman, but with encouragement from Yvonne and Loretta, Linda was rapidly shedding that temporary impediment to her freedom. With her constraints falling away, she discovered that the Grille had a hidden layer, an underbelly that Paul Freeman exposed toward the end of an unusually raucous night. After that night, she understood what the euphemism "going upstairs" meant at the Village Grille.

The second floor of the restaurant, which Linda had never seen, was composed of five large rooms, each with a small bath and furnished with several overstuffed couches, a high-end hotel-style wet bar, a few small tables, and track lighting on the ceiling, controlled by a dimmer switch. When Dolores and Paul mentioned going upstairs and suggested that Linda join them, she readily agreed. She had heard the references to the second floor many times, and her curiosity was piqued more than she expected when presented with a chance to explore. Her first experience at going upstairs turned into her introduction to Paul's magic powder, an introduction that would have been impossible if not for her new outlook on life.

"I hope you'll invite me up again," she said, giggling hysterically, as the Freemans helped her to the car.

Tommy watched the scene from his car several rows back in the parking lot and followed Linda's erratic drive home. He parked halfway up the drive, waited for her to get out, then jumped out.

"Wait a second, Linda. I'll help you," he called out. Linda stopped, a bit puzzled by his appearance.

"What are you doing here?" she asked.

"I saw you come out of the Grille—just thought you might need some help..." He was stammering, trying to come up with some more plausible reason for being there.

"That's sweet of you, Tommy. Really. But I'm okay. And thanks for the dances tonight—you are good, just like you said. Goodnight." Tommy watched her until she closed the door.

# Thirty

*The Divorce Settlement*

SHANE PHILLIPS LEFT THE courthouse hearing swearing. Sam Crawford, the cheapest lawyer he could find, sputtered right along with him.

"It is absolutely outrageous. Wouldn't you know we'd get a female judge? Don't you worry about a thing, Mr. Phillips. We'll fight this settlement and try to get it reversed," Sam said as they reached the parking lot.

Shane glared at him. "You, not we, damned well better get it reversed. That's what I'm paying you for. Call me when you get a date for the appeal hearing. And it better be pretty fucking quick."

Crawford glared back. "I need to tell you something, Mr. Phillips, and you're not going to like it. That judge is making her decisions on what she's given. You gave her a lot by your behavior over the last few months, maybe even years. Judges don't look kindly on a guy who beats up his wife. Now, I'll do the best I can with a reversal, but it may be that a sixty-forty split is the best we'll get. Visitation rights are open to debate, but the kids will have a say in that. Frankly, I don't hold out much chance of improving anything in an appeal, but like I said, I'll give it my best."

The speech had its effect. Chastened, Shane just mumbled a "thanks, and let me hear from you," then shook his hand and headed to his car.

In the car, he began pounding the steering wheel with his fists.

"Son of a bitch! I am really screwed," he shouted at the dashboard. "Something's got to be done."

ALEX PROHL MADE FREQUENT trips to the East Coast. The call from Shane Phillips could not have been timed better. At that moment, Alex was a man with a problem and, judging by the tenor of Shane's voice, he was as well. While his problem involved the rumors of alcohol and drug abuse coupled with gambling issues, especially in Nevada, he wasn't desperate, but a substantial amount of cash could ease his predicament considerably. Controlled violence was a strength of his, a reputation with his colleagues on the road that forced them to use caution in any dealings with him.

After Sam Crawford notified Shane that the final hearing in his appeal was scheduled for the Monday after Mother's Day, two months away, Shane contacted Alex. The truck driver from California would be passing through Hartford in late March.

"I'll listen to what you have to say," Prohl said, "but what I don't need is some hairbrained scheme that's going to get me in more trouble than I am already. What I really need is the cash, and I'll need half before and the other half after, and I mean immediately after."

"Look, uh, Alex, I'm not comfortable with this on the phone."

"Right," Prohl interrupted. "Rest area, just south of Hartford. I'll be there next Thursday from three to five in the afternoon. There'll be a little red ribbon on the antenna."

SHANE FIRST WENT AROUND to the front and stood far enough away so he could see into the cab. When he saw Alex wave, directing him to the passenger side of the vehicle, he moved cautiously. When the door swung open, Alex greeted him with a hearty hello. "Jump in, Shane. Great to see you." He offered his hand as Shane climbed aboard into the familiar setting of a long-haul tractor cabin.

Alex looked as good as ever. He was about Shane's age but could have passed for a future Robert Redford, with rugged good looks and the slender build of an athlete. They shook hands, the firm grip indicative of a firm friendship.

Shane immediately began explaining his mission and ended with a question.

"Have you ever done anything like this before?" Prohl looked at Shane like he was crazy. "Well, you don't, you know, look like..." Prohl chuckled at his awkwardness.

"Hey, hired killers come in all shapes and sizes." He shifted in his seat so that he faced Shane directly. "You think I'd be sitting here talking to you if I couldn't handle the job? From what you told me, this should be a piece of cake. Now, I need you to bring me up to date with what she's done to you lately to deserve this. If I remember correctly, seems like you usually had your way with her."

The question spurred Shane into a spewing of his hatred for Linda.

"I'm sure she screws around. She's going to take my kids, my money, my house, get a fucking 60 percent of everything I own. Who knows how much for alimony, child support, all kinds of stuff. The goddamned judge is all on her side. If she disappears, if there's a permanent solution, then I get it all back. Simple as that. Murder is a desperate answer but sometimes desperate times call for desperate measures, right?"

Prohl listened, then said, "Sounds like excuses for an inexcusable action to me." His comment took Shane back for a moment.

"So you won't do it?"

Prohl's response was a hearty laugh. "Who said that? I'm pretty desperate myself. Luckily, I'm also a nice guy. That's why I get away with murder."

SHANE AND ALEX PROHL visited the Phillips's house twice when Shane was certain that Linda would not be home. Prohl practiced his approach up the stairs leading from the attached barn to Linda's second floor bedroom, once doing it with eyes closed to prove his familiarity with the environment to himself.

"This has got to look like a rage killing, if you know what I mean, Alex. That simple-assed boyfriend, the one she just dumped, has to be the first one they look at after I'm cleared. Are you sure you can do that?"

"Damn right I can do that. Don't you worry about me, just be sure that I get my money like we arranged, all of it, on time."

"And one other thing: She's got breast implants."

Prohl stared at him. "Yeah? So what?"

"I want them cut out. She should've never done that."

"You are one sick son of a bitch, you know that?" Prohl hadn't stopped staring.

"Oh, yeah, this coming from a guy who's going to kill a beautiful woman he doesn't even know for money!"

They shared a conspiratorial grin and shook hands.

DURING THE DAY ON Saturday, Shane called to tell him that the three kids were removed from the house, staying with his mother. The plan was ready to move into the action stage.

After a quick check of the premises early on Sunday morning, Alex knew that Linda must be asleep, and he used his practiced routine to creep up the stairs from the barn. His plan included several fail-safes, none of which he had to use. He efficiently silenced his victim, and stabbed her several times. Despite being unconscious, she wouldn't stop breathing. Fighting back a brief panic, he stabbed her again and again. When he finished, satisfied that she looked like a victim of a volatile anger and rage, he remembered what Shane told him to do with her breast implants. Swallowing hard just as he always did when gutting an animal, he sliced them out. With a disgusted sigh, he skittered them across the room.

After checking her breathing one more time, and convinced she was dead, he removed his spatter suit, mask, gloves, and booties, shoving them into his bag. After a controlled retreat down the front stairs, he exited through the slider onto the veranda.

Twenty minutes later, he dropped his car at the employee parking lot as Shane had instructed and a minute later climbed into his truck. Back on Interstate 84, he watched for milepost 109, pulled off the road, and switched on his flashers, his truck looking just like hundreds whose drivers were catching a nap before pushing the limit of allowable time in a given day. A short walk into the woods placed him at exactly the spot Shane had mentioned. After dropping the bag containing the suit, the knife, and all incriminating evidence into the previously dug hole in a section of thick forest which would likely not see a human footprint for years, if ever, he picked up the folding camp shovel and filled in the hole. After spreading a thin coating of leaves damp from the gathering morning dew, he returned to his truck, on his way to an on-time delivery in upper New York state. His pay for this job was already deposited in his California bank.

# Part Four

## Justice

# Thirty-One

*The Accusation*
*Monday, May 11, 1992*

"I FUCKING HATE YOU!" The message ended with the resounding crash of a phone being slammed back into its cradle.

Detective Parker Havenot, Sheriff Jim Corbett, and Sergeant Sam Olden huddled around the desk in Parker's office, staring at the telephone answering machine. They listened to the message for the fifth time, as if hearing the four words repeated over and over again might provide a divine revelation.

"This has got to be our guy," the sheriff said. Sam nodded in agreement but Parker brought him up short.

"Sometimes it seems like you've got a slam-dunk proposition, but you folks know that things aren't always as they seem." His pronouncement deflated them as surely as air escapes from a pinpricked balloon, but Jim Corbett recovered quickly.

"This guy's been stalking Linda Phillips for months now, and especially over the last two weeks. All of her friends are in agreement about that. I say we bring him in and have a chat."

"Okay. I'll go along with it, but I want it to be voluntary, make it seem like he's doing us a favor, at least to get him in here without issuing any paperwork."

"What about the state police?" Sam asked. "Aren't we going to get into some kind of jurisdictional hassle? They're the ones processing the crime scene."

"Hampton Village is right smack in the middle of our county and I've already spoken with them. We'll be taking the lead with their role just being support. Parker has helped them out before, and I'll guarantee with this one that they'll be happy to let him have it. With his Philly experience, Parker's got more skills in homicide than most of their guys anyway. That won't be a problem but thanks for the concern, Sam." The sheriff turned his attention to Parker. "You're okay with taking this on, right?"

Parker's answer was just to flash a wide grin at him.

"I'll get in touch with Tommy Iverson and have him in here this afternoon," he said. "You guys can watch the interview through the window."

"WE'LL BE RECORDING THIS. That's not a problem for you, is it?" Parker asked, his question sounding more like a statement of accepted fact.

Tommy nodded, staring at the two machines on the narrow table separating the two men. Their knees were almost touching. "I've got nothing to hide. Why do you have two?"

"Just standard procedure; you know, backups for each other. I know I asked you this on the phone, but I'll ask it once more." Parker pushed the record button, and the sound of the whirring tape hypnotized Tommy momentarily.

"This is May 11, 1992. The time is 3:20 in the afternoon. Mr. Iverson, will you just repeat that it is all right with you that we are recording this interview, and that I've offered to postpone it if you wanted to have a lawyer present?"

Iverson scanned the room, his glance stopping at the window exactly opposite him. The stark reflection of the back of Havenot's head and his face told him what it was. "Who else is watching this?" he asked.

"Again, just standard procedure; nothing to worry about. More for your protection than anything. I've got the sheriff in there. Now, if you could answer the question and we'll get this over with as fast as we can."

"Yeah, I'm good with the recording and I sure as hell don't need a lawyer."

"Okay. We'll get started." Unlike most interrogators, Parker always sat while conducting his interviews. He could be equally intimidating with his words and tone of voice as with his body language from a superior standing position.

"So, how long ago did Linda dump you, anyway?" Parker asked the question with one of his confident smiles, the "we've got you nailed" look sparkling in his eyes.

"She didn't dump me. We were just working some stuff out." Tommy Iverson's sweat-drenched shirt belied the fact that the interview was just beginning.

"Come on, Tommy. We've spent most of yesterday and half of today talking with her friends. Everybody in town knows you two were finished. She even told one of her friends that you used to be a friend with benefits but she shut off the benefits."

"She really said that? I can't believe she'd ever say that. We had something special."

Parker reached for the answering machine. He pushed the play button, leaned back in his chair, and watched for Iverson's reaction. It was predictable.

"Is that you on that phone call?" he asked, almost whispering.

Tommy Iverson reached into his back pocket and pulled out a crisply folded, clean handkerchief.

Parker's surprised reaction forced an explanation. "Looks like you just pressed that thing," he said.

"I like my stuff neat and clean. Is anything wrong with that?" Without unfolding it, he wiped his mouth, gathering the droplets of sweat that had formed across his upper lip.

Parker kept watching him as he gazed at the now silent machine. Without saying another word, he hit the play button and the message repeated, echoing off the bare walls. It hadn't finished when Tommy bounced out of his chair.

"Shit," he shouted. "That was the other day. Must've been Friday night." He paced around the room while Parker remained in his chair, waiting for the inevitable letdown. A minute later, Tommy sat down in stunned silence.

"She left it on the machine. Didn't even erase it. Guess she loved hearing your voice over and over again."

"I can't believe this is happening. I can explain that. I was just pissed off, that's all. Wouldn't you be if you saw your girl-friend making out with another guy?" The words ran together as Tommy's voice trembled.

"And just how did you manage to see them making out?" Havenot spoke softly, the relaxed cadence disarming.

"It was Friday night. I stopped by and saw them through the window. I even talked to them on Saturday morning!"

"So, you just happened to stop at your old girlfriend's house and peek in the window. Let's run through this again. Linda dumps you two weeks ago. You don't want to admit it so you keep hanging around, even peeking in her windows late at night. Then, you call to tell her that you hate her. Then, she shows up murdered. You live two blocks away and never left your house that night but no one can corroborate that. You're a hunter and have a hunting guide business with access to who knows how many different kinds of knives and are likely very good with them. You practically lived at her house for several months while you two were going together so you know your way around. Seems like a pretty good combina-tion of motive, means, and opportunity to me."

"First of all, we were still friends. It's not like she hated me or anything. Second, you guys know damn well that it was Shane. He's the fucking ex-husband, for God's sake, and he was thor-oughly nuts about the divorce settlement. A sixty-forty split of all assets? Plus, in two days, actually it would have been this morning, there was going be that final hearing. After that, he was toast!"

The volume of Tommy's voice increased with the realization that the detective was staring at him.

"Shane was fighting that down to the wire and you know it! What about him? He was always threatening her."

"I don't have to tell you this," Parker said, "but I will. He's in the clear. Two of his friends swear they were together at an over-night camping expedition, scouting out some hot spots for deer on the night Linda was killed."

"Then you've got three goddamned liars. That's how I met Shane. I did all his scouting for him. He's clueless in the woods without help. And it's fucking May, nowhere close to hunting season."

"Yep, and all you've got is one liar. Right now, we've got probable cause and I'm guessing about an 85% chance of conviction, even with just the circumstantial stuff. And, by the way, where'd you get those scratches on your hand and face, again?"

"I told you I was doing yard work on Saturday; got into a damned rose bush, and Linda helped me later with some splinters I got picking up brush." The color drained from Tommy Iverson's face as the detective waved at the window.

Sheriff Jim Corbett entered the room and greeted him.

"Hello, Tommy," he said. "Been a while since I've seen you." As he removed a small card from his vest pocket, Iverson reacted.

"You've got the wrong fucking guy. I'd never do anything to hurt Linda. I'm telling you, this is all wrong."

The sheriff began to read from the card, although he had long since memorized the words.

"You have the right to remain silent..."

# Thirty-Two

## A Mess

"You've got to let Iverson go."

Parker just nodded. "You're absolutely right. We've got nothing but circumstantial on him. No weapon, motive is questionable at best—I mean, how many guys would kill a woman they supposedly loved because she bowed out of a one-year relationship? Means? Christ, the guy's got more knives than a hundred kitchens but nothing matches. Opportunity? I guess he had that too, but I'm still going with the husband."

"Oh, come on, Parker. That guy's got the proverbial airtight alibi." Jim Agnew, the lead prosecutor for the Office of the Attorney General, had an infamous reputation with the police in the state. His motto seemed to be "100 percent chance of conviction or no prosecution."

"I'm not going to bring a guy in and look foolish when he produces two credible witnesses that say he couldn't possibly have been in Hampton Village when Linda Phillips was killed."

Parker ignored his reasoning. He was well aware of Agnew's reputation but was insistent in the face of it. "All Phillips has is a physical alibi. We know he couldn't have done it himself but that doesn't mean he's not involved."

"Oh, Christ, don't tell me we have a conspiracy theory. I'll tell you what, Detective Havenot. You tell your actual killer, who has to admit that he killed Linda Phillips, by the way, that I'll give him a great deal if he flips on Shane Phillips. But if you want my suggestion, work on Iverson. Find a weapon. Get a confession. Get something more than an angry phone message. Now, this meeting is over. Let me know when we have something worth bringing to the grand jury, something that won't embarrass me." Agnew stood, his unsubtle hint telling Havenot to leave.

As much as he tried to avoid it, Parker's voice took on an unpleasant edge. "The guy beat her up; according to her friends, he threatened to kill her more than once. He kept harping on the death do us part thing. What more do you want? Isn't that enough to lean on him a little more?"

"Look, Havenot, you're a good detective and a good policeman, but I'm not going to chance a harassment suit. Leave Phillips alone until you have more than hearsay and gossip." The attorney turned his attention to a stack of papers on his desk and began shuffling through them without reading a word.

Parker left, muttering to himself under his breath. "What a fucking mess this is..." he said as he closed the door behind him.

# Thirty-Three

*Getting Away with Murder*

ON AUGUST 10, 1992, exactly three months after the murder of Linda Phillips, Parker Havenot received the summons from Jim Agnew. He had no doubt about the reason for the command appearance.

"He'll be the lawnmower and I'll be the grass," he joked, receiving the requisite chuckles from Sheriff Jim Corbett. "I know it's about the Phillips case and what the hell am I supposed to tell him? We've reinterviewed everybody at least twice. We've done as much with the blood samples as we can. Someday soon, that DNA stuff will be practical but for now it takes so damn long and even then it's not always useful. I can't put the screws to Shane Phillips, the grieving husband and father. I've begged for access to his bank accounts, his phone records, and tried to find out who he hangs out with on the road. So far, it's been permission denied at every turn. I think we can take this probable cause stuff too far. We know a crime's been committed. All I'm trying to do is rule out suspects. If the judge would just let us..."

Jim Corbett interrupted after listening to the harangue, then offered his advice. "If your theory is correct, that it's a murder for hire thing, then the actual killer is long gone, probably was before we even found the body, and along with him went the evidence we need. Frankly, unless we've got more, no judge is going to give us the warrant for those records of Phillips. We don't stand a chance. Maybe we just bring Iverson in. You said yourself that based on the circumstantial only, Agnew would have an eighty-five percent chance of convicting him."

"Yeah, but they're afraid that if he's not convicted, we don't get another shot. Then maybe a killer walks away. Besides, it's not him anyway. My God, the guy's in here seems like once a week and twice on Sunday telling me how Shane pulled it off. He can really be irritating. That profiler claims that a guy who inserts himself into the case, always hanging around with the cops, offering opinions, that sort of stuff, is probably guilty, but I just don't buy it. A gut feeling, but he really seems to have loved that poor woman." Parker grabbed his rain slicker from the coat rack as a clap of thunder roared overhead. "I'll let you know if I have anything left of my ass when I'm done this afternoon."

Corbett once again chuckled but only halfheartedly knowing what Parker would be facing.

"THEY ARE ALL OVER me! This office is fielding calls from people in Hampton Village practically every day, asking what's going on with the Phillips case. So, tell me, Detective, what is going on with the Phillips case?" Jim Agnew had invited his assistant to sit in on the meeting so Parker was outnumbered.

"I can tell you exactly what's going on. Nothing! And it will be nothing unless we catch a break. Something new has to turn up. We can't go back and interview the same people yet again. Unfortunately, some of those folks would like this all just to be over and us showing up on their doorstep again just opens up the wounds again." The depth of frustration in Parker's voice was obvious and Agnew softened.

"Let's give it a little more time, then I'm going to allow you more leeway. I'll just tell the folks and the press that we're working as hard as we can and expect a break anytime now. I'll give the old 'the public is not in any danger' story. I'm sorry to be hard on you but I'm getting it too. You know, someone bites me and I'm looking for someone else to bite. Good luck, Parker. You're a good man."

The brief meeting adjourned with a handshake.

"So, HE'S GOING TO get away with it. It's going on six months now and he's got his house, his kids, his life, and he just walks around free as a bird." Tommy Iverson's refrain was no different than Parker had heard many times before, but his level of exasperation seemed to have him tottering on some brink, an edge the detective hadn't noticed before.

"Look, Tommy, the best thing you can do is get on with your life. This is eating you up but it's out of your control so let us handle it, okay?" Parker smiled, trying to ease the tension, and his little speech did seem to have an effect.

"You're right about one thing, Detective, it is eating me up. I'm figuring I have to do something about that." Tommy paused, thinking, then said, "time to get on with my life, put this stuff behind me, and I think I know just how to do that." He spun on his heels and started to march out of Parker's office. He stopped at the door and turned around. "You're a real patient guy, Detective, you know that? I sure do appreciate that."

TOMMY WAITED ALL AFTERNOON at the Village Grille for Vern Carter to show up. When he finally did, Tommy watched as he found his usual bar stool, then approached him.

"Buy you a beer?" Tommy asked his competitor.

"Never refuse that kind of offer. What's the occasion?" Vern asked, skepticism coating the question.

"Nothing really. Just that with the season starting this weekend, wondered if you got anybody to guide. I mean, I got nobody until the second week. What the hell's up with that?" Tommy slid onto the stool next to Vern as he spoke, then called to Tillie. "Bring over a beer for my buddy, here, will ya?"

"You should know. I got Phillips and his buddies. Guess you lost them, with screwing around with his wife and all before she was killed. He tells everybody you did it, you know? That's all he talks about." As soon as the inflammatory words were out of his mouth, Vern tensed, almost cringing as if expecting an attack. Tommy surprised him.

"Yeah, I know all that. It's fine. He's got his opinions, and I got mine." Tommy segued into another topic. "So, where you taking them for the first day?"

"You asking me to give away my secrets, boy?" Vern laughed. "You know just where we'll go. Your favorite spot if you was the one taking them."

Tommy slapped Vern on the back. "Well, good luck! I got to be going. Enjoy that beer."

HUNTERS OFTEN REFERRED TO the first day of deer season in Monongahela State Park as being in the middle of a shooting gallery. Tommy Iverson was up two hours before dawn. His years of guiding and hunting in the area allowed him to find his way through the woods almost without use of a flashlight. He stood well-hidden in a thick stand of pines well before any other hunters began to find their way into the woods. If Vern was being truthful about where they were to hunt, he and his group would pass close enough on their way to their positions that he'd be able to single out Shane Phillips. Just before dawn, right on schedule, the four men crept by, never knowing that Tommy was watching. Shane was last in line, meaning he'd be the first one dropped off.

Tommy waited until they were well past him, then started his slow circling to a spot just over 150 yards away from where Shane should take his stand. He settled in and waited for daylight.

SHANE WAS GETTING ANXIOUS. Two hours pushed his limit of waiting. He leaned his rifle against a tree and stretched. There had been only silence for a half an hour since the last of a multiple volley of shots had echoed through the forest. He unzipped his blaze orange jacket to get to his water canteen, then removed it and hung it over the barrel of his rifle. He slipped the straps of his camouflage overalls off his shoulders.

"Why the fuck don't they make these things easier to get down," he mumbled as he moved away far enough to relieve himself without ruining the covering scent surrounding his ground stand. He was bent over, struggling with his overalls, when the shot entered his chest and blew out of his back. He was dead before he hit the ground.

"I THOUGHT HE WAS a deer," Tommy said to the Connecticut Fish and Game deputy an hour later. "He was crouched over, didn't look like a man at all. He didn't even have his vest on"

The deputy went over to the rifle leaning against the tree. The blaze orange jacket hung from the muzzle. "I'd think a guide would know the difference between a man and a deer, but this sure looks like an unfortunate hunting accident to me," he said, "but we'll have to wait for the investigators to get here."

THE NEXT DAY, TOMMY stood in Parker's office, looking down at his shoes with his hands folded as if he might be saying a prayer, a silent act of contrition.

"Unfortunate hunting accident, huh?" Parker said. "You're lucky it's not in my jurisdiction or you'd probably be in jail right now."

When Tommy raised his eyes and met Parker's, he smiled. "Believe it or not, sir, I went to Sunday School when I was young. Did you know the real commandment about killing actually says 'Thou shalt not murder?' I take that to mean that sometimes it's okay to kill. I didn't murder Shane Phillips. I killed him, just like I'd kill a deer. And guess what? Nothing's eating me up anymore, Detective. It's going to be involuntary manslaughter or criminal negligence. Either way, three years from now, maybe sooner, I'm back in the saddle again. As I said, I got nothing eating at me anymore."

THREE DAYS BEFORE CHRISTMAS, December 22, 1992, Alex Prohl was driving his rig on Route 84 through West Hartford. It was his first trip through the area since May.

"OH, SHIT," HE MUMBLED when he saw the flashing lights in his side view mirror. The highway patrol car pulled alongside of

him, the patrolman gesturing for him to pull over. He found a wide pullout about a quarter of a mile up the road and stopped. Glancing in the mirror again, he noticed that the officer was approaching cautiously, as if preparing to react to an unexpected attack. He opened his door and climbed out, already adjusting his expression to sorrowfully contrite.

"What's the problem, Officer?" he asked. "I wasn't speeding or anything, was I?"

"No, nothing like that. We've been instructed to escort you to the Covington County Sheriff's Department. A Detective Parker Havenot needs to speak to you. Do you know him?"

"No, actually I don't, and I don't think I'm required to do this." His face took on a reddish tinge, a rising anger replacing the contrite mask of a minute before.

"Well, first off, you're going to get to know the detective, and second, yes, you are required to do this. I've got backup coming to help with your personal escort. We'll just wait in the car until they get here. It's cold out."

"SHANE PHILLIPS WOULDN'T BE dead now if you had put the pressure on and helped me get into his bank records. The fool wasn't smart enough to cover up those two transfers to that California Bank." Parker glared at the prosecutor.

"Yeah, well, it turned out all right after all. Saved us the cost of one murder trial, at least." Jim Agnew smiled. "Good work, Detective."

Parker just shook his head and walked out of the office.

THE SNOW THAT PROMISED a white Christmas for Covington County began to fall at an alarming rate as Parker made his way home. He called dispatch and asked them to connect him with his home phone.

"Hello," Josie answered. The slight quiver in her voice revealed the innate worry of a policeman's wife.

"On my way home, Jos. You were right. There were a lot of cracks in Linda Phillips's wall, but none that should have killed her. She was a good person and deserved to live her life." His voice cracked.

"Hey, I'm off until after Christmas; I say we just stay home and count our blessings."

# About the Author

Duke Southard is a retired educator, having published professional articles in *Media and Methods* magazine and winning an "Edie," the New Hampshire Excellence in Education Award, for his contribution to the school library/media profession in the state.

His educational credentials include a BS from Villanova University, an MA in English Education from Glassboro State University, and a CAGS in Media Technology from Boston University. He is married and the father of three. He lived in New Jersey and New Hampshire before moving to Arizona.

His first novel, *A Favor Returned,* was a finalist in both the 2013 NM/AZ Books Awards and the 2015 Indie Publishers Next Generation Book Awards. His second novel, *Agent for Justice,* was published by Hot House Press and also was a finalist in the NM/AZ Book Awards for 2014. His third novel, *Live Free or Die,* received similar honors in 2015.

The author of two nonfiction books, *The Week from Heaven and Hell* and *The Nick: A Vision Realized,* he has garnered numerous awards for short story and personal essay/memoir entries, including first place in the 2015 Society of Southwestern Authors Writing Contest for his personal essay, "Three Weeks," and two second places in the same contest in 2011.

Please visit the author's website for more information on his works in progress, free programs for schools, libraries and community groups, and contact information.

**www.dukesouthard.com**

CPSIA information can be obtained at www.ICGtesting.com
Printed in the USA
BVOW08s0303080616

451123BV00003B/23/P